Verona in
Autumn

Tom Lloyd

SRL PUBLISHING

SRL Publishing Ltd
London
www.srlpublishing.co.uk

First published worldwide by SRL Publishing in 2023

ISBN: 978-1915073-12-9

1 3 5 7 9 10 8 6 4 2

A CIP catalogue record for this book is available from the British Library

SRL Publishing is a Climate Positive publisher offsetting more carbon emissions than it emits.

Also by Tom Lloyd

The Twilight Reign

The Stormcaller
The Twilight Herald
The Grave Thief
The Ragged Man
The Dusk Watchman
The God Tattoo (collected tales)

The Empire of a Hundred Houses

Moon's Artifice
Old Man's Ghosts

The God Fragments

Stranger of Tempest
Princess of Blood
Knight of Stars
God of Night
Honour Under Moonlight (novella)
The Man with One Name (novella)

Fear the Reaper (novella)

Falling Dark

To my love, Fiona

Prologue

Verona - 1381

'Oh faithless apothecary, thy drugs are false!'

Romeo bows his head, the weight of grief too much to bear. The vial tumbles from his hands, empty but for an empty promise. He slumps against the tomb wall, exhausted by his unwanted survival.

'I feel nothing. No blessed embrace of death, no reunion with my love. I lie here in a cold tomb and yet I live. Juliet is beside me and yet we are apart. But wait – I have my dagger still. Our love will not be denied.'

Romeo draws his knife with unsteady hands. In the lantern's dull light the razor edge gleams with wicked glee. He does not care as he presses it to his lips.

'A kiss I give you, for your potency cannot be denied. The blacksmith was honest in his art, though his compatriot cheated me as he cheated death. Soon my wife and I will be together once again, but before your cold embrace, a kiss for my love.'

He brushes Juliet's cheek. The shock of seeing her this way is as numbing as the chill air. For one moment Romeo wonders if the poison was indeed true. The cool touch of Juliet's cheek is not so awful to bear; as though death has already half-spread its wings over him and warmth is but a fading memory.

That small flicker of hope quickens his heart however and stills the notion. Amid the silence of the tomb Romeo feels it beating in his chest; strong and regular for all that he would wish it to stop. In that moment he knows the poison has failed for certain. He bends to kiss Juliet but pauses an inch away. So close now, as lovers in the darkest hours should all be. At gentle rest with the tiniest kiss of the other's breath on their skin. Romeo finds his own caught in his chest, locked in the cage of his body.

Even veiled by darkness, the lines of her face map perfectly against the image engraved on his heart. He finds himself transfixed, as he was the first moment he saw her. A beauty only glimpsed but seared into his most vital of organs by love's unyielding heat. He brushes one errant curl of chestnut hair back before placing the gentlest of kisses on her lips.

Still he finds it hard to believe. Despite the letter he received, despite the funeral robes and tomb itself. Her pale skin lacks the spectral hue of the dead, her lips the stiffness of an empty vessel.

'She could be sleeping still,' Romeo moans. 'Death itself cannot rob her of the beauty God granted.'

His hand tightens around the grip of his dagger; resolve stiffens his arm.

'My heart torments me. I know she is dead these several days, for all it could be a mere moment ago. My guilt punishes me. For those I have killed I am cursed to imagine those I love still alive. Will I see dear Mercutio look on from the doorway now?'

Romeo looks up as though the ghost of his friend is indeed there, then flinches and touches his fingers to his cheek.

2

'Even the wind mocks me,' he says at last. 'It caresses my cheek like a lover's breath. One last cruel cut from a world that justly blames me. It is not sweet Juliet's breath, though. My madness does not extend so far, for all that this final act will seem more kindness than cruelty.'

He leans back then stops. 'I speak too soon, perhaps I am mad indeed. I would have wagered my life upon her lips parting there.'

Romeo shakes his head and reverses the knife.

'But it is madness only, of that I'm certain. Come, my final friend, cut this tattered soul free. I should have cast weapons aside long ago, before good men died, but this last life taken will only improve the world it departs. I pray my death serves God's Earth better than my life ever could.'

Just as he raises the knife there is the faintest of sounds. Romeo's hand trembles as though the blade hungers for his blood. Madness or not, he heard something more than the lament of the wind. There – again, a sound. A tiny huff of breath. A twitch of the folded cloth on her chest. Romeo gapes and the knife clatters to the ground.

Again his madness breathes and takes greater hold of his mind. Again Juliet's chest seems to rise and her lips part. Romeo stumbles backwards, a faint cry lost in the pit of his chest, but still he hears it more clearly than ever – the drawing of breath.

'What sorcery or sickness is this?' Romeo whispers, crouched at the side of the sarcophagus and clinging to the edge like a child. 'Can I not even go to my death in true fashion? Must there be some final torment visited upon me?'

The breath rises and becomes a wheeze, a cough.

Then, like the blessed light of God shining upon the world, Juliet's eyes flicker and open.

'Is it true? Do my eyes deceive me or is my love returned to life?'

In response Romeo receives a twitch of the cheek then a wan smile. Juliet moans and tries to move, but only feebly until Romeo dives down to gently gather her up.

'Oh my sweet, oh my love – is it really true? Speak, I beg you, Juliet. Am I mad or blessed beyond words and reason?'

'Romeo,' Juliet whispers, 'you came.'

'Came? I...' He finds himself unable to finish. Instead he simply stares at the girl in his arms – as struck and smitten as that first sighting of her.

'Where is the friar?'

'Friar?' Romeo says. 'I am alone. I came to see you one last time. And yet Death's cold heart cannot bear to steal such a jewel from the world.'

'Death?' Juliet winces and tries to sit up but is defeated until Romeo helps her. 'Did Friar Lawrence not send you word?'

Romeo shakes his head. 'He? I received nothing.'

'Then how did you know?'

'Juliet, my sun and stars, I came here to die alongside my wife in her undeserved tomb!' Romeo gestures to the dagger lying in the dust. 'I knew nothing. I came to join you in death, rather than feign to live when such life was without you.'

From outside there is a sudden clatter of boots and voices. Romeo snatches up his dagger and rounds the tomb, but Juliet touches a shaky finger to his arm.

'Hold, my heart, do no more harm.'

Romeo flinches as though stung by a wasp. 'Harm?'

4

he whispers in the voice of a man hell-bound. 'I... it is too late for that.'

The knife falls once more and he points towards the entrance of the tomb, unable to speak. As Juliet struggles to turn and see what lies there, the voices grow louder and closer. Even in his dazed state, Romeo recognises them – Friar Lawrence and his own servant, Balthasar. Before he can summon words they appear at the doorway and stare first at the corpse at the threshold, then in wonder at Juliet.

'What blood is this that stains this place of peace? Oh merciful Jesu – Count Paris, he is dead. Romeo, is that you? Did you kill this man here?'

'I did,' Romeo says. 'It is my sword lying stained with his blood. Are my hands not stained also?'

'What happened?' Friar Lawrence glances back over his shoulder. 'How did you come here this night? Did my message reach you some other way or did angels guide you?'

'Grief guided me, or so I thought.' Romeo turns back to Juliet and takes her hand. 'Now I wonder though. Fortune has intervened in ways I never dared hope.'

'Then... No, no more. I hear voices, there is no time for talk. Come with me, you must away both of you.'

'Away?'

The friar takes Romeo by the shoulders and comes little short of shaking the sense back into him. 'A cousin of our prince lies dead and the watch surely follows on his heels!'

He waves Balthasar forward and slips Juliet's arm over his shoulder. The two of them help her to her feet, still weakened by feigned death.

'Romeo, your sword!' Friar Lawrence hisses. 'You

may yet be forced to win your freedom. I cannot condone violence, but Balthasar and Juliet are innocents in this and I have seen watchmen do bloody harm on all present at a crime.'

'My sword? No, I'll touch it no longer – the blade has only ever brought me hurt. Never again will I wield such a weapon. If I must surrender myself and announce my crimes to stay hasty hands, I will do so. The guilt is mine alone, but I will not add to it unless God himself commands.'

'Guilt or innocence, they will take you if they find you and all love's work be undone.'

'Let us be quick then,' Romeo declares. 'I will carry Juliet, she cannot run yet.'

He sweeps Juliet up in his arms and so burdened seems to stand taller than before. With the friar and Balthasar in his wake, Romeo steps out through the entrance and casts around for the watchmen coming.

'Some wondrous angel's hand has intervened to offer us a second chance,' he says as they set off through the gloom. 'Let us be bold and grasp that hand before it is withdrawn.'

'To my last ounce of strength,' Juliet agrees.

'You must both go into exile then, for Romeo cannot stay. I will see you on the path,' Friar Lawrence says, leading the way with lantern held low to avoid betraying them. 'Then I will return and explain all to your families. Perhaps the same angel will help persuade your parents into sense and ending their feud. For the sake of Verona and their offspring now united, Montague and Capulet must be reconciled.'

'It is in God's hands now,' Juliet whispers. Let the stars favour us this night.'

One

Verona - 1401

A great flock of starlings wheels and dances in the darkening sky over Verona. The city's bridges and avenues are illuminated with lanterns like golden beads. The sky above is a haze of hearth-smoke and autumn cloud, but there is no concealing Verona's slow decline from the heavens. A thousand pairs of avian eyes witness the deeds on its streets, the hunger and the helplessness. Lamentations and entreaties rise in bitter columns of smoke. From such fragile threads the ancient memory of the flock weaves a pattern that tells of better times and current woes.

Unnoticed at first, a carriage rumbles towards the walls of Verona. The flock's vanguard swirls down to meet it, feasting on the insects it stirs up until they sense a change in the air. Then they swoop and dance all around the carriage, welcoming two long-absent children and adding a new thread to Verona's tapestry. Even the flock wonders what will become of Verona now, whether this return heralds rebirth or a final conflagration.

The driver and guard of the carriage, one dark and grave, the other fair and full of cheer, both wear long cloaks against the advancing chill of an autumn evening. They barely notice the starlings that sweep overhead as they chatter all the way to the city gate and are hailed by the soldiers of the Porta Palio.

'From where do you come?' calls the sergeant of the gate, holding his lamp across the roadway. 'The hour is late and the gate is locked at dusk.'

'From your home,' replies the swarthy man while his fairer and fatter companion reins in. 'We bring letters from Milan and passengers, too.'

'How many?'

'Five in all, and one of those not so patient as to submit to interrogation before a warm meal is in him.'

'Their names?'

Before the guard can reply, the carriage door bangs open and a young man swings out. He is tall and broad even for a fighting man, with softly curling brown hair that spills from his head. He wears the smile of a handsome rogue and the scars of one as quick to anger as to laughter.

'My name will be tattooed on your backside, Sergeant,' he bellows, 'if I don't get a cup of wine before the last light has faded. I recognise that voice, do I not?'

There is a laugh from the guard. 'As God is my witness, do I spy the Cattle-dog of Carmagnola? Messer Francesco, is that you?'

Francesco offers a theatrical bow. 'The very same – come to bless this unhappy place with my magnificent presence.'

'Then you are most welcome here, Messer, unless you hide a ravaging band in that carriage!' the sergeant exclaims, laughing. 'Open the gate!'

'I have no ravagers but Rufus and Aylward, both of whom you must know, for I've been tempted away from service for a time, Sandro.'

'You honour me, Messer by recalling.'

'As I do honour all those who stood with us on that dark plain, Sergeant.'

Sandro bows his head in recollection of the dead. 'Your pardon, but I must ask your business.'

'And so you have, Sergeant,' Francesco replies as he steps up onto the carriage. 'If any man questions me on it, I shall assure them you did your duty. Now the day is ended and I am weary from travelling, I will visit you tomorrow and toast those who cannot drink with us. Look upon my companions by all means, but their business is mine and my business is in service of your lord.'

The sergeant bows his head, the bond they share invoked, and waves the carriage forward. Francesco holds open the door, permitting the sergeant to peer into the gloomy interior with his lamp held high.

'A good evening to you all, gracious ladies and honourable gentlemen,' he says in a more subdued voice. 'All friends and companions of Messer Francesco are most welcome.'

'I thank you, Sergeant,' replies a neatly bearded man of middle years, the father of the family assembled. A life of less than noble ease shows on his lean face though his speech is that of a gentleman. 'We are indeed glad to count ourselves friends of this bold warrior.'

'Bold indeed, Messer, and such is the temperament required in Verona. The bravos that prowl this city are a faithless and ignoble breed, whether they be noble-born or hired scum. Like rabid dogs I warn you now, those bound to Montague and Capulet, and just as eager to tear strips off any likely prey. I would caution you as gentle-born to carry a blade whenever you are abroad.'

'I am not abroad,' the bearded man says. 'I am home – and I will carry no blade in either place.'

'You will not persuade him, Sando,' Francesco laughs. 'I've tried all the days I've known him, but he resists every tactic I employ.'

'In which case I will withdraw while my dignity remains intact. I claim no greater knowledge of strategy than yours, Messer,' Sandro says. 'I wish you all well and a good night, be safe in this lawless city.'

Francesco closes the door and raps his knuckles against the frame to signal the driver, Aylward, to move on. The carriage rattles through the gate and up the street where soon they are enveloped in the sounds of a city at its evening revels.

Of his companions, two are in their middle years and parents to the younger pair. Mother and father both look at Francesco with perturbed expressions while their offspring, a brother and sister, crowd together at one window. Each displays that wonderstruck manner of a childhood not so long since left behind. The young man is dark-haired like his father and soon to be of a size with him, but both children owe more in looks to their delicate and fairer mother.

'So, my friends, it is done,' Francesco says. 'We are here, you are returned safe.'

'Safe?' Juliet replies, incredulous. 'You think us safe yet?'

'Juliet, peace,' Romeo says. 'We are here and we are safe. Tonight we eat and sleep after our journey. Let us fear for tomorrow when it comes, there's nothing more to do.'

'Should you wish walls and steel about you, my lady,' Francesco adds, 'you have but to say the word. This writ I hold from our lord, the duke, is all it requires.'

Juliet shakes her head. 'A prisoner is not safer than a free man,' she replies. 'Anonymity is safer still. Twenty years have passed. I would keep our names from being spoken aloud until we have at least taken stock of the city.'

Romeo smiles. 'Then keep that shawl about your head, my love. This beard of mine may hide what the years have not, but your beauty is undiminished.'

'Pah, who in Verona remembers that foolish slip of a girl, beyond her name and parentage?'

'All of Verona – should you doubt it, take one look at your daughter there. Come, Estelle, turn your face this way. Remind your mother of the youthful promise she made good on. Now I may grant there is some tilt of proud Montague about our young model's nose, but the rest is the flower of Capulet that blooms still by my side. Even our friend Francesco can be brought to silence by her regard. God alone knows there is only one man in Italy with such power.'

Juliet is silent a while. She squeezes her husband's hand in acknowledgement of his words, but whatever truth she finds in them perturbs her more than the fear of advancing years.

'Should you wish, mother,' their son suggests with a sly gleam in his eye, 'we could trawl the markets and find you some substitute for father's beard there. None would recognise you even if all the city remarked upon it.'

Juliet makes an exasperated sound and swats at her son. 'Mercutio, you have too much of your namesake's mischief and high opinion of your own wit! While I wish he were here to welcome us, it is perhaps good he is not available to lead you into bad habits. Trouble is drawn to so sharp a wit; our own history is testament to that.'

11

While Romeo bows his dark head at the reminder, Francesco laughs. 'Fortunately our young Mercutio has the pretty eyes of his mother's house. Those will eject him from trouble as much as they imperil the maidens of Verona!'

Before Juliet can reply, the carriage jolts to a halt, lurching sideways as Rufus swings himself off the driver's bench.

'The inn, Messer,' he announces as he opens the carriage door. 'Do you want me to secure rooms?'

'I'll do that, anything to stretch my legs.' Francesco gives his companions an assessing look. 'I'll take these younglings with me too. Their instruction in the art of negotiation is sorely lacking and the innkeeper here is a miser of the first order.'

When neither parent objects the young pair tumble out of the carriage, while the guards set about unloading the luggage. Romeo and Juliet sit in silence together, hands clasped and lips pursed to contain the fears bubbling inside each.

'Are you ready to walk the streets of Verona again?' Juliet asks softly.

Above them the guards clatter away and resume their talk of past battles and lost comrades, casting a protective cloak of noise around those within. Romeo flinches as the trunks crash against each other and wrings his hands. The handsome youth he once was has not entirely fled, yet Romeo the elder is greatly more sober and serious.

'Will I ever be ready?' he replies. 'The warrant of arrest may be suspended, but most in Verona consider me a murderer and despoiler of graves – the worst of all men.'

'Yet they think you alive,' Juliet says, her small laugh

coming close to a sob. 'That much I cannot claim myself.'

'An opinion more easily changed. Your son would hide your beauty behind some scratchy beard, yet one look at your face will be enough for all.' He brings her fingers up to his lips and kisses them. 'Just as it is enough for me, each day, my love.'

Her eyebrow raises. 'Enough, my heart? Oh husband of mine, oh love of mine, I saw you at the tollhouse yesterday. That lady's maid had every man panting like dogs. Not even my noble husband was immune to her charms.'

'Then forgive me, Juliet, for I am a man as any other. You know I was a flitting youth and my eye may wander still, but the rest of me keeps true. My youth and foolishness are one and the same, but slowly my hair turns to grey. My forebears assured me that wisdom would accompany it and the further I am from intemperate youth, the more I agree with them.

'One eye may contain that last scrap of foolishness, but what man is without foolishness?'

'Oh indeed,' Juliet says, less sharp than before. 'None I have ever shared a bed with for certain!'

The gentle jibe brings a smile to Romeo's face. 'My other eye beholds only your light. This sinister bee may flit from blossom to blossom, but the trusty right is yours. I would pluck out the other for the offence it does you if not for—'

'Oh enough, my heart!' Juliet breaks in, won over and laughing. 'You are a capering fool even in your maturity, but I would not spoil the face I love still. Grey hairs become you better than they do me and so I trust your eyes and tongue and lips and fingers. I do not mean to dredge up old arguments, tonight of all nights when we must be of one spirit. An eye cannot fail to see, a heart cannot fail to beat and the drum I hear as I sleep beside you tells me all.'

'It tells you no lies,' Romeo insists, 'of that I swear.'

'Then I am content. I ask no more than a bath to wash off the stink of travelling and clean sheets. We have spent but one night together in Verona, our wedding night. I would take the pleasure of my husband's company here once more. Let our moans chase away the unquiet ghosts that have dogged our steps for twenty years. Tomorrow we begin to put them to rest.'

'So it shall be. Tonight is ours. Verona will wait for the morrow.'

Two

From the balcony of the inn, Juliet and Romeo watch the reaching threads of dawn cast an orange-gold tapestry over the rooftops of Verona. In the sleepy quiet of morning, they find themselves in a moment outside of time. They sit as adults who have lived and loved and brought life into the world, but the ghosts of the children they once were occupy those same seats – the vestiges of those spectral forms almost visible in the early light.

The memory of their romance echoes in the bones of each. It forever marks them, just as its consequences mark the city before them. The mourning drapes and the crumbling walls. The wariness in the eyes of the inn's servants when they see Francesco and his soldiers.

Few could look at the pair they are today and claim life has been cruel to them. They are clothed and fed, handsome and beautiful still for all the faint crinkles of age on their skin. Nonetheless life has not been easy either. Removed from Verona's lap of luxury, they have made their own way and endured the lean times that accompany any such endeavours, the small trials of two lives played out in close confines.

Words are spoken in anger, deeds performed in

haste. They have feared assassins and retribution, poverty and starvation – then worse. Their infant daughter revealed new realms of terror to a pair grown used to wariness. A hidden world they had not guessed at until glimpsed through the veil of fever, of accidents, and the casual cruelty of others.

But even in their darkest times the flame of their love could never be fully quenched. A spark remained and words were withdrawn, pride swallowed, frustrations smothered. Over long years the fire has remade them and bound them, the strands of their souls not merely intertwined, but forged into an alloy quite distinct from the original constituent parts.

As they sit and watch the dawn, fingers interlaced, there is no place where she ends and he begins. Without the other they are bereft, incomplete. Each has sustained the other through the long years of absence – the loss of family and home lingering like the ache of a phantom limb. Now they are returned, both feel a sense of rightness filling their hearts. A burden easing, for all their fears at what may yet come of it.

Caught in a moment that spans the years, Verona at dawn is clothed in the memories of childhood. Stone statues streaked with the tears of rain, tiled roofs tinged pink by the rising sun. The last flowers of summer are not yet extinguished by autumn, the scents and swelling voices unchanged by decades. Verona embraces them to her bosom once more, wordlessly and without reproach – a mother opening her arms to her lost children.

'The day looks promising, my friends,' calls a voice behind them.

Francesco stands at the doorway to the balcony. He stands every inch a condottiero of good means, wearing a rich green and yellow tunic that bears a fighting dog

16

badge. A broad belt detailed with silver keeps his sword at his hip, Francesco's hand resting easily on the scent-stopper pommel.

'But what does it promise?' Juliet asks. Her gaze is inexorably drawn back to the rooftops to where the great seat of the Capulets lies. Her own clothes are understated and plain, the colours of autumn with just a single copper brooch to fasten her cloak.

'On that point it has yet to inform me, dear lady, but promise hangs in the air nonetheless and fortune favours the brave.'

'Fortune is a fickle mistress. You are favoured one moment and her fool the next,' Romeo murmurs.

Francesco raises an eyebrow. 'You tell a soldier this?'

Romeo turns and regards his young friend. 'Forgive me, Francesco. You need no lesson from me there. If any man makes his own luck, it is you, so I trust to your endeavour and your fortune, too.'

'A wise course,' Francesco says with a broad smile. 'Now shall we steer that course to breakfast and chart our path for the day?'

'You have a plan?'

'It is a poor soldier who does not and I prefer to be a rich soldier. I have tried both and there is no profit in the former. Come, your children await.'

'We come anon,' Juliet replies. 'Leave us a little longer to the dawn.'

'As you wish.'

Francesco bows, as though the warrant in his pocket bears a lesser authority than Juliet, and retreats.

Romeo looks at his wife as they once more lapse into silence. The few lines of her face have not diminished her beauty. The delicate curve of her cheek

17

and soft hazel eyes are still arresting to even an idle glance. All the modest hardships of their life have given her a strength of spirit he can only envy.

He sees why Francesco cedes to her will so easily, as though reverent of her wishes, for Romeo is similarly commanded. For a while he simply watches her face – the faint play of emotion and the flit of her gaze from one moment of the past to another.

'Why do you look at me so?' Juliet says finally, uncomfortable under such scrutiny. 'Morning does not favour a mother of grown children.'

'It favours you.'

'Hardly, it is not so long until I am forty.'

'Not so great an age, certainly not when I am older still. Your beauty endures the turn of seasons and winter is not yet come for you.'

'The candle of last night was kinder,' she says with a smile. 'It hides some of the old woman I feel myself becoming. In the shadows I return to the girl you once knew.'

'No less the goddess of my heart,' Romeo declares, kissing the back of her hand with mock solemnity, 'in sensuous dusk or the blazing summer sun. That girl was but a girl. For all that she struck my heart, she was a princess eclipsed by the queen she became.'

'How very regal of you.' The smile wavers on her lips. 'Come now, king of my heart, the night is behind us and dawn has come. Answer me with the clear light of day.'

'Your question?'

She gestures at the waking city before them. 'Us, here, now. Is this madness?'

'Perhaps,' he acknowledges. 'We do not know, we cannot know.'

18

'And yet we risk all for it.'

'I did not drag you here, I made no such demand of you, my love.'

Juliet bows her head. 'Oh, I know – I was as much an architect of this as you, but as I see this map of our childhood follies I have more doubts than ever. We have been gone so long. We had a life in Milan and were safe at our lord's court. Our children know no other home yet we drag them into danger here. Are we mad to do so? Are we fools?'

'Perhaps,' he repeats. 'Perhaps mad, perhaps homesick and foolish where once we were lovesick and foolhardy. But this *was* once our home and my heart tells me we owe it this effort. Verona and the families we left behind.'

'At the cost of our children's lives? We sent letters, to your father and my mother. To cousins who might be sympathetic still, to my nurse and Friar Lawrence. But what did we receive in return? Silence – the deafening void of purgatory that envelops the excommunicated. Not one reply in all those years until well after your father's death and even then my mother dared not write immediately. Some fiction was written against us here. Some will oppose even the acknowledgement of our existence, for I cannot believe none would respond otherwise.'

'We heard of all too much in the years that followed,' Romeo says, lowering his head. 'Beloved Benvolio stabbed in the back; fights and arson, your mother's cousin thrown from a window! Crops destroyed, children and goods kidnapped as though the armies of condottieri were not plague enough.

'Verona has suffered in our absence and for our absence. Those who wished the chaos, who revelled in the violence, have prospered and cut down any who attempt to end it. Our noble houses are mere dens of brigands that somehow wear a coat of arms. A fiction was indeed written, my love. Chapters were added by all those with the pride or rage or self-interest to deny our existence.'

'While we are but a breath in the face of this storm, my heart,' Juliet whispers. 'We drag our children out of innocence and show them their birth right, a city crumbling under the crimes of their inheritance. Children who might – indeed *would* – threaten the positions of those who have profited from this cruelty. Your cousin, Antonio, for one and Reynard too, a Capulet only by marriage but captain-of-arms and heir still. Desperate men, cruel men, with no regard for the lives of children acknowledged by none.'

'Your father set a bounty on all our heads, were they any safer left behind? Would they have kept quiet and obedient in isolation at Pavia? Our children are grown and determined just as we wished they would one day live to become. And who else might unite Verona? Who else might unpick the tangle of this city but the family that ties two houses together?'

'We have a duty to Verona and our families, of that I do not deny, but does it outweigh our duty to Estelle and Mercutio? Verona is a tale to them, nothing more. A story told by the fireside, a play performed in the uneasy dreams of their parents. They do not feel its loss in their heart, birth-right and noble name be damned. Is there any good left in this city that we might gift them with? Or is life in Milan and the chance to forge their own path greater than any reward this madness might bring?'

Romeo hangs his head and is silent a long while. 'I

cannot say,' he admits at last. 'I would not have come here had I thought their lives in great danger. My own perhaps, but I owe this city a debt and it suffers while that is unpaid. I must try to undo the harm I caused, my duty demands nothing less. There is blood upon my hands and it has not washed off these twenty years away.'

'Is your duty to Milan or to your family?'

'My duty is to be a better man than the boy who killed your cousin. Without that I am no better than he – and that boy is unworthy of all the blessings I have been granted.'

Juliet reaches out and brings his hand to her mouth, kissing his fingers with her eyes closed tight. 'Thank you,' she says at last. 'You have stiffened the spirit of this old woman. I should not let fear rule me so.'

'Fear creeps like an evening shadow, so faint we do not see it grow. Without knowing its shade, we are helpless against it.'

'Then let us step out from under this canopy and towards the light of day,' Juliet declares, pushing herself to her feet.

They descend to join Francesco, Mercutio, and Estelle in the inn's dining room, but it is not usual for them to break their fasts so early. Francesco eats heartily while his companions pick at honeyed pastries and cast looks at the great doorway that opens onto the street. The awakening city outside calls to them all, they feel it stirring in their bones as one of Francesco's soldiers arrives back to report to his master.

It is the darker and taller of the two condottieri who accompany Francesco – Rufus. The mercenary offers Francesco a small bow but does not wait to be acknowledged before speaking in a low tone.

'Messer Francesco, the lady is home.'

'And her husband?' Francesco asks between mouthfuls.

'There also, but I'm told it is her habit to visit the cathedral each morning and pray for the soul of her departed daughter.'

'The cathedral? That is a long journey when there are closer chapels,' Juliet says.

Rufus bows. 'Indeed, but it is a journey she must do alone for her husband is elderly and does not walk far. The servants there – ah, forgive me, my Lady, but they speak of his frequent ill temper and the presence of swordsmen who do not deserve the name soldier, yet are that in all but name.'

Juliet nods. 'So my mother escapes each day and we will find her at the cathedral.'

'She is escorted still, but by kin not hired men. Lord Capulet is a man beset by suspicion and his household all keep a close watch on each other.'

'So they may recognise me if I were to approach her – but Romeo cannot go. She wrote to him in desperation, in vain hope. If he appears like a phantom without me at his side, she may react in haste.'

'Estelle would be proof enough,' Mercutio says in a quiet voice. 'She has the look of you, mother – more than enough for a grandmother to recognise.'

'One glance would be irrefutable,' Francesco agrees. 'You would not even need to speak to confirm her hopes as true, Estelle.'

'I would not have either of my children dangled like bait,' Romeo says, a sharp edge to his voice. 'This city is dangerous to all and the more so to us, there must be another way.'

'She will be safe, my friend, I swear it upon my blood.'

'Blood runs freely in a soldier's world, I would you hold Estelle's more precious.'

'More precious than my own, I so vow.'

'I will do it,' Estelle says firmly. 'The choice is mine and I choose not to be a quiet observer when I could help our cause. What would you have me say?'

'Should you have an opportunity to speak to her,' Francesco says, 'and I mean to provide that by means of charm or artifice, give her my name only and a time. Midday at her daughter's empty tomb. If she is pressed, her husband will surely not deny her that.'

'Why not invite her here? She is my grandmother. Surely she cannot bear us ill will?'

'We do not know her heart, not from a letter. It is a rare soldier who can conceal his intent when he stands before me, however. The ranks contain the sharpest and worst of men, well-practiced in armouring their hearts. An old woman's bent I should be able to discern when I look her in the eye.'

Juliet and Romeo exchange a look. Reluctantly, both nod their assent.

'Then we should be up and about ahead of the good dame,' Francesco declares. 'Rufus, fetch your comrade and we shall make our way to the cathedral.' Catching the man's arm as he turns, Francesco gives a small laugh. 'Though it may offend an honourable mercenary, turn your cloaks around before we enter public view. The arms of Milan may serve as armour on these streets, but I would prefer to walk unannounced if we can.'

He stands and lifts his own bundled cloak from a chair as Rufus departs. Unrolling it, Francesco briefly displays the blue serpent of the Visconti to his companions. It is a familiar sight to them all and one that is displayed from the municipal buildings of

23

Verona. Though their lord's rule is hardly popular here, the greatest hatred of Verona is reserved its own – divided upon the familiar lines of Montague and Capulet.

While blood is often shed by the servants of each, anyone displaying Milanese colours is protected. Neither side would risk incurring the wrath of their ruler by deliberately killing those in his employ. The current governor, Ugolotto Biancardo, is one of the many condottiero captains in Milan's service and a man whose record of violence is carved into the hearts of all Veronese.

Quickly fixing the cloak about his shoulders so that the grey interior is displayed, Francesco bows to his companions.

'As a man of great beauty and stature, I shall lead the way and naturally draw all curious eyes to my person, like a comet heralding change. Those who may recognise the youthful faces of old Verona will be occupied by me alone. The veiled stars that trail along behind me thus hidden in plain sight.'

At his words, Juliet and Estelle drape scarves over their heads, to set in shadow features that might stir long memories. Mercutio does not have the same resemblance of his parent, but still he has taken care to dress modestly by the standards of the young nobles in Milan.

By the time they are ready Rufus has returned with his barrel-chested comrade, the smiling archer named Aylward. Both are armed with swords, their cloaks pulled tight around them so the marks of Milan are also concealed. Francesco casts an eye over the whole party and nods briefly.

'Let us be off before Fortune turns her eye from us.'

'Surely not from a man of such beauty and stature,' Juliet murmurs, sparking brief, nervous laughter from her children.

'Ah my radiant friend, even Fortune must avert her eyes from the sun at its zenith,' Francesco replies. 'Come, I leave shadow in my wake.'

'I can only thank God I have my scarf to shade my eyes,' Juliet says. 'Lead on then to Verona's new dawn, noble Francesco.'

Three

The chatter of voices greets them as Francesco leads his company out into the street. A mile to the north, San Pietro Castle dominates the skyline, while closer to hand is Scaliger Castle, the governor's residence with the flags and soldiers of Milan plainly visible. Francesco walks ahead of the others, his soldiers at his heels. All three men are large and draw enough attention that the family following at a remove are barely noticed.

This quiet progression continues until they pass under the archway of the Braida Gate and into the market piazza. There Romeo falters and almost falls behind as memories assail him. A great crowd shifts and pulsates within the square as hawkers call their wares, children play and dogs bark. Every voice seems to be raised and oppressive to a man who has long preferred stillness and quiet.

The riot of sound remains undiminished to Romeo's mind, an unchanging and eternal part of Verona that would exist so long as its people did. Even the pentagonal tower, erected at the gate in his absence, does not change the heartbeat that now assails his ears. But as he stands there, the signs of a city in decline impose themselves until his heart begins to ache with the force of them. Shops that are shuttered, piles of refuse lying stinking on a cobbled piazza floor in significant need of repair. As he moves closer to the market stalls themselves, he realises they are fewer and far from laden with goods. The clothes are threadbare, the wares markedly simple.

'Is my memory tinted by the preoccupations of youth,' Romeo murmurs to his wife, leaning close, 'or is this market meaner in all aspects?'

'It is,' Juliet replies, not so quietly as to hide the worry in her voice. 'These vegetables are small and feeble, that cloth cheap and poor quality. Verona used to offer more to its people, but it seems that is a long time past.'

'Look, there – that merchant,' Romeo says. 'Are Milan fashions so gaudy that even the wealthy here look drab in comparison?'

'No, that is not why.' Juliet breathes in realisation. She casts around. 'What colours are missing?'

'Missing?'

'Even those better off, look at the colours they wear. None in red, none in blue. Fear has drained this city of colour – this is Verona in the eternal autumn of green and brown. None dares wear the colours of Capulet or Montague for fear of stumbling into the feud that festers here.'

Any more reflections between the two are cut short as a loud voice breaks through the hubbub. Romeo glances to their right and sees a tavern where several men are drinking despite the hour.

'Look, another mumbling clerk and his brood gawp at Verona's glory!'

Romeo hesitates then casts his gaze down, seeing the

red of the Capulets on those speaking, though he recognises none.

'Come, children,' he says, ushering them onward, but one of the swordsmen that have made Verona notorious is quicker.

The man leaps from his seat and darts to cut off their path, the smile of a bully on his face. He's a lean man with pock-marked cheeks, not a native of Verona by Romeo's estimation, but a southern mercenary most likely, come in search of easy employment. The troubled times of Lombardy are still less grave than those suffered by the Kingdom of Naples.

The great houses of Verona have made no secret these past two decades of hiring all manner of violent men to maintain their bloody feud. Almost as long-standing are the rumours that such ruffians are given free licence to run the whores, pickpockets, and gambling dens of the city, bleeding Verona dry of money as well as young scions.

The swordsman gives a pantomimed bow. 'Will you not come drink with us first?'

'I regret, I cannot, Messer,' Romeo replies as meekly as he can stand. 'We are on pressing business and must be away.'

'Then you be away and your womenfolk can enjoy our company instead.'

'Womenfolk?' called one of the seating men, a little older than the others with black hair and aquiline features. 'I think you should include him in your description, Giovanni.'

The man stands and gives Romeo a steady look that contains none of his companions' drunken jibes. This one is neither drunk nor unthinking; Romeo feels it in his bones. Though he has never seen the man before he feels a flicker of fear that he is recognised.

'What manner of a man wears no sword on the streets of Verona?' the man says eventually, making his slow way up to Romeo to look him in the eye. He turns to Juliet and then Estelle. 'With beauty walking at his side as though his wife, but surely she is mistress of this wretched creature?'

'Half a man I think, Reynard,' contributes Giovanni and the other nods.

'Half a man indeed. Certainly he is a man without arms and cannot be thought of as anything more. I wonder what else he lacks about his person?'

'Messer, I beg your indulgence but I must pass. My business is on behalf of the Lord Governor and would not wait.'

'In Milan's service? I think you also lack honesty,' Reynard spits. 'Milan's servants always wear his device and there again you are lacking.'

Reynard shoves him in the chest and Romeo staggers while Mercutio takes a step forward, hand on his sword. The other Capulets jump up at this sight and steel flashes into view.

'Oh, the young pup wants to join in the games? Come then, draw your blade. Let us see your mettle. Does it come from the same feeble vein as your father or your mother's, one richer and in sore need of mining I'd wager. Do you wish to join your sire in his lack of manly parts, boy?'

Mercutio looks from Reynard to his father, uncertain and not so hasty as to have drawn his sword yet. There is fear in his eyes and anger, too. He has never before seen his father spoken to in such insulting terms. That it is done in full view of Verona and his family too makes it all the more intolerable, but Milan is no sleepy haven of the peaceful. Mercutio is well aware that once steel is drawn, there is no going back. The time for words will then be forever passed; thought and calm eclipsed by haste and deed.

'My son,' Romeo says carefully, 'please, step back.'

Mercutio splutters in outrage. 'But father! To have him speak to you so—'

'Is my business, though I love you all the more for being willing to make it yours. We want no trouble, our employment demands none, so I ask you a second time, withdraw.'

'Come, boy,' Reynard goads, watching Mercutio with the cruel smile of a cat, 'the cock crows twice for you to withdraw, will you listen? Upon the third you will be dead.'

Mercutio opens his mouth to reply, but Romeo catches his eye and he shuts it again with a snap of the teeth. A crowd is building – keeping clear of any violence but forming a wall of bodies through which there is little escape. Where Francesco is he does not know; the man was striding ahead and is now lost from sight.

Then there is a flash of movement, a jolt of bodies being thrown to one side. Three familiar faces appear behind the front rank of onlookers. But still they are only four against six. If any officers of the city are present they are keeping clear, leaving the violence to play itself out.

'Your name is Reynard?' Romeo asks, a little louder and bolder than before. 'Reynard of the House Capulet?'

'It is,' the man replies, noting Romeo's changed manner. 'But my business is with the boy, not the cheap manhood that sired him.'

'You threaten a boy and you mock another's manhood?' Romeo says, more hotly than he feels in his heart. He has lived his years of exile in close guard over his tongue and has no intention of letting this man provoke him, but feigning rage is simple enough for a man once so intemperate.

'The boy wishes to threaten me, he will get the lesson he deserves. One more word from you and it will be all the sorer for him.'

'Your dispute is with me, Messer,' Romeo says. 'I have no sword, but you are young and unhandsome. No doubt you are well acquainted with the use of your own fist.'

Reynard's cheeks purple at that and in a moment Mercutio's presence is forgotten. He takes a step closer to Romeo and pauses, looking his adversary up and down. He is both taller and broader than Romeo – a large fighting man in the prime of his life, but not such a fool as to be blindly goaded.

'Only a fool and a coward goes without a sword on the streets of Verona,' Reynard says, 'and you are surely both.' He begins to unbuckle his sword belt. 'A lesson you will both receive now and then you'll lie unmanned in the dust while I teach that wife of yours more than you ever have.'

From behind him there is a roar and three or four onlookers fall sprawling into the abandoned space. One collides with a Capulet hireling and knocks him to the ground; the others stumble, howling between Reynard and Romeo. Before Reynard can snatch up his sword again Francesco bounds forward, blade drawn and a bucket in his free hand.

'God's teeth, man!' Francesco bellows at Romeo, 'did I not tell you we are too busy to be handing out lessons to gutless wretches today?'

Reynard snarls and darts for his sword, but Francesco ignores the threat. Instead he steps away and plants a heavy kick in the side of the fallen man, knocking him over once more to leave him groaning on the cobbles.

'Down puppy,' Francesco snaps, 'or you'll feel the flat of my blade.' He casts around at the crowd behind him, affecting to not care about the swordsmen closing on both sides. 'Now, gentlemen and ladies of Verona, who will announce these prancing ponies to me? Come, one of you must recognise them by their effete ways.'

'I am Reynard of House Capulet!' Reynard bellows, enraged, 'the finest duellist in Verona and my word is law among its citizens. Give me your name so I may know who I am about to kill.'

'Duellist? Hah, I spit on duellists!'

'Your name, Messer, I will not ask again.'

'My name? It will mean as little to you as duellists do to me,' Francesco snaps. 'I am a soldier, forged in the fires of battle and afraid of no courtier who waves his prick in the street.'

'So be it. You are a man without honour and you will die such.'

'Honour?' Francesco replies, circling as he speaks to address both crowd and Capulets as he goes. 'To those who deserve honour I offer it most humbly, but cowards have none. To those without honour I offer none, for fear of wasting something precious. A mole knows nothing of flight, a mule knows nothing of intellect, and a duellist knows nothing of true combat.'

'Take your stance and discover what I know,' Reynard says, levelling his blade in the pose of formal challenge.

Francesco hawks up a gobbet of phlegm and spits at Reynard's feet. He continues to circle, arms outstretched with sword and bucket to occupy all the space available. 'A duellist knows nothing,' he repeats, 'only foolishness and empty words. If you wish to fight, let us fight for I will not lower myself to duel.'

'Fight then, damn you!'

A broad grin appears on Francesco's face. 'You hear that, my Spanish friend? He wants a fight!'

Reynard half-turns to Romeo, assuming the words are directed at him. In the next moment a loop of rope flies out from the crowd and drops over the head of one Capulet hireling. The man gives a strangled scream and staggers as Rufus emerges from the onlookers. Off-balance the hireling flails and drops his sword before Rufus kicks his feet from underneath him. The man crashes to the ground, but Rufus is already moving, sword drawn to drive another of the Capulets back.

Just then a second figure appears from the crowd, roaring English curses as he swings his cudgel to fell a Capulet. Then Aylward is stepping over his unconscious victim, brandishing sword and cudgel towards the next foe. The man retreats to Reynard's lee and Francesco hurls his bucket at both. A great arc of water rises through the air. Reynard jumps himself aside, but the other Capulet does not see it in time. Filth explodes over him, provoking a cry of shock and outrage.

The moment of confusion is all that's required. The man finds Aylward's sword at his throat, while Francesco kicks the off-balance Reynard in the groin. The man yowls and crashes to his knees. Francesco stamps down on his sword then shoves Reynard sprawling back. Reynard gasps in pain and disgust as he lands in the spilled water that stinks of human waste, but his pain is such that he cannot yet command his limbs to remove himself.

'A soldier wins,' Francesco snarls at the remaining Capulets, frozen into inaction by the unexpected assault. 'Now throw down your swords or see how a soldier ends a fight.'

They stare at him, fearful and uncertain, so unused to being bested they do nothing in their confusion. The moment drags out, but before Francesco can repeat his demand Reynard struggles up, cursing and spitting, one side of his face smeared with excrement.

'Throw down our swords?' He growls and draws his main gauche. His movements are clumsy and his cheeks pale, but his grip on the dagger remains secure. 'First answer me this, what does a soldier do when he finds himself outnumbered? Do you think we are the only swords Capulet can muster? A dozen more will arrive in moments – do you think your trick will work a second time?'

Even as he speaks there is a commotion coming from further in the piazza. There are shouts of alarm and then the crowd parts and scatters – fleeing from the path of a group of armed men. Romeo feels his breath catch when he sees them, however. A torrent of memories swamps him as the blue of his own House of Montague comes into view.

Reynard's pale face turns sicker at the sight. He casts around for an escape route, but the press of bodies is such that there's nowhere to go. He can only snatch up his sword and turn the point towards his longer-standing enemy.

'What have we here?' calls the leader of the Montagues, a man whose face is familiar to Romeo. In a flash he realises the man is a second cousin, Antonio.

'Have the jesters come out to amuse us all? I see the colours of a clown and the face of a fool. It seems we will have some happy entertainment this morning, my friends!'

Their intent is clear, their weapons are drawn, but before they can cut the vulnerable Reynard down, Francesco steps into the way and the leader comes to a surprised halt.

'Messer, you appear to have strayed into my path,' the leader says. 'Please, move aside and let me about my task.'

'And your task is?' Francesco asks, unmoving.

'Dispatching the criminal, Reynard,' the man replies. 'It appears you have bested him and cornered the wretch, for that you have my thanks and my name – Lord Antonio of House Montague – should I be able to offer service to you in future.'

'You are more cordial than your quarry, Antonio of House Montague, but I regret I cannot step aside. The only service I ask is that you retire. This man is not your prisoner and yours is not the justice of Verona.'

Antonio raises an eyebrow then glances over at the man beside him. 'Did he mishear me?' Antonio asks quietly, a trace of laughter in his voice. 'Was I whispering to the angels or mumbling my prayers? Can the rustic not count swords perhaps?'

'I count as well as I can hear,' Francesco announces.

'Then I say again, step aside else I am forced to become less cordial.'

'I will not and I ask you to retire, my Lord. This man is not yours to deal with.'

'He is my enemy and I will treat him as such.'

'Your enemy perhaps, but *my* captive.'

Antonio peers over towards the remaining Capulets.

35

'Clearly you are new to the practice. My advice in future would be to relieve your captives of their weapons before considering them such. You seem to be outnumbered still, unless you call upon my assistance.'

'I do not call upon you and I say again, retire.' Francesco stands tall and proud in front of the Montague swords, eight men all in the livery of that house. 'Yours is not the authority here.'

'I am the Lord of Montague now my uncle is dead,' Antonio declares. 'None dispute this, and yet you say I have no authority? These streets are obedient to my will and so shall you be, else you be dead.'

'The streets obey you? Then please – command them. That is a trick I would like to witness. Will the cobbles heave up under our feet or is it just the streets you command while the piazzas obey this one?'

Antonio purses his lips, his face losing all trace of the boy Romeo had once known. 'Mock me again and I will become uncivil.'

Francesco shrugs the threat off and turns to look back at Reynard. 'Your word is law on these streets,' he says loudly. 'That's twice I have heard the claim in as many minutes. Do you both accept the claim of your enemy or are you both like crows squabbling over a corpse? You asked me, Reynard of House Capulet, what a soldier does when he is outnumbered? Well I am a condottiero of no modest name and so I do what all mercenaries would do. Spanish Rufus, Aylward, my loyal troops, I bid you turn your cloaks.'

With a flourish they both do so and there is a collective intake of breath. Francesco again looks around, gauging the reaction. With slow and deliberate movements he turns his own cloak to display the crest of Milan on his back.

36

'There is one authority on the streets of Verona and that is of its signore, the duke of Milan. He who claims otherwise should have a care.'

Francesco pulls a folded letter sealed with red wax from a pouch at his waist and holds it high for the crowd to see. 'My name is Francesco Bussone and I am appointed governor of this fair city. I hold here the full authority of Milan – the duke's personal writ charging me to see Verona restored to former glory. I had thought to observe the city a few days, to learn its moods and rhythms, but I see it is sickened indeed and my hand is forced.

'Antonio of Montague, Reynard of Capulet – you will both withdraw or be considered an enemy of Verona itself. Return to your houses and there you will stay until summoned. Be glad no blood was shed here this morning to worsen this shameful scene. You will await my call and pray for my mood to improve if you have any sense of preservation.'

Under the glare of their new governor, the men of both houses shrink back, the Capulets fetching up their downed men, and their leaders are forced to retreat, too. Each gives a look of hatred, as the tattered remains of their pride demands, before they go. The crowd has already begun to melt away and in moments there is no living soul within twenty yards of Francesco other than Romeo's family and his guards.

'My apologies,' Francesco continues in a calmer voice, 'my hand was forced and our plans are upturned.'

Romeo shakes his head and grasps Francesco by the arm. 'My friend – you came to our assistance and saved us injury or worse. There can be no need to apologise, not in this lifetime or the next.'

'Once more, you have our thanks and friendship,'

Juliet adds, offering him a slow, respectful curtsey that her daughter echoes.

Francesco smiles, the faintest pink in his cheeks showing that for all his years of soldiering he remains a young man. 'Something that is always welcome with me. But lady I fear I must steal away your husband, there is much I will need him to do now I have announced my appointment. The governor will have received a letter to expect me, but formalities remain. Would you make your appointment at the cathedral still?'

'I would. We will find a way to pass the message.'

'Then Rufus here will escort you and see you safe, I have trusted my life to him many times.'

'So shall we. May fortune once more turn her eye our way.'

'I demand that she does, since I am now the authority of Verona's streets and piazzas, too. We will see you this afternoon; I will have your belongings brought to Scaliger Castle and apartments readied. Until then, adieu.'

Four

Of all of Verona, it seems to Juliet that the cathedral remains least diminished by the passing years. In the light of the risen sun, its pale stone walls and red marble decoration take on a quality that eclipses the bustle of life surrounding it. Against a clear blue sky it stands apart from the rest of the city, imperious and impervious to the petty cares of the day.

The stark sight is enough to bring Juliet to a stumbling halt as she turns into the cathedral piazza. A breathless gasp escapes her lips, but Juliet is oblivious. Again she feels the ghost of her younger self beside her as time's lodestone draws her forward. Now that ghost reaches out ahead – eager to run to the mother she has missed so dearly. The mother within Juliet remains reticent however, a tangle of fears.

The piazza is modest compared to many in Verona. There is no market of wares, only the clatter of labourers about their work and the chatter of passing servants. A pair of red-feathered griffons stand guard at the entrance to the cathedral, their hawk eyes seemingly fixed upon a murmuration of black-frocked priests.

'Mother?' Mercutio inquires. 'Are you well?'

She nods. 'I am, but it has been twenty years and many miles between then and now. I find my feet grow heavy these last few steps.'

Mercutio slips a hand around her waist. 'What is a son for but to lean on when the years burden you?'

'Thank you. I need but a moment to compose myself. It would not do to call out or embrace her. My wits must rule my heart here.'

'Shall I go ahead?' Estelle asks. 'Rufus, come with me. It should prove no great feat to identify my grandmother while these two keep to the shadows. I shall ensure she sees my face as I kneel to my prayers. With Rufus to cloak me with Milan's protection, her attendants should steer clear.'

'They may yet, Estelle. Remember they are not servants but kin charged with watching my mother.'

'Doubtless there are both,' Rufus agrees. 'I was told she is only permitted to make the journey in the company of relatives – Capulets who will feel no fetter to their actions, should they wish to confront an unknown girl in public. But there will be others, the honour of a house at war demands it.'

'What if they recognise her?' Mercutio asks.

'What is there to recognise?' Juliet says with a shake of the head. 'My father's belief is cemented by years and fear. It is a fact long established that I died as a girl and my body was stolen away. Should Estelle resemble a cousin of theirs it is no great thing, we are all of Veronese blood so they will think nothing of it. My mother's reaction is what we must fear for this will come as a great shock. She cannot know to steel herself this morning of all mornings.'

'I wager the lady of a great house will keep a tight rein on her public face,' Estelle says. 'It is likely she will find a way to approach me and we can speak. If not, I have the name of the inn and our new governor already written down. I need but leave it for her to find.'

'And if she does startle at seeing you? Draws the attention of her attendants?'

'Then Rufus will see me right. I will be in a house of God – should I desire to leave no man will stop me. They may pursue me outside, but my assumed name I have known as long as my true one. While that takes place Mercutio may slip over and whisper the message himself.'

Mercutio nods. 'Francesco is no longer resident at the inn, but by midday she will have heard all that transpired. It will be simple work to fashion a private meeting.'

'Then the plan is formed,' Juliet confirms. She takes a deep breath and stands straighter, pushing her son's arm away. 'I am recovered, my resolve restored. My mother was always in the habit of rising early, let us proceed before she is finished and away.'

Estelle nods and turns with a determined sweep of the dress, Rufus falling in behind her in the manner of all bodyguards. Juliet watches her daughter walk without hesitation past the priests, several of whom pause to watch her until Rufus twitches his head their way. Then they all duck down, embarrassed, and shuffle away.

Pride swells in Juliet's head at the sight of Estelle, barely more than a girl in her mother's eyes yet so serene and assured. The worry remains, lurking deep in Juliet's belly, but for that moment, pride outshines all. The shadow of her girlhood trails behind and fades to nothing as Estelle enters the dim magnificence of Verona cathedral.

Mercutio takes Juliet's arm once more. 'Come, we

must find our seats for this performance.'

'Would that it were just a performance,' Juliet says. 'There is no rehearsal here, no script but Estelle's wits and the audience all bear knives.'

'I would pit Estelle's wits against both bears and knives,' he replies, gently squeezing Juliet's hand. 'And even if I would not, look up.'

She does so. 'At what?'

'The cathedral itself!' Mercutio laughs. 'All of Verona may be changed – both great houses may be diminished in numbers and honour – but the house of God is greater than they ever were and has endured worse. The centuries have made little mark upon this house. Is it any less magnificent than in your youth?'

Juliet shakes her head. 'It is unchanged.'

'As all who enter it know. Whatever dull grievances a man might carry in his heart, they are nothing compared to the shining glory he will find inside. To raise one's voice in such a hallowed silence would be to challenge God's majesty. No man in Verona, not bold Francesco nor arrogant Reynard, would so dare.'

'Then nor do I,' Juliet replies. 'Let us go silently and with all humbleness. God alone will judge our mission worthy of success or not.'

The swift and ready smile returns to Mercutio's lips. 'Then it is fortunate we are in the correct place to ask his favour.'

*

In prayer the pain increases. Lady Capulet presses her forehead onto her clasped hands, hiding her expression from the eyes around her. Easing her weight to one side lessens her discomfort, but she cannot hold herself that way for long. Soon she is half-slumped against the side of the pew box, thankful for the sturdy wooden screen her husband had erected to eclipse the stalls of the Montagues.

She takes long, slow breaths and waits for the ache to subside. It dims only a little, but that is enough and she straightens, aware her attendants are ever vigilant.

Always you watch, she thinks, glancing at the pinched features of her grand-nephew and jailor, Gennaro, and plump cheeks of Lucrezia, her lady-in-waiting and widow of Gennaro's cousin. *You see it all and God will judge your silence.*

Finally, she returns to her prayers. The words in her head are a jumbled mess, however, and she can only hope God understands. If he does, nothing comes of it. He grants neither strength nor respite. Each morning she prays here yet it bears only withered fruit.

At first she took to visiting the cathedral only as a way to escape her husband's ire, his movements hampered by gout. The shell around her soul had petrified long before. The seed of her faith was a dry and dead thing. It took several years for light to pierce that husk, for her to feel anything more than emptiness when she visited the cathedral.

Yet as my prayers fall unanswered, what light I once felt inside drains ever away.

She looks up at the altar – at Christ on the crucifix behind and the saints looking down from the painted dome above. Bloody light smears the white walls behind. The saints she will not pray to, they are mere men and their imperious faces cannot move her. But Christ himself bears no such pretensions. Beaten and bloody, he hangs on the cross and does not hide from his pain. For that, Lady Capulet finds love in her heart

43

for him. There she sees understanding, for all that her years of prayer go unanswered.

Is that why I come here still? The quiet is little solace when I am always alone and my prayers are just empty words. When I leave, the shadow of my husband's rage will still hang over our home. His cane will still strike as true as once his sword could, his tongue just as sharp.

She shifts again and considers pushing up to sit rather than kneel, but she does not wish Lucrezia to see the pain she is in. Lord Capulet's age matters not when she is just as old and this morning his temper has almost cracked her rib. Some cruel voice at the back of her head hates her for giving him just what he wants, to cry out and cringe, but she has never been strong enough to deny him.

Nor to flee, nor to throw myself into the river, Lady Capulet reminds herself with bitterness. *God would not grant me that strength and now I no longer ask. My hopes are humbler now. I pray for a letter to be received. I pray for a glimpse of the girl I lost.*

She bows her head once more.

I pray my husband to have strength, not I, that he may end this as I cannot.

Eventually she looks up again and across the nave to where the Montague stalls stand empty. There are others in the cathedral, many the same faces each morning and she notes them now that her empty prayers are done. The ancient woman who wears a mourning shawl over the deep lines of her face and has done throughout every long year Lady Capulet has been coming. The thin man who wrings his cap as he prays with a fervour Lady Capulet can only envy. The dark girl with the broken tooth who simply sits and stares towards the altar each day. The fat merchant's wife whose fine silk shawl never fully conceals the threadbare clothing underneath.

Those and half a dozen more are Lady Capulet's family now. Their faces are dear to her and their pain is her own. She charts her days by the tidal moods she sees in their faces, the waxing and waning of grief followed like the phases of the moon. As Christmas approaches she will give each a small gift – not enough to induce others to come day after day as they do, but she hopes enough to give some small comfort in the winter of their lives.

Her accounting of this broken flock is almost done when something catches her eye. Lady Capulet stiffens and a stab of pain makes her moan softly, bringing Lucrezia scuttling to her side.

'My Lady, are you well?'

Lady Capulet gives her a baleful look that makes the lady-in-waiting pale and briefly lower her gaze.

You know. 'It is nothing, leave me.'

'You will be expected back soon,' Lucrezia replies, not moving.

'Leave me.' *I will not be cowed by one such as you. I am not yet so broken.*

After a long pause Lucrezia bobs her head and steps back. The ghosts of memory flicker through Lady Capulet's mind; a babe in arms, a young girl clattering towards her with arms outstretched, a young woman abed as though asleep. Through blurred eyes she casts her gaze again, searching for what has snagged her thoughts and dragged them to where her woe resides.

Her heart lurches and jolts like a kite caught by the wind when she finds it. In the second row of public benches there is a girl, half-a-decade older than the daughter Lady Capulet lost. She wears a simple dress of green wool, but elegantly cut and modestly decorated. A grey cloak hangs from her shoulders and a russet silk scarf has been slipped back to reveal hair braided in the Milan fashion. All this Lady Capulet notes by unconscious habit, the instinct of one who has presided over Verona's highest society for decades. It is the face that makes her breath catch.

She finds her hands closing like claws around the raised front of the pew. Her aging knuckles pop and ache, but she cannot move or even draw breath. The rest of the dim cathedral seems to recede from view and her heart tolls fearfully in her chest. It is the only part of herself she is aware of, a hollow echo that threatens to burst her eardrums.

And then the girl looks up and the spell is broken. Lady Capulet gasps – given strength once more by the intensity of the gaze that settles upon her. She shudders both with effort and emotion as relief and fear clash violently inside her. This is not her daughter nor the spectre of the girl she lost, but there is so much of Juliet there the meeting of their eyes can be no coincidence.

For one long moment she stares at the girl then feels tears roll from her eyes. Through joy or terror she cannot say, for both ring out from her heart, but her mind screams with exultation.

Juliet is alive! The letter spoke true, my girl is alive. May Hell's legions take me if I have so forgotten her face to mistake her daughter.

Lady Capulet hardly notices the tears trickling down her cheeks, but Lucrezia does and scuttles forward once more. Gennaro looms in her wake.

'My Lady!' Lucrezia gasps. She receives no reply but the fixed gaze on Lady Capulet's face is enough. She follows it to the young girl just as she looks away.

'Who is she?' Lucrezia asks urgently. 'I do not recognise her.'

'I have never seen her before,' Lady Capulet says in a whisper, 'but she is lovely. My soul is restored by the very sight.'

Lucrezia straightens up, a frown of confusion on her face. She is a woman of little wit and fewer wits, easily set adrift on the tide when faced with the unexpected. She wrings her hands and looks left and right as though this is a test of some sort. Only when the girl gets up to leave does she decide to act.

Lucrezia marches across the nave, barely pausing to curtsey as she passes the altar. Her hand is already outstretched to grasp at the girl's arm when a figure slips between them. Gennaro growls and follows as a burly foreign soldier blocks Lucrezia's path. He's a darker man than most Italians – a Spaniard, Lady Capulet would guess – with a twisted black tattoo on one cheek and a sword at his hip. Lucrezia falls back with a gasp and Gennaro takes her place.

Lady Capulet for one short moment wishes that he does not stop, that Gennaro ignores the unspoken threat and carries on to his death. By the time the Spaniard speaks, however, she has cursed herself for the thought in such a place and time.

'Far enough, Messer,' he says, quiet words that cut through the hush. 'My lady wishes to be left to her prayers.'

He speaks well for a foreigner – a common man's accent for sure but properly learned unlike the English mercenaries who can only to shout garbled demands for beer.

'Get out of my way,' Gennaro demands, astonished

that any mercenary would block the path of a Capulet. He doesn't even see the style of clothing that tells Lady Capulet the foreigner's cloak will likely display Milan's blue serpent.

'I choose not to.'

Gennaro takes a step forward only to be shoved bodily back. He is a large man, taller than the Spaniard, but is rocked on his heels. Lady Capulet can see his cheeks redden and his hands tighten into fists. He glances to his right and summons their two guards with a look, the men scampering forward pulling cudgels from their belts.

Lady Capulet can only watch the whole scene with astonishment. She barely notices a second stranger slip across her view as Lucrezia glares at the startled onlookers. Younger even than the woman, the man does not look at Lady Capulet. He simply strides past and whispers 'Francesco of Carmagnola,' before heading back towards the door while Lucrezia and Gennaro are occupied.

Lady Capulet blinks once as the words filter through her brain – she knows no one of that name. She opens her mouth to call after him but catches herself. There is something familiar about the young man and she has to fight the urge to watch him go, instead allowing the mercenary's distraction to snare her, too.

'My name is Gennaro Capulet and I would speak to the girl,' Gennaro repeats in a low, angry voice. 'Get out of my way or be dragged from this place and beaten you until you beg our forgiveness.'

By response the man shifts his feet to better see the advancing guards and places his hand around the hilt of his sword.

'You would dare profane the house of God?'

Gennaro gasps.

'You profane it with your presence already, Messer,' the man replies with quiet assurance. 'Molest the lady in any way and I'll cleanse this house of you.'

'May God strike you down for such threats of death before the altar.'

'May God strike me down if I cannot cleanse this temple without killing.'

Gennaro turns to the guards and points to behind the benches where onlookers are retreating. 'The girl, there! Hold her.'

'Do so,' the Spaniard says in a louder voice, 'and you both will hold nothing again – I will take your thumbs in Judah's judgement.'

'You speak the words of a good Christian, but threaten bloodshed in God's house?'

The foreigner makes no reply so Gennaro glances back and points again at the girl. Before he can speak, however, the Spaniard's hand darts forward at the offending digit. With a swift jerk he dislocates Gennaro's index finger and her grand-nephew crumples to the floor with a wail.

'I'll shed no blood,' the man declares, 'not in this place, but the blows of a bishop will serve me well enough.'

'Damned and twice damned you are!' Lucrezia gasps in a shrill voice, hurrying to Gennaro's side and dragging the man up. 'The House of Capulet does not forget such an offence and God's judgement will greet you after.'

'God is not so prideful that this offence surpasses acts of battle,' the man replies. 'Whatever horror awaits my soul for those, the pride of the Capulets holds no such terror.' With that he turns and sets off after the young woman.

Lady Capulet sees her lady-in-waiting twitch at the mark of Milan on his cloak. To her surprise, however, it gives Lucrezia only modest pause before she whispers to Gennaro. With gritted teeth she nods and sets off after the young woman and her guard. Lucrezia hurries over and takes Lady Capulet's hand.

'My Lady,' she says firmly, 'you must leave now.'

Lady Capulet looks up at the Christ, enduring his pain for the sake of others. She nods as she pushes herself to her feet with a revived sense of purpose. 'Yes – I believe you are right. The time has come.'

Five

No longer a girl, Juliet thinks as she watches her daughter leave the cathedral. *As the moon and stars turn, so our children take our place in the world. Once I taught her to be brave, now she shows me as I become the child my of fears.*

Estelle does not rush. She walks in stately fashion without looking back, as majestic as a queen before her subjects. Rufus is on her heels while the Capulets – none of whom she recognises – loiter like startled wild-dogs. The guards are both foreign sell-swords and neither is anxious to test himself against a seasoned fighter such as Rufus. Gennaro, perhaps a distant cousin who was a squalling child when Juliet fled Verona, seethes and boils with frustration, but he cannot go alone. He knows his damaged finger makes him all but useless against a trained swordsman.

Juliet is content to linger too. Of the two dozen worshippers in the cathedral only Mercutio has left. The rest stand in shocked silence – their refuge from the city's troubles suddenly violated.

'Come, Lady Capulet,' the lady-in-waiting says loudly, taking her charge by the elbow and hustling her forward.

Juliet forces herself to draw further back into the shadows as her mother is manhandled and complains loudly of such treatment. For all it pains Juliet to witness that and do nothing, she realises it is a ruse. The years have been hard on her and old age has her firmly in its claws, but the mother Juliet knew would not speak so in public. In exaggeration however, she can win a few more moments for her granddaughter to escape.

Eventually the Capulets follow and the more ghoulish of penitents follow them out into the light of day. Anonymous behind her scarf, Juliet follows those and slips into the burgeoning crowd outside. There, Rufus again draws all eyes to himself while Estelle and Mercutio disappear from view, heading towards the bridge.

Gennaro and his guards have stopped a safe distance from Rufus who faces the cathedral door, sword and dagger drawn. To Juliet's horror, however, the nobleman is in the midst of calling to a group of men in Capulet colours at the mouth of a side street. As he instructs them to follow Estelle and they move to obey, Rufus takes a few steps their way. The men hesitate, but it is plain to all that Rufus cannot delay them without turning his back on the others.

Gennaro nods and draws his sword with difficulty, transferring it to his left hand while his guards pull their weapons.

'You would draw against Milan?' Rufus declares loudly.

'I would draw against a villain in a cloak,' he replies. 'One who has made threats and drawn first. Clear your lowborn hide from my path or make that cloak your funeral shroud.'

Again Rufus checks around, keeping himself in wary movement while he assesses the situation. The other Capulets are gone from the piazza but the two guards stand on either side and it is not easy for him to keep both in view. Juliet opens her mouth to shout for peace but catches herself in time, knowing that she cannot draw their attention.

He is trusted by Francesco and has no high-born pride to satisfy, she reminds herself. *However brave Rufus might be, he will not cast his life away.*

'Do you yield?' Gennaro calls again. He raises his sword unsteadily, but it is enough to run through a distracted man and they both know it.

'I will sheath my blade,' Rufus replies after a short pause. 'But should you intend to molest my mistress still, that I cannot abide.'

'I wish her name, that is all. Her presence disturbed my noble kin and I am charged with her safety.'

'The noble lady is safe.'

'And your mistress flees like a dog. We have had cruel imposters send messages to my lady here, fanciful claims of kinship and demands for money – criminals who would prey upon an old woman's grief.'

'My mistress is neither.'

'Then tell me her name?'

Another pause. 'I am bound not to give it.'

'A masked identity,' Gennaro scoffs. 'That great harbinger of honest intent. Do you put up your sword?'

Rufus nods and with no great haste returns his weapons to their sheaths. 'It is done,' he states. 'Now leave with your charge.'

'I will have words yet with your mistress,' interrupts the lady-in-waiting, pushing forward.

Rufus shakes his head. 'She has no words for you. I

tell you now her business in Verona is neither criminal nor bears ill-will to the Lady Capulet, but you may not accost her.'

'I will be the judge of that.'

At that moment, the Lady Capulet Juliet remembers steps forward. 'In the shadow of God's house, we do not presume to judge,' she declares in a firm voice. 'Lucrezia, I am fatigued and we will return.'

'But—'

'I said we will return. When the reaper finally brings me to harvest and you are blessed with our Lord's gentle affections, then you may make such demands. Until that day, as my breath persists so does my will.'

Lucrezia's mouth tightens in a line. Juliet can see that her mother's position is far from absolute, but who in the city could fail to recognise the Lady Capulet? Whatever forceful reminder of her position she receives in private, in public she remains mistress of a great house and her command is to be obeyed.

'What about the men I sent?' Gennaro asks sulkily, cradling his injured finger.

'Run after them if you wish,' she replies airily. 'Leave them to their fate if you do not.' She pauses. 'Wait – they are headed towards the bridge are they not? Well then, run to the near bank and whistle for them. Call my husband's dogs back to their kennel. The over-eager hounds are gored by the boar, the properly trained will obey and survive.'

'Boar?' Gennaro asks, looking confused.

'The swine that root on the far shore of course,' she replies. 'Our house's enemy claim that district, be quick or you will explain their loss to Reynard.'

*

A breeze whips up off the river and lashes Estelle's back with spray as she flees across the bridge. Rusty leaves swirl on invisible currents and spots of rain fall like the city's weary grief. The scourging wind spurs her on and she runs as best she can for the far shore, panic gnawing at her belly. Mercutio is just behind her; she can hear his measured feet and muttered oaths. She glances back and sees men in red pursuing them, more than Mercutio could ward off alone.

A prayer for Rufus' safety runs through her mind before her brother gives a cry and points past her.

'There!'

Estelle looks and sees a knot of figures wearing the blue tabards of Montague retainers, four faces turned their way.

'Keep going!' Mercutio adds. 'They will sniff a fight and be eager for it.'

Estelle does not reply, too concerned with keeping her balance. Not since she was a girl has she run like this and the fashions of Milan do not encourage such activity. When she risks a second glance behind she sees the Capulets are almost upon them. Mercutio realises it in the next instant and he stops, drawing his sword with a shout.

'No!' Estelle shrieks.

The Montague men are still a way off, but as Estelle stops she sees them break into a trot.

'Wait, check your blades!' she implores them all as the three Capulets draw steel and Mercutio stands with dagger and sword ready.

They are militiamen in Capulet colours. Estelle can see from their faces how young they are. Three dark Italian boys; not seasoned mercenaries, more likely farmhands not long ago. As the city suffers and periodic plague rolls like a barbarian horde across the landscape, so more fodder for the feud is drawn from the countryside in search of a wage.

'You must come with us,' the older of the three demands.

He is a few scant years older than Estelle herself, but a broken nose and wide shoulders suggest him the most experienced fighter there. Age means little when men like Francesco go to war at twelve. Nonetheless, she knows he will not wish to cross swords with a nobleman like Mercutio, trained in combat as all young men of good birth are.

'You have no hold on us,' Mercutio warns, sword and dagger held out in anticipation of attack. 'Withdraw and let us go in peace.'

The man glances past him and grimaces. 'You will come now!' he demands, waving his companions forward to encircle them before the chance was lost. 'House Capulet demands it.'

Mercutio and Estelle edge back but then the clatter of boots heralds some measure of salvation. Four Montagues appear on their right, so alike their enemies they could swap tabards and Estelle would have little certainty of who served what.

'House Capulet has no claim on us,' Mercutio insists loudly.

'Our orders say otherwise.'

'Your orders come from a worm-ridden old fool,' joins the leader of the Montagues. 'Pursue them and the worms will have you, too!'

'This is none of your concern,' spits the Capulet, but he draws back a shade all the same. 'Withdraw and leave us to our business.'

The man laughs. 'My concern goes to anyone forced to deal with curs. You are outmanned here, tuck in your tails and run.'

'Montagues do not count as true men,' the Capulet replies, retreating still. 'They whine at the doors of their whorehouses, begging to lick up the scraps.'

'I'll take your balls and take your life now!' the Montague cries, but before he can close the ground enough to strike a blow there is a loud whistle from the further shore.

At the end of the bridge Estelle sees the Capulet nobleman, Gennaro, who had attended her grandmother with his two guards. Gennaro is waving them back and the Montague laughs loudly. One moment of inaction is all he needs and he darts forward to deftly slice at the Capulet's buttock with his sword. The wounded man cries out and leaps away, not badly hurt but face flushed red with rage.

'A coward's touch!' he howls. He swings his sword wildly and the ring of steel echoes out.

'The only touch a Capulet understands!' comes the reply.

Estelle sees the further Capulets start to run, hearing the clash of blades, and the Montagues spread out across the width of the bridge. Mercutio retreats towards her, ushering Estelle back, while in the distance she sees the distinctive shape of Rufus advance too and she gasps in relief.

Outnumbered, the Capulets begin to give ground. As the Montagues drive them back a strange animal shriek cuts the air and makes every man recoil. Estelle gasps as a dark ragged shape rushes between them. A hooded grey figure throws itself at the reaching blades – heedless of the danger.

57

The howl is unrecognisable as the words of man, but it conveys fury as palpable as a thunderstorm. Mercutio puts himself and his sword between his sister and this new threat, but the crazed apparition ignores both. Estelle can see no face beneath that hood – little trace of humanity at all in the clawed, filthy fingers that emerge from within a torn and stained robe. There is no doubt, however, their ire is directed at both houses without favour.

The hirelings hold their ground for a moment before one essays a cut at another and steel rings on steel. With no thought to safety the figure leaps at the crossed blades, screeching wordlessly with such intensity it hurts Estelle's ears. One sword nicks its arm, but the figure pays it no care and shoves the blade aside before flailing at the one who struck first. Under such a furious assault the Montague punches his attacker, but the blow is ignored. He finds himself slapped and scratched, a thin fistful of hair yanked clear out, until he scrabbles clear with a yelp.

The figure finally turns Estelle's way and she glimpses the mad wide eyes of a man – a monk she realises – beneath the shadowing cowl. His beard is straggly and unkempt, his face a mess of scars while his jaw hangs slack to expose broken teeth and a mutilated mouth. He stops as he looks at her and goes suddenly, terrifyingly still.

For one long moment Estelle is convinced that he is going to pounce upon her, rend her with teeth and nails. Mercutio clearly thinks the same and levels his sword, but the monk's crazed wailings diminish to the yowl of some wounded creature. He wavers and staggers, now more an old man than the elemental force he appeared as, but his gaze never leaves her.

One Montague is emboldened by the change and swipes a mailed fist across the monk's cheek. The monk stumbles and almost falls, but some part of his furious strength remains and he slowly turns to face his attacker.

The Montague glances back at his comrades, a bully's grin widening on his face, and he swipes at the monk again. This time the monk does not stagger, he takes the blow full on his face. When the fist is drawn back again he spits a mouthful of blood back.

Cursing, the hireling raises his sword, but before he can strike there is a shout from behind. Estelle turns and sees a crowd of citizens watching – anonymous in their dull browns and greys, keeping clear of the feud playing out once more on their streets. From somewhere within that mass, safe from retribution, a voice cries "shame" and the call is taken up by the rest. The Montague's arm falters and before long the man leading them has grabbed it and pushed the weapon away.

'This is done,' he announces. 'Let the dogs lick their wounds.'

He gestures to the blood dripping from the buttock of a Capulet and his comrades laugh feebly. They withdraw, the Capulets already retreating back across the bridge to the protection of their late-arriving comrades.

Soon it is just Rufus standing there, a bewildered onlooker, while Estelle and Mercutio are left alone with the monk. He makes no move towards them, but does not leave either. He stares at brother and sister with searching eyes while the hesitant common folk of Verona creep past unnoticed to resume their day.

'You have our thanks, Messer,' Mercutio says in a croaked voice.

He offers a stiff bow. Estelle can tell her brother is nervous and unsure, but they were both raised to act a

59

certain way. She finds herself curtseying without any conscious thought. The monk makes no sign he has noticed, but at last he shuffles forward and raises a thin, scarred hand. Mercutio tenses but it is clear the monk means them no ill. Slowly, as though approaching a skittish colt, the monk approaches Estelle and shifts the scarf to better show her face.

The monk reels at the sight and the strength falls from his limbs, like a puppet with its strings let loose. Somehow he manages not to fall. His bloodied and ruined mouth now hangs open in wonder, not rage. Estelle finds herself spellbound as she watches emotion cascade across that horrifying face. Before either she or her brother find the breath to speak the monk's face turns to sheer terror.

He backs away, hands raised like a sinner before the gates of heaven, then turns tail and flees. In moments he is lost in the crowd. By the time the spell is broken and Mercutio takes a few steps to follow, he is gone.

*

Juliet follows the crowd that had gathered at the end of the bridge. The people of Verona are well used to abandoning places until the blood is spilled and honour has drunk its fill. She passes the Capulets with downcast eyes, but they are not looking for her or anyone else. Once they are gone she catches the sleeve of an old woman carrying a basket of eels.

'Good woman,' she says in an apologetic tone, 'do you know what happened?'

The woman eyes her suspiciously, noting the cut and colour of her clothing before she replies. 'You are new to Verona?'

'I... yes.'

'Just the usual trouble that – or have you come so far you've not heard talk of the plague upon our houses?'

'The feud I know of,' Juliet replies, feeling a pain in her chest as she speaks. 'But how did it end there?'

'The last man of this city to live without fear and made mad because of it,' she says. There is bitterness and shame in her voice. 'The last fragment of Verona that once was.'

'Mad?'

She nods. 'A monk – none know his name, but they say the city speaks to him and that has broken his mind. He hates the great houses and will not stand aside when they fight, but he is the only one.'

'Where does he live?'

'He sleeps in the shrine Lady Capulet built in her daughter's name, at the entrance to the graveyard near San Fermo.' The woman hesitates. 'Best you do not go there, my Lady, he's a wild one – a lunatic. They say he tore out his own tongue when the city began to whisper in his ear.'

'How long?' Juliet asks, a wave of dizziness breaking over her.

'Years, my Lady. Decades. They say he was called to the city when Lady Capulet built that shrine. He's been here ever since. He spends his days walking the river-bank or the city itself.'

'But he is a monk?'

'Perhaps once. He wears a friar's habit, but no men of the church dare go near him. He shames them, my Lady, for they do not speak out against the violence.' She hesitates and her voice gets quieter. 'He shames us all – for the fear we hide in our hearts. Folk say when the last true man in Verona dies, the city will die with it.

The families will tear each other apart and God's judgement will come down upon us all in sword and flame.'

Juliet feels the weight of that judgement upon her shoulders and takes a few wobbling steps to the side of the bridge to steady herself there. She hardly notices as memories of a grey friar's habit strike her with the force of a stooping falcon.

Lawrence.

Six

As the wings of dusk stretch across the sky, Francesco stirs from his desk and goes to the window. He watches the sweep of birds hunting for insects in the last of the light, but his thoughts are elsewhere. More than once he makes to return then stops, too restless and distracted to look through any more papers. He curses under his breath, coarse words in a refined room, and watches life continue outside.

In the courtyard below he can see soldiers, clerks, servants and stable hands – some in the livery of Milan, but all brisk and purposeful now that Scaliger Castle has a new master. A brief smile appears on Francesco's lips. What stories have been told about him, he can only imagine. Aylward is a master of many trades. The man's careless talk is as skilfully guided as the arrows he shoots. Every man, woman and child in the castle will tread carefully and work dutifully after hearing Aylward holding court over a cup of wine.

'The myth of a man can be shield and sceptre both,' Francesco says to the evening air. 'But this is no barracks and there is a city beyond these walls. Some are enemies, some are fearful of power. All will need to trust me before this can succeed. Yet it is in the barracks I know my place and the place of all things. There I was raised and my heart beats to its rhythm. Now I step away from what is allotted and find myself fearing what may come of such temerity.'

Behind him stands the great desk that once belonged to Prince Escalus, flanked by standing lamps of worked brass. A thick rug in the Ottoman style occupies the centre of the room. Low-backed settles occupy two sides of the rug while old throne-like oak chairs flank the fire. The walls are dominated by the portrait above the fireplace – a large and imposing image of Verona's true lord.

Gian Galleazo Visconti, Duke of Milan among many other titles, is a man whose stern visage gives away little in the flesh and the artist has captured that inscrutability. Francesco knows not to mistake the trust and faith placed in him with great affection. He is a servant of his lord and no man is more than a single thread bound within the fabric of life.

He returns to the view and something catches his eye: a soft note of calm amongst the bustle. A woman with her back to him, wearing a plain grey cloak. By her carriage alone, Francesco can tell it is Estelle. Though young, she bears a quiet grace that marks her from the crowd. She stands less erect than most women of high birth, each step seemingly considered and placed so as to avoid disturbing the ground. He knows the years of Estelle's childhood taught her to walk softly, aware of a distant threat, even as those same years instilled the ferocity of motherhood in Juliet.

Francesco watches Estelle go to the garden below, enclosed from the rest of the courtyard by hedges and potted orange trees. A fountain stands at its centre and there Estelle sits on a bench to watch chaffinches bathe in the fountain. Once settled she remains very still, lost in the capering of the birds with her hands clasped tight in her lap. He watches her a little longer before a slight shiver trembles her shoulders.

Driven by a sudden urge for fresh air, Francesco snatches up his sword and leaves his study. His great boots echo loudly on the vast stone staircase down to the ground floor, clerks and servants alike stepping aside from his path. On impulse he snatches fruit from a basket carried by one young girl, a pomegranate, and carries that outside. As the first lamps are lit around the courtyard, Francesco enters the enclosed garden and hesitates inside the gloomy threshold.

There is no reaction from the figure on the bench, head still covered by her cloak, so Francesco steps awkwardly forward – caught between a desire to speak and an unwillingness to disturb Estelle's thoughts. At the movement she flinches and draws back, but the surprise lasts mere moments before Estelle gives him a wan smile.

'Oh my faith, you startled me,' she exclaims, rising from the bench to curtsey. She pushes back the hood of her cloak to reveal the neat braids of her hair.

Francesco waves the gesture away, embarrassed by such formality.

'My apologies,' he says. 'I intended nothing of the sort.'

Estelle's smile widens. 'I should hope so. Startling the young ladies in your service would not be seemly to your position, My Lord Governor.'

'I shall try not to disappoint you, my Lady.' He pauses. 'I... I came to see if you were well. After the shock of earlier.'

She inclines her head. 'I thank you for your concern, Governor.'

'Please, Estelle – I would not wish our friendship to wither into formality because of some temporary appointment.'

'Nor shall it,' she assures him. 'But your friendship to us all is valued sufficiently for formality. We would not wish the city to see your attendants forgetting their place.'

'The city is not watching us.'

She glances back up at the windows overlooking the courtyard. 'Some part is, of that I am certain.'

'Surely we can sit and talk still?' he says, indicating the bench. 'My splendour will no doubt suffer worse before the day is ended.'

'Oh indeed,' Estelle says with a twinkling grin. 'The evening meal is not yet upon us, after all.'

He gives her a mock frown. 'A little more formality, my Lady, if you please? I am governor of an entire city after all and carry the grandeur of Milan with me.'

'My deepest apologies!' Estelle laughs as she sits, leaving space for him to join her. 'I had thought that a pomegranate, but I see now it is the grandeur of Milan.'

He glances down at the fruit in his hand then holds it out. 'Ah yes, this. I had thought to give it to you. A shock can upset the appetite just when the body needs feeding all the more. You seemed pale and ate little earlier, something sweet may revive you.' He shrugs. 'Now I am less inclined to such a gift. I would not want the city to think I was giving away Milan's grandeur.' He sits beside her and turns the fruit in his hands. 'Perhaps my lord can spare half, however.'

'Then I would thank him for his munificence.'

With practiced swiftness Francesco draws his eating

knife and makes a few deft cuts. Breaking it open he offers over the glistening red chambers.

'Does the duke's generosity extend to spoons?' Estelle enquires.

'It ah... no, it does not,' Francesco says with a short laugh. 'He prefers his subjects do not depend so heavily on the state.'

'Very well, my Lord Governor, I am suitably chastised by public policy.'

With her finger and thumb Estelle plucks a few seeds and pops them in her mouth before delicately licking her fingers clean.

'It is delicious, thank you.'

They sit in silence a little longer; small Estelle neat and composed; great Francesco discomforted and shifting.

'I could not spare the time to speak to you earlier,' he says at last. 'For that I am sorry.'

'Oh Francesco, do not think of it. It was a shock certainly, so soon after the confrontation with Reynard, but we are safe. Rufus served us well and I am recovered. You cannot take on the demands of a city and also worry over a frightened girl.'

'I can do both,' he says, hand twitching towards hers before halting, 'and one is more urgent than the other. Verona's woes will linger through to morning and beyond. There is little more I can do until I meet with the heads of Montague and Capulet. I have had many moments of fear in my life and often few friends to share the burden with. Had I been able to come to you sooner, I would.'

She nods in understanding. 'I am grateful you are here now. No more need be said. In truth my head is still awhirl, but I now feel I will be able to sleep tonight.

I pray the new day will refresh all. I do not wish to repeat the experience, but I am not so sheltered that I forget it was mild compared to the trials of this city – compared to those first terrors you experienced. Verona sees worse than that each day. The experience will armour me for what may come.'

'What may come.' He sighs. 'I would spare you of that sight if I could.'

'Do you fear it must end in violence?'

'To end a decades-long feud in mere weeks? That is no simple task for any man. Hercules himself was not asked to turn hearts in his labours. Eight years a soldier makes me a veteran, though I'm as young as you. Veteran enough to be useful, young enough to be discarded should my value be done.'

'Francesco, you should not think that way. You are valued by your lord.'

'Yet not too highly. I do not mean it as complaint. I am a young lieutenant of low birth in my captain's company. There are more experienced soldiers, men with lineage who might be here in my place. It is not ability alone that has placed me here – though I do not begrudge the chance to prove myself. I have ascended further than anyone in my family and my dreams are of higher still.'

'Your captain and his peers have a brutal way of war,' Estelle counters. 'Theirs is not the touch required in Verona.'

'And nor is mine, in truth. Your father can govern this city, your mother can reunite it, you and your brother can offer it a future. I am here for other purposes. It is incidental that I am afforded the chance to prove my worth.'

She touches his hand and speaks more gently. 'You

68

think less highly of yourself than you should. Than those around you.'

The words falter in his throat for a moment. 'I thank you,' he says at last in a hoarse voice. After a short while he shakes the mood off and forces himself to sit taller, facing the world with a broad smile once more. 'Rarely have I been accused of thinking too little of myself. Perhaps you could assure your mother of this?'

She shakes her head. 'By those who do not know you, perhaps. My mother would give you short thrift if she thought you naught but wind and bluster.'

'A good soldier is always cautious, Estelle, and it does not do for a man of my low birth to dream too hard. Though the stars may look inviting, only a fool stretches to reach them.'

She says nothing at that, eyes downcast and sitting very still. Just as he fears he has insulted her, Estelle takes a deep breath and smiles up at him. She places his hand between both of hers and squeezes it tightly between her small palms.

'Fortune is a fickle mistress,' she says gravely, 'but not always is she cruel. As your friend I beg you not to always mistrust. Never forget there are also others who look up at the stars and wonder what might be theirs.'

'Some may reach further than others,' Francesco replies. 'God has placed them upon the high ground. I am a man of ambition, of that I shall never deny. Cowherd of Carmagnola is not the title I shall die with, of that I promise you. But a man does not climb mountains by reaching too far and trusting to fortune. He makes sure of his standing and moves without haste.'

He stands, more abruptly than he intended but feeling the weight of expectation bearing down.

'Haste can see a man cast down again,' he says,

looking down at Estelle. 'For those of us used to the low ground, it is all too easy to crave the mountain top, but the top itself is not always the prize. I should leave you now, I have more to prepare for the morrow. I bid you good evening, my Lady Estelle.'

She nods. 'Good evening to you, my Lord Governor.'

*

From a window across the courtyard, two people stand in the twilight of an unlit room. Their shoulders rest gently against each other's, the comfort of long years pressed close.

'How long has this been brewing I wonder?'

'You read much into a look and a quiet word, my love.'

Juliet turns to look at her husband. 'There is much to read, my heart, should one possess a learned eye. A man of strength and wit, a woman of intellect and grace – it is no great leap to admiration and friendship becoming more.'

'Nor is it inevitable, even at an age when romance more easily blooms.'

'Bah, so speaks the boy who fell in love at first sight – the boy who had seen enough of infatuation to know the difference, yet was so smitten he could not think or eat.'

Romeo smiles. 'The boy who had little enough sense, but knew what he saw was unlike anything he ever had before.'

'Indeed, my heart,' Juliet says with the quirk of a smile. 'It was lucky for you, perhaps, that no rugged soldier also attended that particular ball, a warrior whose charms might have eclipsed your own in the eyes of a young, impressionable girl. At least admit they make a noble pair, close in each other's company while the world turns about them.'

'I think one is noble, the other not.'

She frowns. 'You would forbid her because of that?'

'Forbid?' Romeo says with a shake of the head. 'I would fear for them, nothing more. She is proof incarnate that love may chart a better course than the plans of parents.'

'She is older than we were,' Juliet says, returning to the sight of her daughter alone in the garden. 'Possessing greater wisdom than either, too.'

Romeo gives a small laugh. 'Not you I think. However, we are no model for others to follow. I would not stand in her way, but nor would I encourage her to take a similar path.'

'We have encouraged her all her life – son and daughter, both. The path they choose is the one they must take and we will not judge. How could we raise them any other way?'

'How easily might we have been torn asunder, in those first years?' he counters. 'How easily might I have turned to drink? Have lacked the courage to be a father?'

'I had faith in us. Even in the dark times.'

'As did I. It was a certainty that sustained me, strengthened me. Two young saplings, pleached by some divine plan and only strong enough to survive what was to come by the presence of the other.'

'Still you fear for her, my heart?'

'Still I fear for her,' he confirms. 'I know no other way to be a father. Our love had the disapproval of all, yes, but we were not so different, our families equal however opposite.'

'Francesco's station has not stopped him being your friend. He has won your trust through actions and deeds. What more would you ask of him?'

Romeo shakes his head. 'I ask nothing, my love, it is not my place to ask. I like Francesco, I respect him – yet it is a truth undeniable that his upbringing was quite apart from hers. His life has been very different, not only his station but the violence that is his livelihood. There will be pressures on us all over the weeks and months to come that none can guess at yet. What they feel may prove enough, or it may not. Only Lady Time can tell and her whispers are too soft for the ears of men. The course of history cares little for our hopes and dreams.'

'Neither are we entirely helpless before it,' Juliet declares. 'For all that we may not cast the final dice, we are players not pieces on a board.'

'You would involve yourself? Encourage her even? Francesco is my friend, *our* friend, but also a mercenary – a soldier and killer of men. His life is not his own and peril marches in step with him.'

'I would be there for my daughter, no more and no less. I would not have my child fear my disapproval and have that affect her actions. We have both seen how that turns out.'

'It did not all turn to disaster and ruin, my love.' Romeo laughs gently. 'I hope you do not regret every moment of what followed.'

She raises an eyebrow at him. 'I have two fine children, that much I will admit. But the greater truth, o husband of mine, is that there followed ruin beyond the lives we lost in our youth. Hurt done to those we never even knew. The course of history is not ours to change, but if we simply allow events to play out as they will, can we truly object when the mistakes of the past are repeated?'

'Let us see if we might undo some of those past mistakes,' Romeo says with a nod, 'for the sake of all our futures.'

Seven

The following morning, the heart of Milan's authority in Verona is laid siege by fog. When a horn announces each of two deputations from the city, Francesco goes to the balcony to watch them emerge from the gloom. From there Scaliger Castle resembles an island, set apart from the rest of the city by that veil of mist while a low, dull sun illuminates little. Of San Pietro, the fortress that overbears the city and houses many of Milan's troops, there is no sign.

The Montagues and Capulets come in a blaze of colour – bright liveries and house symbols clearly delineated from each other, both emerging from a grey and ghostly city. To a soldier it is almost comical, servants and high-born bullies playing a child's imitation. There are no more than a dozen on either side, but they are carefully arrayed and emblazoned to leave their allegiance in no doubt. No tiny flash of red is to be seen on the Montague side, no sliver of blue betrays the Capulet line.

Francesco looks down at what passes for his own uniform. There is no place for his much-repaired hauberk and gambeson here. Instead he wears a quartered silk tunic of white and blue that fits close around his body. His sword remains a warrior's weapon however finely crafted, no doubt far less ornate than those worn by his guests, but there is a message there, too, should they have the wit to read it.

It takes a few minutes for his guests to be admitted and Francesco forces himself to sit at the great desk while he waits. Having been summoned, neither party wishes to rush to this young man's order – certainly not in the presence of their old enemy. But an order it is and an officer of Milan he is, so presently the impish figure of Felipe, steward of Scaliger Castle, heralds the appearance of five figures to Francesco's office.

First to come, by dint of seniority or unbending resolve, is Lord Capulet – an old man beyond his years who leans heavily on his cane. His hair is entirely white, his body stooped and spare where he once had been tall and strong. The gimlet-eyed lord fixes Francesco with a look of unveiled disdain, the familiar sight of a nobleman forced to endure the presence of a commoner.

Finally he eases his way inside and permits the Lady Capulet past, with the darkly scowling figure of Reynard behind. The underling of Capulet is freshly scrubbed and attired, every inch a nobleman, but behind Francesco's smile is the memory of Reynard befouled and beaten.

'My Lord Governor,' Felipe declares in a voice seemingly too strong and bold for a frame as slight as his. 'It is my honour to present to you the Lord and Lady Capulet, and in attendance on them, Captain Reynard Capulet.'

'My Lord Capulet, Lady Capulet.' Francesco bows low to them, receiving little more than a grunt from the former. The lady bears an altogether different mood, try as she might to restrain it, and Francesco sees a flush to her cheek that he fancies has little to do with him.

'Lord Governor,' Lady Capulet says with all courtesy. 'We thank you for your invitation. I'm sure you are—'

'Invitation?' Lord Capulet interrupts, his voice rattling and harsh. 'It was no such thing. A demand, nothing less – call it no prettier than it is.'

The man's irritation is plain to see and Francesco wonders how insistent Lady Capulet was on joining this deputation. To wait in the courtyard would not serve her purposes, but her husband is renowned for his ill temper.

'I will call it an invitation then,' declares the man who follows at a slight remove, 'and offer thanks to he who extends it.'

Felipe coughs and hurriedly speaks up. 'Furthermore I present the Lord Montague and Sir Paolo Bruno.'

Fairer and broader than Reynard, Lord Antonio walks with the same lightness of step, but his expression betrays no animosity from the last time they met.

'An invitation and a welcome one, for I was uncivil when we last met, my Lord Governor. You have my apologies, both personally and to the court you represent.'

Here is a man more comfortable in his power, Francesco thinks as he bows once more. *He knows he loses nothing by withdrawing from the quarrel and gains in the eyes of an honourable man. What twist of fate is it then, that I have brought his downfall in my hand?*

'Lord Montague, I thank you,' Francesco acknowledges as he returns the bow. 'And Sir Paolo, welcome to both of you.'

'Congratulations upon your appointment, my Lord Governor,' says the older man. 'May it prove peaceable and profitable for all.'

Sandy-whiskered and bear-like in size, Sir Paolo is a grizzled man in his fifties who wears the colours of Montague though he is not of that house. Instead he is father-in-law to Lord Antonio and by all accounts the younger man's closest advisor. His manner is similar to Antonio's – a man who knows his own worth and does not pretend to know more. With a regal bearing, great size and a hard look in the eye, Francesco immediately warms to the man.

'Peace and profitability for all is my wish, too, though it may go against the grain for a man raised under a mercenary's wing.' Francesco pauses. 'However, the augurs are not favourable and my humour precarious, so let us not yet declare victory.'

Again he hesitates and looks directly at Lady Capulet. 'My Lady, may I ask you retire to the solar where my servants might attend you? I am a man of blunt words and would speak frankly to the lords of the city.'

The surprise on her face is no less genuine than that of her husband's, but Lady Capulet wastes no time in acquiescing.

'Of course, my Lord Governor. I venture you would not offend me with plain speaking, my home has had the aspect of a barracks for many a year, but I am happy to be at your service.'

'Thank you, Lady Capulet. Felipe will escort you and see you are provided with refreshment.'

She leaves without haste or meeting her husband's eye and soon the five men are left to warily eye the other factions represented in the room.

'Gentlemen, please be seated,' Francesco says after a strained moment of silence. He fails to do so himself and stands with one hand resting on the back of a tall armchair, watching the four men uneasily take their seats.

Again he waits, just a fraction longer than is comfortable for those attending him. The youngest man in the room by a decade, Francesco is all too aware he must make the most of what he has, else he undermine any authority he might wield. Before the hush becomes unbearable, Felipe returns with a footman in tow, bearing wine and five goblets. With brisk efficiency, the wine is poured for each man, then the servants retreat. Francesco raises his goblet in toast to each pair attending him.

'Your health, Messers.'

He drinks deeply, his words returning only in muted echo as the four men sip, but Francesco pays that no mind.

'I thank you again for attending me so promptly,' he continues, undaunted. 'I have been sent by my most wise and honourable lord, Duke Visconti to—'

There is a cackle from Lord Capulet. 'Boy, let us not pretend in private,' he declares. 'Should you lord be overburdened with honour he would not be Duke of Milan – indeed he would not be alive. That he is a man of greatness I do not deny, but honour is a vestment like any other to men of power. You are too young to remember events of a decade past, but I assure you it is graven on the hearts of every Veronese citizen.'

Francesco takes a slow breath. 'The Duke of Milan is a man of honour,' he says carefully, 'that much I would not debate with words alone. He is not however a man of excessive forgiveness. When dealing with those less honourable than himself, he is not so weak as to stay his hand. You remember that terrible day and I grieve too for those lost, but my lord also remembers why Biancardo and his troops needed to be sent here. But you ask me to speak plainly and so I shall. Do you know who I am?'

There is quiet from the room as he looks from one face to the next. Eventually Lord Montague clears his throat.

'You are Francesco of Carmagnola; lieutenant in the company of Facino Cane and soldier of Milan, now Lord Governor of Verona.'

'Correct, Lord Montague. I was born a cowherd and raised a mercenary. I bring no noble lineage to my position, no wealth or agenda. I am paid to fight by a man who knows my value and rewards those he deems able, but he is not one to brook failure or betrayal.'

'Does the duke mean to insult us with your appointment,' Sir Paolo asks in a measured voice, 'or is it threat alone?'

'We have had enough of both with Biancardo acting as governor and captain-general of Verona,' insists Lord Capulet. 'Or is Cane's dog sent in its master's place, to offer a taste of what may follow once the German Emperor is seen off?'

'Among the count of our lord's virtues,' says Lord Montague, 'is numbered not lowering himself to insult.' He smiles coldly. 'Other than to the sons of cats that is.'

Francesco blinks as he recalls the term, one used mockingly by the duke towards a haughty young lord of Padua. Its intended target also recognises it, he sees, but Reynard ignores the barb and makes no reply.

Francesco leans forward, the sturdy back of the chair

faintly creaking under the pressure. 'In the Milanese state a man's abilities are recognised and employed just as an architect may utilise a variety of materials. Choose to be insulted or threatened at your leisure, my lords; it does not change the fact that I am here with very specific instructions. We all know Verona is a city beset by its past, plagued by violence and enfeebled by its divisions. No architect could brook such fissures and flaws should they threaten to bring down a wall. My lord has tolerated your squabbles long enough and declares them now over – for the greater good of Milan and all cities that fly the biscione flag.'

'Over?' Lord Montague says carefully. 'You ask us to forget those we have lost? The oaths we have sworn?'

'I ask nothing, my Lord. Verona has languished this way long enough, I intend to see her rise once more and will accept no opposition. The past is done with, there is enough blood spilled on either side to satisfy the hungriest of ghosts. I will see no more.'

'No more?' declares Lord Capulet, angrily striking the floor with his cane. 'Would the world be so simple, Governor. The hearts of men are not so easily turned.'

'Hearts that are stone against words are mere flesh against swords. Look at me, my lords – I am no diplomat, no statesman or merchant. Duke Visconti offers you his hand in friendship and honour, but make no mistake – this title I bear is the velvet glove of his forbearance.

'I do not care for what may be grown or built. My trade is in death and my apprenticeship was to a man whose reputation is known to all of Italy. Do you think anything of your feud will shock me? Do you think any of your excesses beyond me?'

He stops there to allow his words to sink in. These

are men unused to being spoken to in this way, but he is satisfied in what he has seen of the city and his lord's judgement. A soldier's discipline is what is required in Verona and that is something Francesco knows as well as breathing. Nothing gentle will stir them from their violent habits, only the certain threat of brutal punishment. The English devil himself, John Hawkwood, could offer no greater savagery than Francesco's tutor in war.

'So this is the true face of Milan's rule?' Lord Capulet says at last. 'A threat indeed. The iron fist raised above us all.'

'These are the wages of sin,' Francesco replies. 'Has there been any great change to the laws of Verona? Was Prince Escalus more indulgent of the discord between your houses? My Lord Visconti has only one apology and that is to the citizenry of Verona. For too long has he been loath to intervene, to impose his will so firmly on a vassal state that welcomed his flag and has been largely faithful in its obligations.'

'That is your message to us?' Lord Montague asks in a more composed manner. 'Obey the law and all will be well?'

'Is it so difficult a request?'

'Indeed not, yet I cannot help wonder what is left unspoken. In politics and the game of houses, a simple message is rarely just that. I have learned to be most wary of those who come with empty hands and humble professions.'

'You put me in a bind, Messer. A man who holds a surprise for you would hardly announce it ahead of time. What use then are denials to me here?'

'My apologies, Governor, I meant no insult.'

'Then none is taken. The duke's message is simple

in itself, the complexity lies in keeping to it. He wishes Verona to be whole and strong, to be a jewel in the crown of his domain. This feud diminishes all it touches, Milan's interests as well as yours.'

'A jewel in his crown?' Lord Capulet barks. 'There is the truth to it. Duke Visconti is no longer content with the title he bought, he would be a king I wager. Does he value Verona or see our struggle as a stone in the boot that marches upon Florence?'

Francesco spreads his hands apologetically. 'Again you ask things a humble soldier cannot know, in a manner that suggests refuting your words would instead confirm them.'

'A humble soldier would hardly see such a distinction.'

Francesco smiles at that. 'I confess you have me there, my lords. I am not by nature humble, nor am I a dullard brawler. But I do not pretend to know every thought and motivation the duke may hold close. Better men even than I have found themselves snared and stumbling as they attempt to predict him. All I have is my task at hand and it is considerable enough. For Verona to recapture its glory, all my efforts will not be enough. It is dependent upon your houses, your wills, to see this done.'

He pauses and lowers his head a touch. 'Before this spirit of endeavour may be embraced however, the ghosts of the past must be laid to rest. I am told grand balls are a thing of the past in Verona, that the last sparked an escalation in the feud between your houses. In which case, to mark the beginning of our future I have decided such a tradition must be revived before new life can be breathed in this city.

'One week hence, there shall be a ball held here and

you are all invited. All noble born sons and daughters of Verona, greater and lesser houses, will attend to celebrate this city's future.'

Silence follows his words. Francesco sees they have all gone still with shock – just as he knew they would. Those Milanese sent to Verona have reported this back more than once, the tacit omission of those days when two young noble offspring met and fell in love. Though it fuelled the years of feuding to follow, the events themselves are never spoken of in Veronese society.

'You dare to presume?' Lord Capulet rasps. His face is scarlet, his knuckles white. 'You stand before me and idly speak of things you know nothing about? Devil I name you, coward I dub you. My younger self would have killed you where you stand and you only speak knowing my strength fails me. Blood and breeding reveals all once more. Low-born you are, base you shall always be. Run back to the dog who taught you to kill, to prey on the weak and vulnerable. You are good for nothing more.'

Francesco stares down at the man, resisting his own anger at words he anticipated. 'I am going nowhere,' he says in a calm, quiet voice, 'and it is cowardice that has held this city back all too long. The dead must be honoured, but to revere them such that words cannot be spoken is madness, it is cowardice of its own. Yes, cowardice – a fear to face the future without them. A desperate need to cling on to the memory of what was lost. But no longer will I allow that in Verona, not while I have breath.

'A ball there will be, here and once a week hence. Every noble house of Verona who wishes to be part of her future shall attend. All the city shall witness the joyous interment of its long-lingering sickness. Capulet men shall dance with Montague maidens, the injured shall speak no ill of those who have wounded them, the elders of each house shall stand side by side and toast the city's future.'

Lord Montague does not allow Capulet time to respond. He stands and looks Francesco directly in the eye. 'One week hence,' Antonio confirms. 'The feast of St Luke. House Montague shall attend, my Lord Governor, with the maidens serving as our vanguard.'

Francesco bows. 'I am grateful to hear it. Now, there are also matters of taxation and revenues that the duke wishes for me to discuss with you.' He sits and indicates the settle. 'Please, indulge me a little longer.'

Eight

After gladly departing her husband's presence, Lady Capulet is shown down the corridor by a servant. There they enter the upper hall that forms part of the governor's private quarters and the servant bids her to wait for the governor's aides to attend her. A fire burns at one end, but otherwise all is still as the servant leaves and closes the door behind her, leaving Lady Capulet alone.

She inspects the room while she waits, attempting to calm the swirl of thoughts running through her mind. A long oak table occupies much of the solar, while at the fire stands a pair of tall chairs and two goblets of wine on a table between. Above the fire hangs the serpent flag of Milan, with lesser devices on the longer wall. Spaces traced in soot show where the previous governor's personal possessions have been removed.

Lady Capulet walks to the chairs just as the door at that end opens. When a figure steps through and lifts hesitant eyes to behold her, something catches in Lady Capulet's chest. Time itself holds its breath.

No longer a girl, but not so different still, Juliet stands in the doorway as transfixed as her mother. Taller than when they parted, she stands with the strength of years supporting her, where once she was a willowy child too easily bent and bowed. The lines of her face are unchanged, the depth of her beauty a promise fulfilled. Her grey dress is that of a woman of modest means, but the cut and cloth is of a finer quality than most Veronese will wear.

Then the spell is broken and Juliet's face seems to crumple as the tears spill. The wind is driven from Lady Capulet's chest and as she reaches to embrace Juliet, she falters and stumbles. The pain in her ribs, gift of her husband, flares.

'Mother!' Juliet gasps, gripping her arms to steady her. 'Are you well?'

'My child, I am blessed beyond words,' Lady Capulet whispers, almost afraid to admit it aloud. 'I... It is you, it is really you! I had almost given up hope. I knew it though, I knew when I saw her. I knew her face before ever I saw it in the cathedral. She could only ever be your daughter.'

'It is me,' Juliet says, smiling through her tears, 'and she is my daughter indeed!'

Juliet ushers her mother to a chair and pulls the second close. She takes Lady Capulet's hand, encases it in her own two.

'I am here, we all are.'

'You *all*?' Lady Capulet finds the strength to smile again and her heart becomes a step lighter. 'Your... your husband, too?'

Juliet nods, her voice wavering. 'Your granddaughter, Estelle, and grandson, too. Mercutio was the one to deliver the note to you. Both as wonderful as any parent could hope for and desperate to meet their grandmother. I begged them allow me to greet you first.

It is a filial indulgence they understand, but they wait impatiently just beyond that door.'

Lady Capulet gasps. 'They are waiting? I beg you bring them through. I will not have long to spend with you and would not miss a moment.'

Juliet jumps up to fetch her children, motherhood not robbing her of the girlish grace that haunts Lady Capulet's memory. She darts to the door and in moments two young faces appear. She blinks at them twice as she tries to bring order to the tempest of her thoughts. Too slowly does she find herself able to rise and take in their faces, both so brimming with nervous excitement they can hardly keep still.

'Estelle,' she says in a hoarse whisper. 'Mercutio.'

Unable to speak more she sweeps them both into an embrace they gladly welcome. When finally she does release them, there are tears on the faces of all. Her mouth is so dry she can hardly speak, the breath squeezed from her chest. A sip of wine and a moment's pause is enough to restore order to her mind, however.

'Come, allow me a proper look at you both,' the grandmother in her commands, rising from the deepest part of her soul like a kraken finally unshackled.

Estelle and Mercutio stand back and present themselves, struggling to contain the surging cross-tides of emotion within them.

'Tall and strong,' she whispers, touching each's cheek with reverence. 'You have your mother's beauty, Estelle, and I see much of her in you too, Mercutio. I had believed you dead for so long, Juliet. I have known only despair for so many years it is hard to remember what happiness is... and yet, in my dreams I have glimpsed these faces. The family I lost, restored after countless prayers.'

She pulls them close again. Juliet embraces all three for a long tearful moment before stepping back.

'I had resigned myself to never seeing this day,' Juliet admits as she attends her eyes. 'After the assassin came for us, we were certain it would never come.'

'Assassin?'

'A long time ago now, before we established ourselves in Milan.'

Lady Capulet's stomach grows cold. She can scarcely find the strength to reply, but the sight of Juliet has restored much in her heart.

'Sent by your father?'

'We could only assume so. We had sent letters before but received no reply. Balthasar came once, but my second cousin, Andrea, had been killed not long before. He was warned he would be killed even approaching any Capulet.'

'So he would have been,' Lady Capulet says, remembering the terrible days that had followed. 'His face was known as loyal to Montague.'

She pauses and looks again at her grandchildren. 'So strange,' she says, taking their hands, 'to see you both now, to know you are the closest kin I have and rejoice in your touch, but you are Montagues, too. I do not hate you for that I assure you, nothing of the sort, but to live in Verona and feel such love for a Montague...' She smiles at her daughter. 'Well, there is only one other in living memory.'

'And look what trouble it got her into,' Mercutio says, finally breaking his silence.

Estelle scowls at her brother's flippancy, but Lady Capulet only nods.

'These twenty years and more the very notion has been preposterous. Outrageous, yes but also unthinkable. Better to claim the sun has chosen to rise in the west, for then the ridicule would not be accompanied by contempt.'

She bows her head. 'Juliet, I am so sorry. I was mad with grief, your father too, and you were dead – of that we were certain. We saw your body, cold and absent of all that was precious to us. When at last I did receive a letter from you, I could not believe it. It was a forgery, it had to be, the devil's own torment. Despite the handwriting, the details, it could not be true.'

'The ploy was a desperate one,' Juliet admitted. 'It brought about the death of Paris and only the hand of fortune saved us.'

'I have never come to know if your father believed those letters, whether he could permit himself to. At first we were of the same mind, I am certain. As the clouds of grief eased and I began to wonder...' Lady Capulet shakes her head. 'I do not know. His rage has run unabated all this time, it is the lodestone of all he is. I doubt he is able to believe anything else now, even should the evidence be put before his eyes.'

'Surely he must?' Estelle insists. 'When he sees mother, what choice could he have?'

'I fear the answer to that,' Lady Capulet replies. 'Rage is what drives him, every beat of his heart and taken breath, and it robs him of reason. A rabid dog cares not for the sense of its actions and nor will he. There are few left who recall the face of my young, deceased daughter to bear any certain witness, fewer still brave enough to do so.'

'We will be cautious,' Juliet says. 'But for their insistence, these two would not be in Verona at all.' A small smile appears on her lips. 'I am afraid to report, mother, that your grandchildren are determined and wilful, not averse to bold action once their minds are made up.'

'Verona shall not be inherited by the meek,' Lady Capulet says solemnly, 'but I counsel you both to restrain the hastiness of youth. The factions of this city are boulders grinding against each other. Anyone caught between becomes just so much grist. I failed your mother once before and forced her to extreme action, I would not have our past repeat itself.'

'It will not, mother. Romeo and I desire only to heal the divisions in Verona, however best that can be accomplished. There has been so much violence in the wake of our departure, we must try to end it and Duke Visconti supports our effort. If we cannot, we will return to Milan and the life we have built there.'

'Your husband is here?'

Juliet nods. 'Elsewhere in the castle. He thought it more than enough for you to meet the three of us.'

'I am not so old and infirm as that.'

'Then you are stronger than I. Just waiting to see you has proved exhausting for me.'

'I understand. I would meet him too, see the man he has grown into – I remember only a handsome, restless youth.'

'He has changed,' Juliet says. 'Romeo is a good husband and a loving father.'

'But not nearly so handsome as mother claims he once was,' Estelle adds impishly. 'The ladies of Milan prefer Mercutio's looks I think.'

Lady Capulet waves her hand. 'But of course, the Montagues have always grown thick and bovine in manhood.'

'Will you tell us more of them as children?'

She places a hand on her granddaughter's. 'I will,

but not today. There will be time in the weeks to come. Please, would you give me a few moments more alone with your mother? I doubt I will have much longer, your grandfather is irritable on his better days and the new governor is, I hear, a low-born mercenary. I doubt they will remain civil for long.'

The pair smother their disappointment and nod, offering the proper respect to Lady Capulet and depart without a word. When the door is shut behind them, she takes Juliet's hand.

'They are a credit to you, my dearest girl. I am glad to have met them even if it has proved later than I would have wished. It must have been difficult to raise them without family or much money, fearing retribution all the while.'

'We sent you a portrait, years ago,' Juliet says hesitantly. 'Of Estelle when she was but a little girl. I have wanted to bring them to you so badly, but the risk was too great. I thought to give you that would be proof enough. You have the picture of me at a similar age and she looked so alike.'

'I never saw it,' Lady Capulet whispers as though a part of her has been stolen. 'But that means he must have known you were alive. The servants must have given it to him and he would have recognised it... he ordered me to take down your childhood portrait, too. It must have been at that time, he found he could not bear to look at it and I was made to pack it away.'

'I...' Juliet's words die in her throat as there is a knock at the door behind, leading to the main corridor, and the maid who showed Lady Capulet in enters.

'My Lady, your husband calls for you.'

'I come,' Lady Capulet says, nodding formally to Juliet. She had stepped back as the knock came, not trusting the servants with gossip that might kill her and her new-discovered family.

'My Lady,' Juliet says for her part, curtseying low. 'It was a pleasure to make your acquaintance.'

'I am glad. I trust it will not be too long before we meet again. Good day.'

Though it pains her, Lady Capulet turns her back and makes her way to her husband's side without a backward look.

Nine

As the grey afternoon begins to turn to dull autumn
dusk, the side gate of Scaliger Castle creaks open. It is a
gloomy and narrow street that four figures step out onto,
overlooked by the battlements of Scaliger Castle on both
sides. On a chilly day it bears a dismal mien and the first
two figures pull their cloaks tight around them before
they head east across the city. Passing the great and
ancient stones of the arena, where rooks fill the air with
sound and the swirl of wings, they head towards the
church of San Fermo and the graveyard that lies over the
river from it.

Behind them follow two soldiers, armed but without
livery or any markings of house – their leathers carefully
drab in a city where colour may signal allegiance. The
day's business is largely completed and what citizens
they pass keep clear, even as the Montague and Capulet
retainers watch them carefully. Crossing the river they
turn south to follow a sward at the river's bank a short
way. As the evening draws in and the last chorus of
birdsong vies with clattering bursts of sound from
taverns and brothels, they come to a graveyard. Before it
stands a shrine, which it is said can be seen down the

length of a city street from the house of Capulet.

A wide river path runs between the lichen-flecked graveyard wall and the water's edge. The dull lap of water is overlaid by clear high voices of birds, hunting the evening breeze. The press of houses is not so tight out across the river so they feel a sense of lightness as they walk. An easing of the city's burdens as they step from beneath its looming shadows.

Making their way around a horse and cart that lumbers down the path, Juliet and Romeo halt at the shrine. Orange flames spill from a great iron bowl that sits in its mouth. No more than three yards across, the shrine is a square construction with a pitched roof, brick-built and weathered older than she whose memory it serves.

The principal feature is an alcove before the fire-bowl. There stands an alabaster statue of the Virgin, unpainted save for her robe which is red. A stone ledge runs beneath this around the three sides of the shrine; a tattered bedroll tucked under one part while driftwood is stacked neatly under the rest.

'And the monk himself?' Romeo asks, scanning around.

'If this is where he sleeps, he will not be far.'

'The woman said he spends his days walking the riverbank. Perhaps he is not yet returned from his patrols.'

Juliet nods. 'Then we will await his return.'

'We owe him as much and more,' Romeo agrees. 'For the vigil he has kept and the long years of pain endured. Verona has many dead to pray for, some small vigil of our own would not be time wasted.'

They kneel together before the statue of the Virgin, feeling the warmth of the fire on their backs. The two foreign mercenaries who have escorted them, Rufus and Aylward, step to a discrete remove at either side. Romeo glances back and gives Rufus a brief nod. Their goal is not to make the shrine look under guard and clearly the common folk of the city hold its resident in awed regard.

As Romeo bows his head to the statue he sees his wife has not yet done so. Instead she stares directly at the face of the Virgin as though seeking the answer to some question.

'Is all well, my love?' he asks softly.

Juliet blinks for a moment. 'It is,' she confirms. 'I am merely struck by the strangeness of this. This shrine is a symbol to the city of my death – a memorial to the ghost I left behind. How many have prayed here? How many have spared me a gentle word or charitable thought as they made their peace with God here? I feel humbled and guilty about something beyond my knowledge or control. How does the blessed Virgin see me here? As some sort of deceiver? As an undeserving recipient of prayers? The deceit of my death caused pain to those I love and surely that is part of the sin of suicide? The pain you bring to those around you in addition to the insult to God's own work? Will I answer for it the day I die?'

'God is merciful, my love. The young and the innocent hold a special place in his heart and you were both.' Romeo's head sinks a little lower. 'What words might be spoken at my judgement I am less sure of. Is there such a defence to muster? I carry the guilt of my actions each day. Each day as my son and all noble men hone their skill at arms, so I train my anger to cut with words alone.'

'God sees your heart,' Juliet says with greater assurance. 'He sees your penitence far in excess of fighting men or princes who scatter baubles before his door. He will know your efforts to restore this city's fortunes, my heart. He will lift the burden you have placed upon your shoulders.'

Romeo nods. 'No true sinner believes he deserves to be saved.'

'And no man in the robes of penitence may conceal the true colour of his soul at the final judgement. It is not our place to speculate on God's unfathomable will, merely to live as the deserving should.'

They lapse into silence and finally the words of prayer return to Romeo, parting clouds of doubt to shine forth. His heart feels lightened by speaking his fears and regrets aloud, though Juliet already knows them as well as her own. To offer confession without the comforting cloth of sanctity brings clarity to Romeo's mind, slipping free from the bonds of private cares.

Immersed in a dreamless, timeless state he feels his spirit rise from his body. It ascends through the evening air, caressed by the last golden glimmers of light as though touched by God's own hand. Only the soothing snap of the flames and the faint whisper of Juliet's prayers keep him tethered as the gloom and chill furtively envelop his mortal form. How long he kneels, Romeo cannot say – mere moments or many minutes until a soft cough from Aylward drags him back.

'My Lord,' the mercenary murmurs in his rough way. 'He comes.'

Romeo blinks owlishly as his wits return, sparing one final look for the Virgin before pushing himself to his feet.

'Ready, my love?'

Juliet gives a wan smile. 'Could we ever be ready?'

'That I doubt, but we must face him nonetheless.

This is only the first of many hard reunions.'

She inclines her head in agreement and rises, too. The couple remain within the small privacy of the shrine and wait for its resident to appear. It does not take long for footsteps to become audible. Romeo realises with brief alarm that there is more than one person approaching, but ahead he sees Aylward do nothing more than offer a small bow of respect to the newcomers.

Two figures appear out of the gloom and jolt to a halt. Romeo feels his breath catch as he sees the wild-haired hermit of Verona, no different to how he was described but still unexpected. Though the man's hood is pushed back, Romeo can see nothing of the man he once called friend. The flesh has withered to a spindly collection of bones, all clothed in the torn and stained rags of a beggar. Prominent eyes dart with nervous energy from within a nest of lines and scars. Dirty grey hair hangs ragged and long over one side of his face. A fitful line of broken teeth is exposed by the slack jaw, drawing all eyes to the wretched stub of flesh inside his mouth.

The air is driven from Romeo's lungs. It is all he can do to remain standing and before he can recover, a thin wail breaks the silence from the monk's companion. Such is the anguish in the sound that Romeo's shock is dismissed instantly and he stumbles forward on instinct as a woman falters before him.

'Merciful saints,' Juliet whispers from his side. 'Can it be?'

The monk's companion is as old as he, a small woman in a plain smock and servant's scarf over her head. She seems to crumple under the burden in her hands, a bowl covered by a trencher of dark bread.

Without thinking Romeo steps forward and slips a hand under her arm, keeping the woman from collapsing. He takes the bowl from her and sets it aside, but she finds her strength as he does so.

A second more piteous sound escapes her lips as she takes a tentative step forward. Juliet reaches her hands out towards the old woman as though in supplication and the spell is broken. The woman sweeps forward and wraps her thin arms around Juliet's shoulders, pulling her head fiercely against her while sobs break from both women.

The words that follow are garbled and meaningless in all but the emotion they convey. A dam of years breaks in both and from it the inexorable flood bursts. The old woman is smaller than Juliet but she handles her like a child, turning her head to kiss her cheek again and again, brushing back her hair and tilting her chin to bring her features into the light.

'My sweet child, oh my dearest girl! Can it really be you? But how? Has God answered my prayers? Have I stumbled beyond the veil?'

'Nurse, nurse!' Juliet cries, laughing and sobbing. 'It is me, as alive as you and never so glad to see a face as yours!'

'You are truly alive? I had not dared hope, not even when Lawrence first returned and told his story. It all seemed a cruel prank. I found you dead, I laid you out and washed your cold skin.'

Juliet gasps and pulls herself back from the embrace. 'Lawrence,' she says in a choked voice, looking at the ragged sparrow that flits uneasily behind her aged nurse. 'You... I, I do not have the words.'

'Lawrence?' Romeo says uncertainly, still unable to recognise the man after such terrible changes.

Hearing that, something seems to click in the monk's mind. He pauses in his twitching and shifting, raises his head and finally looks Romeo directly in the eye as a man might. Broken and haunted the man might be, that one moment is enough to reveal the spark of who he once was. Romeo takes a step then hesitates as Lawrence shies back, before the anguish and guilt he feels drags him to his knees before his former confessor.

'My friend,' Romeo croaks. 'What have they done to you? I am so sorry.'

Lawrence eyes him warily before reaching out a thin, claw-like hand. Romeo does not move, he does not wish to startle the man. In truth he is unsure if he could summon much strength to react in any way. With awkward movements, Lawrence touches one finger to Romeo's cheek then snatches it back. Once more he does that before the digit lingers and prods, scratches at Romeo's beard, tugs at his coat.

All of a sudden it seems too much and Lawrence scuttles back, out of reach and clutching fearfully at the wall of the shrine.

'My Lord,' Juliet's nurse whispers, 'let me.'

She disentangles herself from Juliet and retrieves the bowl. With the shushing sound of a parent to their baby, she hands it to Lawrence and coaxes her arm around him. Slowly she urges the man down to the bench with his meal in his lap. There is a steady assurance to her now, the movements of a routine long practiced. Even in the presence of Juliet her own thoughts are set aside in favour of her charge. In that moment Romeo sees it as a true holy duty, her obligation of care eclipsing all. It is humbling to witness and the shame of his part in the cause burns hotter than ever.

Lawrence is soon calmed, Juliet's nurse as practiced

and assured as a stable-master with a skittish colt. He does not eat but perches on the stone bench on the far side of the shrine – no more than two yards away, yet it seems enough for his troubled spirit.

'He does not know joy,' the nurse says gravely as she straightens and stands before Juliet and Romeo. She puts herself between the fire and Lawrence, casting a protective shadow across him. 'His torment has been too great. Without fear or regret he will throw himself between clashing blades, but any reminder of the past tears at half-healed wounds.'

'There is much we have to thank him for, as if thanks could be enough...' Juliet begins, but her breath seems to falter and her words tail off.

Romeo slips one arm around his wife and takes up her cause. 'There is more to be said than either of us know how, but one recent act must come first. Our children were caught between Capulets and Montagues, only to have Lawrence bare the steel of his soul and prevent any great bloodshed. Thank you, Friar, for that newest mercy. Even before you recognised something of Estelle, you did not hesitate as most good men might.'

'You have a daughter?' the nurse says, clasping her hands to her breast. 'The very image of her mother I trust?'

Juliet nods and takes her nurse's hands. The pair sit side by side on the bench beneath the statue of the Virgin.

'A daughter and a son, Estelle and Mercutio,' she says with a smile. 'Both flowered into adulthood and better in most every way than the flighty wretch you were forced to chase after.'

In reply the woman kisses Juliet's hand with motherly affection. 'More often a delight, my lamb. It is the joy which lingers longest in the mind, that much you will know if your children are grown. I shall measure their worth against a high bar, though I am sure they will match the standard set.'

'And both shall strive their hardest to do so,' Romeo joins. 'For yours have been the standards expected of them over the years. I have no doubt there are some manners and habits that will have endured flight, exile and the passing years to yet be recognised with approval by you, good woman.'

'Then I shall be content. But are they in the city too?' Her eyes widen with sudden fear. 'Each of you is imperilled by your presence, but your children are strangers to all Verona and more vulnerable for it.'

'They are here,' Juliet says, 'and party to our undertaking. They come in full knowledge of what it might mean, but our small family is one that will stand together. We each are of the same mind that Verona's walls should no longer separate parent and child.'

'Your undertaking? Ah, but do you come with this new governor from Milan?'

'The House of Escalus is no longer a force in the city, the greatest power resides with the Montagues and Capulets. Only we can bridge the divide between our houses, and for the sakes of all those we left behind we must try if there is the smallest chance for Verona.'

The nurse shakes her head in violent distress. 'Your families will never allow it. The grief remains too strong for Lord Capulet, the heat of feud is undiminished by the years!'

She points towards Friar Lawrence who flinches under the attention and shrinks over his as-yet untouched bowl.

'Do you not know the evil act your father wrought

upon the messenger of good tidings? His rage has not quieted since. It has hardened into the lodestone of his soul, but remains as furious and unrelenting as the tempest.'

'What did happen, back when the friar returned?' Juliet asks.

There is a long silence, the nurse's small frame sagging under the weight of memory.

'It was a terrible time,' she admits at last. 'Blood had been shed, the Montagues were assailed by your father and Prince Escalus both. Friar Lawrence came to the Capulet household one night under cover of a rain storm. It was not his wish to foment trouble, not when the city might yet be brought back from the threatened state of war. He begged a private audience and was granted such. I was serving as a maid to Lady Capulet in the wake of your loss and found myself present to overhear.'

For a few moments she can say no more as tears begin to fall from her eyes. When she summons the strength to continue it is without heed to the trails on her cheeks that trace a well-worn path.

'I could not believe his words and nor did your parents, though I now know he spoke with God's own truth. For all that I knew of your marriage and might lend weight to such conversation, I knew you dead and that clouded all. Though Lawrence claimed it a ruse, I could not dare to believe my prayers were answered so readily. He spoke with the honesty of the true believer though and I was poised to step forward and risk my lord's wrath.'

'But you did not have the chance?'

'He had not finished speaking,' she says with a miserable shake of the head. 'There was such passion in his voice I was more congregant than lay-speaker. But your father did not allow him to finish. Before I knew what was taking place, Lord Capulet had flown into a fury to surpass anything the days and weeks before had held. He spoke the basest things, he struck the good friar... Lord Capulet beat him until Lawrence could speak no longer, but it was not enough for his rage.'

'He saw only an emissary from me,' Romeo breaks in. 'My words, my lies come to taunt him in his darkest hour.'

'I believe so. To accept the dead are not dead when we have seen them cold with our own eyes – malice was the better explanation.'

'And I far from a credible source,' he agrees. 'Son of his enemy, slayer of his kin, intemperate and foolish youth. Had we not feared his wrath, Juliet would have returned alone.'

'I thank God and all his angels that you did not!' the nurse exclaims with a gasp. 'Truth would have meant nothing to him, the pride of man burns hotter than all things. Though he did love his lost daughter, Lord Capulet would have seen betrayal before relief, his own wounding before his own love.'

'He would not have torn out my tongue,' Juliet murmurs, 'that much I know. A hiding for certain, perhaps disinheritance or a demand that I get to a convent, but not mutilation. He could not have held me forever, our marriage was legal and—'

'And he would have cared not a jot for it,' her nurse interrupts. 'When the business of rich men and their reputations is at stake, the law and God's word itself are twisted to purpose. Prince Escalus was not so secure in his position to care and his brother showed little regard for the rule of law when he murdered Escalus to succeed him.'

'Your father's actions are not yours to bear the guilt of,' Romeo says. 'Lawrence himself agreed a friar would be safe from Lord Capulet's rage in a way you were not. If your father rejected the sanctity of the church all bonds of loyalty would likely be cut from his heart, too.'

Juliet opens her mouth to speak but abruptly Friar Lawrence stands. Both she and Romeo are stilled by the intensity in his eyes; a sharp clarity amid the wild storm of his affliction. For a moment he does nothing, he merely stares at Juliet without moving an inch. When he does stir, his normally twitching and trembling fingers are slow and purposeful. He takes a few dignified steps forward and runs a finger down Juliet's cheek, a caress full of wonder and fatherly affection. Then his hand drops and takes hers. Lawrence bows low and kisses the back of Juliet's hand before touching his own throat and making an almost apologetic gesture with his free hand.

In the next instant the spell is broken and Lawrence retreats to his bench, taking up his bowl and finally starting on the meal inside. Romeo feels the breath driven from his chest and sees a single tear slide down Juliet's cheek.

'Thank you,' she whispers. 'I am sorry still, beyond all limits of word and deed, but thank you.'

Romeo finds himself nodding, too. The gentleness of Lawrence's actions speaks volumes, more than Romeo himself knows how to respond to. They sit in silence for a long time, the night drawing close around them until the fire begins to dim and Romeo moves to feed it more wood.

'The wound was grievous,' Juliet's nurse says as he does so. Her voice is hesitant. She struggles to speak the words, such is the burden of memory they bear, but it is clear she must say them however great a toll it takes.

'Lord Capulet ordered his guards to do it before Lawrence could say any more, could spread any further lies. He stood over Lawrence while they worked their cruelty. It took two strong men to hold him down, despite the beating. Your father watched it all without saying a word. He showed no anger then, nor pleasure or anything else.

'He said nothing more. When the tongue was cut out he cast it into the fire himself and turned his back. Once he was gone, your mother ordered them to cauterise the wound and take him to the priests at San Fermo. They were to say he had been found attacked in the street and they did not know his name.'

'Did he not accuse Lord Capulet after he had recovered?' Romeo asks.

She lowers her eyes and he can see the pain in her face as she remembers that time. 'It took many months for the injury to heal. The pain sent him half mad. He came close to starving and a fever set in. The priests spoke the last rites over him three times, but each time he turned away from death's door. The monastery at San Zeno took him in once he was strong enough to move.'

'Did the Franciscans never claim him as one of their own?'

Another shake of the head. 'Either Lord Capulet told them lies about him or they were angered by his abandoning of his duties when you fled the city. They did not lift a finger,' she says bitterly. 'I carried a gift from my mistress to the Abbott of the Benedictines, which ensured his care lasted as long as required. For a further year he raved, was a danger to himself and others. When Lawrence climbed from that pit of madness, he was a shadow of who he had once been, but more human than beast once again.'

'Yet he sleeps here and walks the streets all day?'

'He will take no greater charity than a bowl of stew and wood for this fire,' she confirms. 'The monastery cast him out, he would not stand for the failings of man even when his senses returned – most especially those of the cloth. What he saw among God's folk often caused him to fly into a rage. He has rejected all worldly things. The loss of his speech was forced upon him, but so much else he has gladly renounced to better serve God.'

'And you? Are you still in my mother's service?'

She shakes her head. 'Pensioned away,' she explains. 'Not long after Lawrence returned. There was no role for me there after your loss and my presence served as constant reminder. I keep house for a shopkeeper's family not far from here, kind and God-fearing people. It is enough to keep me busy and their children have proved a blessing over the years. They are understanding of my wish to make an extra meal each evening, too, and embrace the expense as the duty of charity. I am content in my place and having seen your face again I would have only one wish before I met my maker with an easy heart.'

'Estelle and Mercutio?' Juliet says. 'Little could make me gladder than to bring you all together. It grows late tonight however, we must return. Come tomorrow, I will send you a message to arrange when. Shall I send them here?'

Her nurse nods. 'I would not wish to trouble the Bruni family with such matters, life is fraught enough for the common people of Verona. Send your message here and I will make what arrangements I need in the evening.'

She rises with Juliet and embraces her once more, kissing both Juliet and Romeo on each cheek with fulsome delight. They have no words for Lawrence when it comes to parting and for his part, the friar is unable to look them in the eye. Only the soothing hand of Juliet's nurse on his shoulder brings Lawrence from his shell. He bears it with some discomfort as both kiss the back of his hand with reverence.

Night has fully drawn in by the time they set off back to Scaliger Castle, banks of cloud advancing from the south to deepen the gloom. Under the promise of imminent rain the four hurry back across to safety, Verona's citizens following suit as they abandon the streets to darkness. The hammer of rain on tiles accompanies them as they attend dinner in the solar and silence reigns as they eat. The toll of the day is clear on the faces of all present and none take much pleasure in the fine meal laid out.

Afterwards Juliet and Romeo retire to their bed, weary and fearful of what the morning might bring. The rain continues above them as they try to sleep, not soothing but a more insistent reminder of all that lies beyond their room. Only when the storm begins to ease and the castle is quiet do they finally slip into a peaceful rest, holding each other close like shields against the cares of the world.

Ten

In the fitful hours before dawn, Lady Capulet shifts and turns as rest eludes her. It has been years since night was a friend, since sleep was a kindness, and while the discomfort of her ribs has eased it lingers yet. The welcome hours of solitude leave a void around her, one swiftly filled by the shadows of fear and creeping regret. This night however there is a new, jagged shape lurking in the darkness of her bedroom, one that only deepens as the glow of dawn's first light appears.

In her mouth there lingers a cold and bitter taste. Thoughts swirl and clash in her mind, spinning around one kernel of iron certainty. Whatever the consequences, whatever the burden on her soul and horrors she might endure, her path is clear. Lady Capulet can see it no matter where she turns her face. The terrible weight drags at her head, a gravity that draws her in with inexorable patience.

Eventually she accepts the time has come. With tired, stiff limbs she lifts the blankets from her body and eases herself upright. It is still dark; only the suggestion of day lurks on the horizon, and there is a deep chill in the air. It prickles her skin as she slowly lowers herself to the floor where a thick rug keeps the bite of cold stone away. Careful to make no sound, Lady Capulet stands and surveys the path her mind has traced a hundred times or more across the night.

She ignores her robe. Barefoot and chilled, she takes one careful step and then another. Age has robbed her of her balance and she uses the foot of the bed to steady herself until her reluctant legs can be trusted. She crosses the room and stands by the door, massaging her fingers until the tremble is gone from them. The hinges of the door are freshly oiled, the latch polished and silent as she opens it. Once she would lock it as often as she dared, but in recent years she has hardly bothered. There has been no need and few care to disturb the rest of a woman who sleeps little.

The door opens towards her. From the doorway she surveys the gloom beyond, allowing the lines of shadow to resolve into their familiar shape. Faintly there is the sound of breath and she listens to its rhythm with a practiced ear. The tiny snuffle that heralds it prompts a distant revulsion, the contempt of the over-familiar. The inhalation that bears a slight gasp of struggle, the exhalation of weary, almost surprised, relief then a long moment of silence.

Lady Capulet takes a step inside, silent and steady in her resolve. The breathing does not change. It persists with stubborn regularity. With each breath the silence between extends just far enough to prompt a tantalian flicker of hope before it is dashed again. She walks forward, not feeling the cold on her skin. She can make out little of the tangled bedclothes from here, but there is only one person buried there, the breathing tells her that much.

As silent as a spectre she approaches the bed and

looks down. The faint light outlines a shape there, a face turned slightly away amid an untidy nest of pillows. There is the ashy wisp of stubble on his sunken cheek, deep fissures in the skin around his eyes. A vein traces its jagged path down his temple, all the way to the bulbous lump of an ear. What noble line there was once in his jaw is gone. Drink has scarred the bridge of his nose. The skin is withdrawn and tight against the line of his skull as though contorted by decades of disdain.

He sleeps deeply, better than her it seems for there is no justice in this life. What ailments are visited upon him do not come close to what is merited. There is a sour smell of sweat overlaying the stink of the chamber pot somewhere beneath, sweet wine from the cup beside the bed. Mud from the tramp of boots lingers sadly in the background like a lonely ghost.

She inspects the face a while longer. It is not disturbed by her presence; her regard makes no impact. The brass wine cup is almost empty, but a trace of dark wine remains. He has been drinking all evening, chasing the ghosts away with an angry determination.

An oil lamp sits behind it, the rounded glass bowl shadowed with soot. She contemplates these, but her attention is drawn to a pillow his nightly flailing has pushed to one side. She blinks at it several times before moving, almost surprised at the sight. With all the care she can muster, Lady Capulet lifts the pillow and holds it high. She gazes once more at the face below her, then brings the pillow down onto the face of her husband.

He is slow to react and for a moment Lady Capulet wonders if he has somehow died in that moment. She does not withdraw, however, but straddles her husband's limp form to bring what weight she can to bear down onto his bony chest. Finally wakefulness stirs his thin, wine-enfeebled limbs and they begin to lift and tug at the blanket covering him. It is pinned by her knees however, and then the panic sets in.

She grits her teeth and awaits the pain in her joints as Lord Capulet begins to properly fight his fate. She is not a big woman and he almost dislodges her in the first spasmodic burst. Distantly she wishes she had indulged herself over recent years, overcome the urge to eat and drink only sparingly as she prayed for God's gentle touch.

Lord Capulet tries to turn and almost frees his head, but she manages to twist the pillow and clamp it firmly to either side of his head. With no care for herself Lady Capulet pulls herself further up, keeping the blanket tight with her knees as she squeezes the last scrap of air from his lungs. He bucks again but weaker now, his strength so diminished the weight on his body is too much to shift.

With his arms free, she knows her husband would have the measure of her still, but he cannot heave her away and Lady Capulet fights the urge to scream her defiance at the last. Instead she closes her eyes and remembers times long past. The hot summer nights when he had been a true husband and she had taken pleasure in his strong body beneath her. The assured touch of his hand as they entered a ballroom and felt the collective breath catch. The embrace of his arms as she cradled their daughter, the rock she wept against in Juliet's bedchamber.

When he falls still, she does not notice straight away. There are tears on her cheek, her head is filled with heat and shame and anger, too. It is the surging pain in her shoulders that makes her open her eyes, that makes her finally recognise something has changed beneath her.

She does not move for a long while, indeed can hardly command her aching limbs.

Fingers clawed, back hunched, arms tight – her whole being is about this one act regardless of what may follow and she is exhausted by the effort. Trying not to cry out in pain she slowly unpicks her fingers from the pillow and gasps for air. She comes close to sinking down upon the bed beside him, spent of energy, but the fear that he is somehow not yet dead spurs her on. With short, stiff movements she clambers to the edge of the bed and sits, panting and light-headed. He does not move, does not cough and jerk awake to accuse her as her terror expects at any moment. He is still, silent. Dead.

Lady Capulet has thought no further than this point, had resolved herself to give not a moment to what may follow. Now it has come she cannot think what to do. A long moment of quiet follows as she stares at him. The distant first chirps of the dawn chorus intrude little on her thoughts at first. Only when the hammer of her heart fades does Lady Capulet feel the world return around her. The song of dawn fills her mind then, sweet voices that ring out through the dark.

With an effort she straightens and stands. Though she wants to simply flee or be discovered and allow all things that follow to be of another's choosing, she reaches shakily out and removes the pillow. Lord Capulet lies still beneath, staring and open-mouthed. She restores the pillow to where she found it and, though it revolts her more than she can understand, closes his eyes again, restores his jaw to some semblance of normality.

The rumpled sheets she straightens a little to something more akin a peaceful night's sleep and then she steps back.

'I...'

Her whisper fades with nothing to follow. She has no words; what can there be? With a note of sad emptiness in her belly she turns away and returns to her own bedchamber, at last remembering to take one final look at the scene for clues that might betray her. She finds none and cannot find the strength to search long.

Fate shall take me as it pleases. If justice has finally returned to Verona, I shall bow to it. If justice is dead here, its killer lies dead now too.

She retreats to her bed and makes to say a prayer but again she has no words. Instead she simply slips under the blanket. Nestled within the trace of warmth that remains there she shivers once and closes her eyes.

To her surprise, she sleeps. When the screams and shouts begin, Lady Capulet wakes startled and confused – rising from a deep and dreamless slumber to the sharp insistence of the waking world. The fright she takes as her door bangs open is genuine. Her incomprehension at the servants' cries proves far from the affected shock she had distantly planned. Grey dawn light washes across the room, spilling through the open doorway. More shouting follows, harsh and deep as the house guards appear. Swords are pointlessly drawn as angry and alarmed men search for the enemy, but there is none they can find. The curtains in the room beyond are hauled open and the scene is laid bare.

Lady Capulet finds herself unable to move, staring through the open doorway at the foot of her husband's bed. There are more shouts and footsteps but she remains still – blind to the milling figures, deaf to their barked calls.

'He... he is dead?' she whispers.

If anyone hears they make no effort to reply. In this private scene of horror she is left a mere bystander. She is only half out of bed, her thin and pale legs exposed to ungentle view until her maid, Julia, finally comes to her senses. Julia shuts the door again, ignoring the outrage on the face of the liveried thug behind it, and sweeps Lady Capulet's robe from a chair. This she wraps around her mistress's shoulders before kneeling to fit her silk-covered slippers onto her feet.

'He is dead?' Lady Capulet repeats as a treacherous voice in the distance of her mind marvels at her act.

Julia averts her gaze. 'My Lady... I fear it is so.'

With her maid's help, Lady Capulet rises and goes to the door. When she opens it the room falls still. For a moment she has their entire attention, a glimpse of times passed, before eyes turn downward.

'My Lord Capulet.'

The words hang in the air like sad memories. In the faces there she sees a strange acceptance, as though they have heard something profound in her words at this turning point in Verona's history. She has nothing more to say, however, no great epitaph or even kind words. Her husband lies dead and she feels nothing, as though she has died at his side.

Such is the curse of old age. This city and family have moved on without me and I hardly recognise either. I haunt the streets of Verona, touching nothing, rooted only to the places of my past. My Verona no longer exists, it began to crumble the day my precious Juliet was found dead and now nothing remains to rebuild from. This was my last true act of life, whether or not I am accused of the crime. Perhaps I will retire to a convent and pray all my remaining days, but never shall I repent.

She approaches the side of the bed. Her body feels like a marionette she must direct, jerky and uncertain movements. Lady Capulet commands her hand to reach out and brush the cooled brow of her husband. It is what a wife should do, she believes, when confronted with her deceased husband.

He looks at peace, the tension of rage gone at last from his face. The sight is strange. She has forgotten what he looks like at peace, it has been so long. But now the lines fade, the effect of age diminishes. For the first time in years she sees the face of a man she once cared for, the father of her child.

'Lady Capulet,' calls a voice behind.

She turns and sees him. This at least she has expected and her body finally obeys as she has planned.

'Captain Reynard,' she acknowledges. 'He... our lord is gone.'

The man hesitates. She can see it on his face, the calculations and suspicions that whirl through his head, but there is only the slightest of pauses before Reynard bows his head.

'You have my condolences, my Lady,' he says with rare humility. 'All of Verona will mourn him. He was the lion of our times.'

A loud roar does not a lion make. 'Indeed, Captain.'

She pauses again then lowers her head, as though the weight of grief bears heavily upon her aging frame.

'I do not know how we will manage without him. I... Captain, would you see to the arrangements? He held you in the highest of esteem, you were first among his confidents. In lieu of any heirs, I ask that you shoulder this burden.'

Reynard covers his surprise well and bows low, but she knows he is beaming on the inside. They both knew this day might come and her words are clear enough before witnesses. By asking this of him, she is showing Reynard she will not oppose him – relinquishing her claim on control of the family and its wider interests.

'Of course, my Lady,' he replies in a voice enriched with authority. 'I will see him honoured as only a lord of the Capulets deserves.' Turning to one of his attendant guards he adds, 'Niccolo, send word to the governor about Lord Capulet's passing – the Podesta, too. Verona's chief magistrate must also know.'

There he pauses and approaches the bedside, servants retreating from it in the same instance. With as much care as is possible he lifts the bedclothes and inspects underneath as much as decency and dignity permit.

'Inform the podesta we do not believe the circumstances are suspicious, but we have summoned Lord Capulet's doctor and he is welcome himself at his convenience. The rest of you will leave. I will not have our lord's passing dishonoured by the neglection of your duties and the Lady Capulet does not need your intrusion on her grief.'

Lady Capulet wishes she could applaud Reynard's new-found stateliness, but instead she merely nods.

'I thank you, Captain,' she says in a quiet voice as the room's occupants flee. 'I know you will attend to all.'

He offers her a deep bow, something that just a day before would only ever have proved grudging.

'I will leave you, too, my Lady. I know you will wish to pray at your husband's bedside.'

'That I do wish, Captain.' She waves to her maid who fetches the padded stool Lady Capulet keeps in her room for prayers. 'I thank you for your consideration.'

He closes the door behind him without a word and Lady Capulet kneels, hands clasped.

Enjoy your days of summer, Reynard, for they will be few. My husband never believed the letters nor Lawrence's testimony – he thought it all cruel malice directed towards our house. The portrait, perhaps that did sway him, but he preferred to put her from his mind. He never thought to exact a more calculating revenge. My daughter remains legal heir to all he possessed. I shall enjoy seeing her crush you in due time.

Eleven

When the knock at his door comes, Francesco finds himself hesitating, unable to call out. He sits at his desk in the governor's private study. His hands hover just above a folded letter, the wax of its broken seal still faintly malleable. He had woken not long before, the letter arriving as he broke his fast alone on bread and wine left over from the previous day. Juliet and Romeo follow the usual practice of the nobility and refrained, but Francesco was raised a fighting man so he ate alone.

Once Francesco had opened the letter, all thoughts of food had left him. The scant sentences within were enough to send his mind awhirl. Reading it once had been enough for him to bark a summons for his advisors, but for one terrible moment he could not remember what names he had used.

Only his two trusted soldiers, Rufus and Aylward, knew their true names. The risk of word getting out was too great to have it otherwise. To the servants and officials of Scaliger Castle and certainly the mercenary garrisons of San Pietro and the southern citadel, they were Renato and Sabina Esposito. Duke Visconti was renowned for employing an army of lawyers and civil servants, waging war in the courtroom as often as on the battlefield. Few in Verona would pay much heed to two more.

Only the lack of surprise had reassured him, the immediate bow and departure by the servant that surely would not have followed a summons for Juliet and Romeo Montague. The moment of panic had startled Francesco into action, however, and he had swept into his study to be alone with his thoughts.

'Come,' he calls at last.

First Romeo appears, with furrowed brow and cautious steps, but there is enough of the lordly youth remaining in him to drive him forward. Juliet lingers, however, eyes wide and searching as though an ambush is to be feared even here. She holds the door open, wary and alert, until Francesco asks her to close it.

He rises and picks up the letter before discarding it again and rounding the desk. His hands itch to hold something, letter, pen or sword, and he clasps them together to avoid bunching them into fists.

'My Lady Juliet,' Francesco says. 'I fear I bring ill tidings. Your father, he died this morning.'

She gasps, but any response is drowned out by Romeo's exclamation.

'Oh merciful God, murdered? Was it Reynard or my kin?'

Francesco raises a hand to quieten his friend. 'Please, wait a moment longer. I would have you say nothing right now.'

'Nothing?'

'I am governor of Verona,' he says in a slow, patient voice, 'and you are my advisors. This is not news that should greatly alarm or upset such persons so we must be calm and quiet now more than ever.'

119

'Calm?' Romeo demands, but Juliet catches his hand.

'My heart,' she says weakly, 'listen to him. Francesco is correct.'

'But—'

'Hush, no more words.' She looks at him with pleading eyes. 'Sit with me, hold my hand.'

Romeo blinks once then nods. With his wife's hands in his, he leads her to one of the governor's sofas and they sit together. Francesco can see Juliet's hands trembling faintly, but he reminds himself of his duty and continues.

'I have received a letter from Lady Capulet,' he says, fetching it and brandishing the offending document. Neither makes to take it from him and it ends up folded and clutched tight in his hands. 'She writes that her husband has passed away quietly in the night. No sign of violence upon his person or chambers, merely the effect of age. The podesta has been informed also so he may make judgement on the city's behalf. The letter... it goes on to say that she has withdrawn to her chambers to pray and entrusted Captain Reynard to administer Capulet affairs in the meantime.'

'It must be murder then,' Romeo growls. 'Reynard fears for his position of influence if hostilities are at an end. What need would Lord Capulet have for such a man in times of peace? A Capulet by marriage he became, but it was as a mercenary he first showed his worth. Without the need for a strong right hand, nobler minds might have come to the fore of Lord Capulet's favour.'

Francesco says nothing in reply. Though he nods in understanding, he looks away for a long moment before he can find words.

120

'I fear you are right,' he says. 'Such is the way of the world. There is no doubt Reynard is capable of this and more, we have all had occasion to take his measure. Unless there is someone within the household willing to testify to the deed however, what can I do? Perhaps the podesta will make a ruling of murder, but the lord was old and weak in body. It would have taken little violence to achieve and a skilled man will leave no trace.'

'For the sake of all Verona we must find a way to stop him. Reynard has no interest in peace – Lord Capulet may have been architect of the city's strife, but Reynard was the mason who oversaw it all. It is all he knows. He will not abandon his years of work for some other craft.'

'For the sake of Verona...' Juliet gasps, her hand going to her mouth. 'Oh merciful God!'

'What?' Romeo demands. 'What is it?'

'Do you not see?'

Both men look at her in confusion as the shock intensifies on her face. 'Can it be true? Is this another burden we are to suffer? Are the heavy hopes of a city all placed upon our backs, that we must carry them in penitence?'

Francesco frowns. 'You believe it was not Reynard who killed your father?'

'I...' She lowers her head and crosses herself, grief bearing down upon her. 'I do not know. Perhaps it is shock, perhaps it is some devil of pride within me.'

'Pride?' he echoes. 'You believe this death to be about you?'

She shakes her head. 'I do not know – that much I must be clear of.'

'My Lady, you speak now to your friend, not the governor of the city – to a man who holds your whole family in the highest esteem.'

'I speak to both, for they are the same and would both be lesser were they to pretend otherwise.'

The statement stops Francesco in his tracks, but now his mind is upon the path he sees clearly enough the direction it leads. 'As governor,' he says slowly, 'I understand, you do not offer proof, yet I hazard that as my advisor you might still responsibly air a suggestion. One that in another forum would be considered baseless gossip and as such unworthy of passing to the podesta, whose solemn duty is to investigate crimes.'

'It is so,' she replies weakly. 'I cannot know the circumstances of my father's death, I must make that clear as you say. I have heard no confession or admission, nor been privy to his will. I can only state that he was a proud man, one consumed with anger. Grief consumed him when he thought his child dead, her body stolen. I was his only heir and I had been taken from him – this he knew and any suggestion otherwise caused him more pain than he could bear.

'A man's pain leads swiftly to rage. His was great enough to have a man's tongue torn out, unable to bear the words they spoke. To be confronted with undeniable truth, the pain of twenty years might erupt, and rage might once again become his response. A man who feels the sting of betrayal reaches equally for the sword and the pen.'

Romeo nods, understanding all at last.

'A returned heir might nullify anything stated in his will – where grief may have cast a shadow over his written words of inheritance.'

Juliet takes a long breath, her hands trembling. 'Who better to know how grief's shade affected him than his wife, his companion in loss? Who better to know how he would react to the sight of his child, grown and bearing the name of his most hated enemy?'

'And who could be more willing to risk her life and immortal soul for the sake of the child she lost once?'

Twelve

Veiled by cloud, the sun hides its face as Verona wakes to the news. There is shock on the faces of many, a dull haze of understanding that dawns only fitfully. No tears fall, no great peals of anger or grief ring out, but nor does it brighten any mood. As Juliet walks to the carriage and they set out through the city's dew-slick streets, she sees her own numb detachment reflected in the faces they pass. Noble and commoner alike, they fear for what might follow, but shock still reigns. Lord Capulet's influence has touched every life here across generations. For good or ill his existence has been one constant amid a sea of troubles.

'They say the death of Lord Montague prompted celebrations,' she says, as much to herself as her companions.

Juliet remains lost in the view out of her window. Wrapped tight in a heavy shawl she still shivers and curses herself for feeling so cold inside.

'Not for long,' Francesco replies in a heavy voice. He is dressed formally, as befits the governor on official business. 'Many were beaten by Antonio's men and the following day there was a skirmish between Montagues and Capulets. Four died there, more as a tavern was burned and Capulet workshops pillaged. Those who thought they saw the end of this feud marched instead towards a city aflame.'

'And now?' Mercutio asks in a subdued voice.

'Now they do not know,' Juliet says. 'Now they fear the worst, for what else have the years taught them?'

'I will celebrate,' Mercutio says. 'In my heart I cheer it.'

'Mercutio! He was my father!'

Her son bristles with the full force of seventeen years alive. 'And he tried to kill you! What sort of man could do that? He would have done all he could to murder us both, our whole family, had he known we were here.'

'And still he was my father,' Juliet says. 'For that much I honour him as the Lord tells us to. The man I knew as a child was one I loved deeply, I beg you to remember that still. I do not forgive him for what came after, not when it endangered all I hold most dear. A parent must cherish their child – and scold them when they are wrong, as he felt I was – but cherish and protect them before all things.'

'A man who sends assassins after his daughter and grandchildren deserves no tears, no memorial at all,' Francesco remarks. 'An unmarked grave should be his rest, lost out in the fields where none will remember.'

'I do not argue with you, for all that we cannot make it so. But my son, my beloved son, do not cheer his death either. Do not open your heart to the bitterness that consumed him. All you knew of him was as a threat to your life, a distant fiend you had to fear.

'I will not ask that you forgive or mourn him. I do not know if I could manage such a thing myself. I ask only that you learn from his failings – see his example of a soul sickened by hate and anger, and resolve never to lose yourself that way.'

Mercutio frowns, lip caught between his teeth just as Romeo does when he tries to think before speaking again.

'I shall,' he says eventually. 'He was a man who had only malice in his heart for us. I would not want that poison to take root in my own, that would be a final victory for him.'

Juliet bows her head in thanks and again turns to the view of Verona from her window. The streets are quiet still. They pass the blackened skeleton of a burned-out house, soot-stains spread across its neighbours like plague, and a ragged funeral procession of servants who stand aside for the carriage to pass. Two dogs fight over the scraps of something rotten in an alley, a colonnade of trees leading to the market droop as their yellowed leaves fall and rot beneath.

The streets pass like a memory. Etched forever into her mind, Juliet hardly sees the buildings as they now are. Their destination fully occupies her mind. Her stomach tightens with every clatter of the horses drawing them before suddenly there is one lurch to the right and the carriage jerks to a halt.

Through the window she sees changes, the streets around her family home so familiar but bearing sharper edges too. An arched gate has been built across the road, sealing off the house and more from the rest of the city. As men in red livery approach she draws back from the window.

'Lay hands upon the governor's carriage and you will rue the day!' Aylward roars from the guard seat above them.

'All visitors must be checked,' the man replies in less

bold tones. 'Those are my orders.'

'Your orders mean nothing before the flag of Milan,' Aylward replies. 'Touch that door and I'll put an arrow through your eye.'

Juliet turns to Francesco, alarmed, but the young mercenary merely shakes his head.

'I trust my man,' he says quietly, 'and they will see sense.'

'Then you must wait here,' came the reply.

'Damned if we will! We convey the Governor of Verona, come to pay his respects to Lady Capulet. Open the gate or you'll bring further woes upon this house.'

Juliet cannot hear what more is said, only a mutter of conversation further away, but in moments the creak of wood and jerk of the carriage brings them up to the familiar courtyard. She can see the gates just behind them and past those a crowd of onlookers. At the forefront stands a figure she can recognise only too easily. Afforded a respectful distance by the others, Friar Lawrence's tattered habit twitches in the fitful breeze. His face is barely visible and she can discern nothing from it, but still she feels warmed by his presence.

Francesco exits the carriage, leaving Mercutio and Juliet within. They have brought only four horsemen as escort, and Rufus and Aylward stand at his heel in the livery of Milan. The badge of that city, the blue serpent devouring a red man, suddenly looks terribly out of place.

The courtyard is dull and grey compared to her childhood memories. Gone are the pots of flowers and the herbs basking in the sunshine. The threadbare rose that clings to the wall looks sickly and small where once it reached the rafters. As Francesco heads towards the door it opens and Juliet sees her mother appear, similarly diminished.

Lady Capulet is draped in black and moves with heavy, awkward steps. Where others might see the weight of grief, Juliet sees only the strain of events – of fear and more besides kept behind a mask of dignity. None would expect an old woman to wail and mourn, certainly not a Capulet of high standing.

'Lady Capulet, I come to offer my condolences for your loss, and the condolences of the magnificent state of Milan,' Francesco declares with a bow. 'Your husband was a lion of great renown. Duke Visconti spoke particularly of his strength and character as he appointed me to my position. I met him only once, but he was all I have been told to expect and more.'

'My Lord Governor,' she acknowledges with a nod of the head. 'I thank you for your words and your presence here today.'

Her eyes barely flicker towards the carriage, but Juliet knows she has seen her daughter at the window. She eases back only a little. With a scarf over her head and in the shadow of the carriage, only a mother would recognise her at that distance. Certainly not a relation whose memory of a young girl is dimmed by twenty years.

'I will not disturb your grief long, Lady Capulet. I trust the podesta is satisfied and all is well within the household?'

Lady Capulet seems to stand a little straighter as she replies. 'It is so. He agrees my husband died peacefully in his sleep.'

Juliet fancies her mother is relieved by the courteous detachment shown by Francesco. It would be well within his right to probe further and a bold mercenary would not hesitate to do so should he wish to.

'I am glad. Is there any service I might perform for you?'

Lady Capulet inclines her head. 'My husband's will has been misplaced in the years since he wrote it. Until such a time as it is found, might you permit my witness as to his wishes?'

'Certainly I would.'

'Thank you, my Lord Governor. In lieu of a direct living heir, my husband appointed Reynard Capulet as head of the family and inheritor of his estates, subject to a modest pension for myself.'

Francesco hesitates a moment before he bows to Lady Capulet. Although Juliet knows full well this was anticipated, for him to accept it without pause might cause onlookers to question why.

'Very well, it does not serve the city to exist in a state of confusion. In so far as my position allows me to formalise such appointments, I so rule that pending discovery of your husband's will and in lieu of any living heir, Reynard Capulet is acknowledged as successor to Lord Capulet in your stead, my Lady.'

Juliet watches the faces around the courtyard, blood relations and mercenaries who serve them or have married in as Reynard did. There is little surprise, little anger either. It is clear Reynard's grip on the family remains considerable without her father.

'They will accept it?' whispers Mercutio.

'They will,' she replies. 'All they see is an old woman who wishes to live out her days in peace – not to exist as a frail obstruction to the true power within the family.'

'And with the Governor's blessing, there is no need to have the will ever come to light?'

'Indeed. I am sure it will be kept safe in case some

rival is foolish enough to attempt forgery, for who would gamble on the contents?'

'I can think of one person.'

She turns to her son and places her hand gently on his arm. 'Perhaps so, but let that be a last resort.'

Before Mercutio can reply there is a commotion behind them. Juliet opens the tiny port-hole window at the rear of the carriage, but all she can see is the disorder of movement as Capulet soldiers rush toward the gate. The clatter of hooves rings out then comes to a halt as a man bellows for the Lord Governor. His tone is coarse, his accent of Savoy.

Juliet watches Aylward push his way past Capulets and call the rider forward in affectionate tones. The rider – a low-born soldier by his garb and weapons – greets Aylward and slips from his saddle, abandoning his horse to his friend as he marches on towards Francesco.

'My Lord Governor!' he calls out. 'I bring a message for you!'

'News of battle?' Francesco claps a hand on the man's arm. 'Tell me then, soldier.'

'News of victory I bring, my Lord. I... the message is to you personally from General Cane, however. It is perhaps not fit for noble company.'

Francesco smiles, more comfortable around the bawdy ways of mercenaries than the quiet grief of the nobility. 'Very well, you will follow us back to Scaliger Castle and deliver your message there. My Lady Capulet, with your permission I will leave you to your mourning. If there is some service I might yet perform, send a message to my offices and I shall assist you in all things.'

'You are most kind, my Lord Governor,' Lady Capulet says in a quiet voice. 'I thank you for your accommodation.'

'Until I may welcome you to my autumn ball then. My Lady Capulet, my Lord Reynard, good day.'

Thirteen

As he orders a return to the castle, Francesco is terse in his commands before flinging himself back into his seat. He stares out of the window as the carriage clatters briskly on, lips pressed together and his sword-hand closing and opening.

Mercutio looks from his mother to the bullish mercenary, clearly puzzled. 'Was the news not what you hoped for?'

'All that and more,' Francesco says.

'Was it Reynard then?'

Francesco gives a curt wave of the hand. 'All is well, Mercutio.'

'I...'

'Peace, boy! Leave a man with his thoughts, will you?'

Juliet lays a reassuring hand on her son's arm. He mumbles an apology and sits back, looking down at the floor of the carriage instead. Chastened but ignorant of why, Mercutio has the sense to say no more and leave an explanation for later. When they lurch back into the castle courtyard Francesco does not wait for it to pull to a halt before flinging open the door. He is out and trotting across ground in the next moment, beckoning forward the messenger as he calls over his shoulder to Juliet.

'Bring your husband, attend me in my study.'

Francesco does not wait for a reply, but Juliet nods all the same.

'Did I do something wrong?' Mercutio asks her, eyes wide with anxiety.

She knows how greatly he admires the big, fearless warrior and can see the relief when she shakes her head.

'Even in victory, men die. He will not celebrate until he knows the fate of those he loves. Remember, my son, Francesco has lived near half his life in the company of Facino Cane. Many of those mercenaries will be brothers in more than arms.'

Realisation brings a flush of embarrassment to Mercutio's cheeks, but he is not so young as to let it daunt him for long.

'I understand,' he says. Mercutio steps out of the carriage and offers his hand to Juliet. 'I will find Estelle and let her know the news.'

Here he falters, fearing he has revealed a secret if Juliet is any judge of her son's manner. Her children trust each other completely and whether or not Estelle has revealed her feelings to her brother, Juliet knows she will not have taken pains to hide them.

'That would be a kindness,' Juliet says. 'Estelle would not want to be ignorant of this and Francesco would not wish to snap a second time.'

Mercutio races off and Juliet goes to enquire on her husband. Directed to him, they embrace without words before she leads Romeo to Francesco's study with a promise of news. When they arrive, the soldier has finished relating General Cane's words and she sees a more relieved governor. Francesco stands over the smaller soldier, one great arm resting on his shoulder while they each raise a cup of wine. The soldier hastily downs his drink when he sees Juliet and Romeo, a guilty look on his face.

'Aha, my faithful advisors,' Francesco declares. 'Come, join me in a toast of my captain.'

'The news is good then?'

'More than good – General Cane has delivered a hammer-blow to the German pretender at Brescia. From his account it must have broken the back of Emperor Rupert's invasion. Milan's security is assured once more.'

'And the part that was not fit for noble ears?' Juliet enquires as Romeo fetches them wine.

Francesco laughs and claps a heavy hand against the soldier's back, rowdily ushering him towards the door. 'You may leave, friend. Have the steward arrange food and supplies for your return. As for General Cane, my Lady, he bade his messenger deliver his words exactly. There was some brotherly ribaldry for a lieutenant who was absent at his captain's great victory. I believe the general was in the highest of spirits at the time, or perhaps sunk into a vat of them!'

'But the Germans are well beaten?' Romeo asks cautiously. With mercenary armies it was common enough to claim greater credit in the hope of additional payment. Truth takes longer than mercenaries to traverse a ravaged countryside.

'So it appears. Given the manner of Cane's report, I do not doubt it. He would incur the duke's wrath soon enough if he lied. Milan's eye may once more scorch a path south, so my captain claims without hesitation. With no general fit to replace Hawkwood at the head of

Florence's forces there is little to stop Duke Visconti.'

'Does he send Verona's garrison south?'

'Not yet, but I would prefer to have good news for him before winter comes. I have no great stomach for governing a city. This office is one I will gladly surrender to you when circumstances permit.'

Juliet cocks her head at him. 'You fear victory will be so swift it may outstrip you?'

He laughs again but she sees a certain hunger in his eyes, one born of more than the lure of riches.

'I am a soldier who sees the advantage and cannot pursue it! I would hold myself in cheap regard if I had no ambition for this coming campaign. We must not be hasty I admit, but I was made governor ahead of others of higher station so I can be more easily replaced. Our lord wasted no breath or dignity feigning otherwise.'

Romeo sets his cup aside. 'In which case, we should proceed apace. I have drafted your proclamation regarding the amnesty and the ball to signal Verona's new era.'

'A quick step it must be, yes,' Francesco says with a smile. 'It seems a rare first move towards war however, declaring an amnesty and the festivities to celebrate it. But come, let me see my wise words before they are posted throughout the city.'

He takes the parchment eagerly from Romeo, though he is a man less than comfortable with letters. Juliet knows he is learning however, while many in his position leave such work to wives and clerks. Francesco's great brow furrows as he concentrates on the text, but after a short while he gives up and hands it back.

'Most learned and lawyerly to be sure. I am a better son of Milan than I had realised, my friend.'

135

'We must set your aspirations high, my Lord Governor,' Juliet says with measured humour. 'You are a man who would be bored unless he were reaching for the stars.'

The comment draws a pause from Francesco, but he recovers quickly and offers her his best smile – one that has won many a heart, one closer to her own than others. 'I shall endeavour to meet all your expectations, my Lady.'

'Of that I have no doubt, my Lord. This does mean however that I must depart. There is a ball to arrange and a lawyerly pen will not suffice there.'

*

The days that follow the death of Lord Capulet move swiftly from one to the next. Bursts of autumn sunshine give way to glittering showers then reclaim the heavens once more. A gusty breeze sweeps across the city and seems to lend its energy to the inhabitants of Scaliger Castle and the city beyond. The warring families take heed of their governor's warning and a spell of peace adds to the new sense of hope. Verona knows as well as any city of Italy that all peace is temporary so any chance to breathe freely is all the more welcome.

Estelle finds herself swept up in preparations for the ball and embraces the charge. Unable to explore Verona with the ease her brother might, Estelle turns her energies and Milanese sensibilities to the service of her parents' design. From the servants she hears much and chatters merrily as they work. Before long even those who might be wary of her station, modest though it appears, are won over and the mood of the city begins to be unveiled before her.

While the Capulets draw inward and Lord Reynard consolidates his position, the Montagues have proved most careful in their restraint. The harvests are modest, but any calm within the city permits them to be brought in without trouble. Estelle gladly reports to Francesco during the moments he can spare that for the first time in many years, the people are hopeful for what may come. Though only a glimmer on the horizon, it is welcomed by all as a first step.

The ball is to be masked and Estelle takes it upon herself to secure costumes for her family. Amid a sea of nobility and wealth they will not be greatly remarked, but anything that makes them stand out could yet prove dangerous. For her mother, a songbird mask with short purple feathers; for her father, a fox with stout whiskers.

Her brother, Estelle hopes, will emulate the angelic visage she has selected for him and find no time for argument with Verona's hot-headed youth, while her own bears only curling webs of green. For Francesco, she has chosen something rather more magnificent, a great lion's mane and roaring visage that will command the room as he must.

As the day of the ball arrives, the great hall of Scaliger Castle is decked in the colours of autumn. With a dozen tasks to hand, Estelle finds herself unexpectedly alone and takes a moment to inspect her work. The ceiling is hung with paper vines and Venetian glass decorations that sparkle in the light. Vases of red, orange and yellow flowers adorn the walls, filling the air with a heady sweetness, while ribbons wreath the musicians' platform.

'May I invite you to dance, my Lady?' whispers a voice through the hush.

Estelle whirls around to discover Francesco lounging

in a doorway. She smothers a laugh and curtseys prettily. 'I fear that would not be seemly, my Lord Governor.'

He shrugs and pushes off from the jamb to cross the open floor. 'There are no servants here. No eyes to see and tongues to wag.'

Francesco's boots sound crisply on the wooden floor and echo around the room. He is tired, she can see that in his eyes, but the light of his smile warms her cheeks.

'None at present,' she corrects him. 'But in moments they are likely to return.'

'Do you deny your Lord Governor?' Francesco asks.

She clutches her hands to her heart. 'Never could I presume to occupy his valuable time.'

'You occupy his time nonetheless, both waking and sleeping.'

He takes another step forward, almost as though to embrace her only to step smoothly aside. She follows in kind, a slow facsimile of a dance where only their regard meets.

'My Lord is most kind to favour me in his thoughts.'

'The earth, sun and stars all favour you,' Francesco says softly. 'Man is an imperfect beast, not in step with such natural rhythms, but we can aspire to follow such an example.'

'I fear you are dazzled by the sun, my Lord, for what woman could match the ideal you have conceived?'

'You, my Lady.'

She turns away with a sigh. 'You ask too much of me. None of us can come near to such perfection. Pretty words I have heard before, my Lord. Milan is full of them. Pretty words I have been warned of before. I beg you, Francesco – soldier though you be, you are noble of spirit and kind of heart. Do not raise me so high, do not cast flattery all about me and call it honour.'

'What should I do then? Have I offended you? Estelle, you are dear to my heart I swear it!'

She pauses and glances over her shoulder. 'I know, my Lord, and I hold you in the same esteem. But I have seen where excess and exhortations may lead and I wish none of that. You are a good man and a strong leader, I admire all that you are and I embrace all that you are not. Do not cover your eyes from all that I am not, that is all I ask.'

He stops, his feet falling heavily to rest, and bows his head. 'You are correct. I apologise for letting my heart run away with my tongue. In this place I see the glamour that has been cast and drink too deeply of it.'

'There are no apologies needed, my Lord,' Estelle says. She reaches out and brushes his hands with her fingers. 'I am glad your warrior heart can be moved to such sweet melodies.'

'Perhaps we may dance tonight, in the privacy of my heart if not before all of Verona.'

'I will gladly join you in that dream, my Lord,' Estelle says, three quick steps taking her neatly around Francesco before she starts to walk briskly down the length of the hall. 'In my heart we will dance until dawn's first light.'

Fourteen

'Lord and Lady Reynard of House Capulet.'

The guests turn in one neat step, this a dance every person present knows. Feathered gowns ruffle nervously as the city's highest tier comes into view; chirrups of conversation wither to nothing. In a room of music and merriment, all Juliet can hear are the footsteps of the newcomers and the cries of house martins feasting in the last of the light outside.

For a moment she imagines the crowd parting and Reynard recognising her for who she is – her thin mask no protection from his regard. Her chest tightens at the thought, her heart stutters in fear. But it does not happen. Her view of Lord Reynard and his wife is limited behind a screen of Verona's nobility. When she is afforded a glimpse, Juliet sees a man basking in his new-found position not seeking prey.

A mask of red and black stripes does not hide a tigerish smile as he surveys the crowd. His wife, Isabella, is tall and elegant in a magnificent gown that glitters purple, red and white. Hers is the bearing of a ruler, Juliet notes. The husband who married into the Capulets is first and only a predator still. There have been rulers of his ilk across Italy, most notoriously in Milan until the current duke deposed his uncle.

Our lord will never stand for Bernabo Visconti's image to gain prominence in Verona, Juliet realises as she watches Lord Reynard. *History itself warns you, Reynard, but I do not see here a man able to hear such words.*

'Did you know her well, Lady Isabella?' Romeo whispers in Juliet's ear.

She shakes her head. 'She was just a child, a second cousin who I rarely saw.'

'And now she is the Lady Capulet. Is she the true power here I wonder?'

Juliet shakes her head. 'Perhaps she believes so, perhaps she had only hoped of it, but I see otherwise.'

'She has the bearing of a duchess,' Romeo contends. 'See how they all watch her every movement?'

'A duchess may give a tiger commands, the tiger chooses what to obey. They warm to her, but they flinch at him.'

Behind the rulers of the Capulets, more of their house filter into the hall. Those are not announced, not when it is a masked ball, but their colours remain obvious. The Montagues appeared earlier, Lord Antonio at their fore and most welcoming of his host. Both had known Lord Reynard would make the grander entrance. That Antonio made no effort to antagonise his enemy was something Francesco pointedly appreciated.

'Musicians, play!' calls Francesco as he strides forward to greet the Capulets. A lively tune is struck up and the moment is broken as dancing resumes. Those not of either faction – the Milanese, the merchants and landowners, the city officials and guild leaders too – have all had Francesco's expectations laid gently out.

The ball marks a turning point for Verona and they are all expected to keep the merriment going, the tensions eased. Romeo goes to play his part and takes the hand of one young lady to lead her out, sparing a last smile for his wife as he does.

'My Lord Capulet, welcome,' Francesco says in a loud voice before bowing to kiss the hand of Lady Isabella. 'My Lady, you look magnificent.'

She curtseys and thanks him, the pleasantries formal but no stiffer than Juliet had feared. Lord Reynard is slower in his response, but has sense enough to shake off the memory of their first meeting and speak with all the grace he can muster. After presenting the apologies for the dowager Lady Capulet, whose ill health is already expected, Reynard introduces a half-dozen of the leading Capulets, each one sour-faced and at least a decade his elder.

At a look from Juliet, those who have been deputised to service descend and begin to tease the faction apart, diffusing the red of Capulet through the colours of the ball. Before long it is only Francesco and Reynard standing alone, the two men lingering on the cusp of awkwardness. By then, however, Juliet has smoothly swept Lord Antonio up from where he watches it all and ushers him to their side. She departs with as little ceremony as she arrived, keeping close in case she is required and ready to dissuade those who might intrude.

'My Lords, I thank you both for attending,' Francesco begins as the music and clatter of feet afford them some modest privacy. 'I hope this night will indeed serve as a turning point for Verona's fortunes.'

'Do you mean to so easily draw a line under it all?' inquires Antonio. 'How easily the dead are erased from our hearts.'

'Would you prefer the alternative?'

'There is much that I would prefer, my Lord Governor,' he replies, eying Reynard all the while.

'No doubt Lord Reynard would wish something similar, but it cannot be so,' Francesco says before Reynard himself can respond. 'To seek some full measure of justice would be to tear down the two great families of the city and undo all that we might hope to achieve.'

'Yet enmity still exists,' Reynard says, 'no edict or amnesty can erase that.'

Francesco inclines his head. 'The amnesty offers some foundation without which there will be no future for either of you. Mark my words, my lords, the first to break it will suffer my wrath. There will be peace or lives shall be forfeit. The man who cannot contain his house shall suffer, too.'

'You make such a threat?' Antonio asks, astonished. 'What man can be held responsible for orders he does not give, fires he does not light?'

'He who commands troops must answer for their actions,' Francesco replies simply. 'Should they engage in hostilities again and again, a captain must answer to his failings wherever they lie. This advice I do offer, as a man who has served once and likely shall again as a mercenary throughout Italy. A company of free men is not fixed, its numbers ebb and flow according to the tides of war. The most loyal are retained even in periods of peace, the unruly cut loose as needless expense.'

'You would disarm us now?'

'I would see you attend to the life of the city. You are landowners and more besides, but few of your needs can be fulfilled by soldiers. Some have shown

143

themselves greater than their initial employment – you Lord Reynard are testament to that and I am a man who wholly agrees with such elevation. Many will not follow such an august path however and will perform poorly as men of industry.'

'Should we be without guards entirely?' Antonio asks. 'Should we unbar our doors, offer our daughters to the rabble, perhaps?'

'Unrest and disorder ever shadow the horizon, I am well aware of that, yet each of you can call upon a hundred fighting men. More even, should you summon those houses aligned to you. My lords, this state cannot endure. Where fighting men gather, fighting shall naturally follow.'

'Hired hands do not contain wounded hearts,' Antonio says. 'The enmity between our houses will remain without them. The fires of hate will burn as strong.'

'I cannot give orders to your hearts, for what man can extinguish hate? My words are to your heads, to reason and self-interest before all things. There are many who are employed as threats and provocateurs to your foes. It does not take a soldier to know fewer swords on the field lead to fewer deaths. You need not like each other, but Verona is crumbling and this feud kills more than those of each house.'

'That much I do not deny,' Reynard breaks in, 'but twenty years and more of this feud is not so easily ended by either of us. Certainly not by one who is new to his position and knows there are some willing to undermine him. We both have rivals, I am sure, eager to tear us down.'

'I leave to you how you consolidate your positions,' Francesco says coldly. 'My concern is order within the city and an end to your hostilities. There is amnesty granted to all crimes and violent acts between members of your houses. I do also extend grave warning as to the consequences of further acts. This city will remember the rule of law whether it takes one young fool to be hanged or many. I cannot control how others may choose to test my resolve.'

He takes a breath and bows to them both. 'Tonight is a first step, nothing more need be resolved so long as we remain one yard closer come the morrow. Should Montagues and Capulets exist in a single room without injury done, the city will take note and we may all hope for what will follow. I thank you for your attendance and invite you to enjoy all we have on offer.'

Juliet watches Francesco leave them and the hush that follows in his wake. At last, Reynard and Antonio incline their heads to each other and part – no insult done, no violence instigated. She is far from the only one to be watching and all note the cordiality. Finally Juliet finds she can breathe once more, but just in that moment a man appears suddenly at her side. She gasps as the man clears his throat, but as she takes a proper look at him, there is no glimmer of recognition.

'My apologies, Madam, I did not mean to startle you.'

He is a fleshy man in his fifties, with thinning brown hair and the practiced servile stance of a merchant among the powerful. His small mask lies across only the bridge of his nose so as to keep clear of his waxed moustache.

'No, Messer, the fault was not yours,' Juliet manages

to say after a blank moment. 'I was lost in thought, there is no fault for you to bear. May I assist you?'

'I merely wished to introduce myself, Madam. I see you are an advisor to the Lord Governor. My name is Arturo Malacrolla. I am a merchant of Mantua.'

'It is a pleasure to make your acquaintance. I am Sabina Esposito,' Juliet intones with the blank formality of someone serving in their professional capacity.

'And you are one of the governor's principal advisors? I would be most interested in securing a meeting with him in due course – or perhaps with you, if his availability does not permit such a thing.'

There is an edge of suggestion in his voice that causes a pricking of her thumbs. Though they both wear masks, Juliet sees lecherous intent in his manner and wonders whether it hides further motives.

'My husband is the governor's principal advisor, Messer. I merely assist where I can and at a ball a lady may more easily direct. I am sure Renato would be glad to offer you an appointment. He wears a fox mask – I would gladly point him out to you.'

'A most noble partnership to be sure. Do I have your husband to thank for this truce between houses? The feud has been most disruptive of trade in recent years.'

'Yet you still make the journey?'

'My contacts are here,' he explains in apologetic tones. 'While there remains profit to be made, however modest, I must pursue it. Tell me, did yourself and your husband comprise the entirety of the governor's party?'

'We are his only advisors – his two most trusted comrades in arms accompanied him too.'

'Ah, I see. I ask because I see a young woman unknown to me, there, at the doorway. She strikes me as

146

most elegant and graceful – beautiful too, perhaps, in the opinion of the governor who surely knows her beneath that mask.'

Juliet follows the line of his gaze and indeed there is Estelle, her dress decorated with green silk ribbons and her painted mask framing the curve of her cheek. She is remarkable perhaps to a young lusty man, Juliet is sure, but less so to a merchant older than her mother. What instead has snagged Malacrolla's notice is the manner of Lord Francesco. The governor stands distracted from his conversation, gaze drifting time and again to a young woman half hidden behind a whirl of society beauties.

'That is my daughter, Estelle,' Juliet says in a tight voice.

'Your daughter accompanied you on this assignment? Do you intend to establish yourselves in Verona for several years?'

'The duke instructs us, we go at his pleasure.'

Malacrolla nods, gaze resting firmly on Estelle. 'Naturally. An unmarried woman should not be apart from her family for so long and the problem of this feud cannot be ended in one night. Ah, but do I see a suitor for the young lady appear at her side? Surely not long since a boy however, no match for a woman in the full bloom of beauty.'

'Indeed not. That is my son, Mercutio.'

'Then you are most blessed, Madam. He has a noble bearing, though in these parts his name is considered ill-omened. You favour Verona for the first time?'

'We do, Messer.'

Finally he bows to Juliet. 'I thank you for sparing me your time, Madam. At your direction I shall send word tomorrow to your husband, Messer Esposito, to request that appointment.'

Juliet watches him go with a troubled heart. Once Malacrolla has disappeared into the crowd she prepares to distract Francesco's notice so that few others will have occasion to remark upon his preoccupation. Before she can move however, the governor recovers himself and returns fully to his conversation while Estelle is coaxed into a dance by one young man in Capulet colours. The pace of the music increases and more pairs move towards the open space in the centre of the hall.

Surveying the room, Juliet spies the merchant speaking closely with a Capulet lady, but before she can see what transpires she is entreated into dance by a cordial white-haired knight of the city. Two circles are formed as the musicians finish their introduction with a flourish and then Juliet is swept into a lively dance between the knight and a Montague she does not recognise.

She can only glimpse fragments of the room beyond, trusting her feet to the steps of the brisk dance. Francesco stands deep in conversation, Romeo laughs as he passes her, part of the other circle that turns in the opposite direction. Of Malacrolla, she sees nothing, her attention drawn instead to Lord Reynard. The man stands well back from the whirling rings, watching all with a predator's regard while a cohort of Capulet red flanks him.

Some of the dancers are already a little drunk and they stagger in the middle of the dance, causing the circle to lurch sideways. Juliet is forced to haul upon the hand of the Montague beside her to keep her feet. To her relief he responds with practiced grace, raising his arm to take her weight. Just as she recovers her balance, however, something slams into her heel and her foot is swept from underneath her.

Juliet tumbles with a shriek and pulls the Montague down half on top of herself. Distantly she hears a shriek of surprise followed by laughter and cheers from those watching, but all is eclipsed by the stinging blow of the Montague's elbow against her shoulder. Juliet is thrown to one side and hits the white-haired knight who has her other hand.

The pair sprawl across the floor as more stagger and the ring of dancers bursts apart. Men rush forward; the clatter of feet surrounds her. Juliet feels hands underneath her arms and in the confusion her mask is knocked from her face. She recoils in shock, falling back a step but securely held by those who have come to her rescue. Steadied, she feels the hot prickle of a host of eyes watching her as her mask tumbles away.

For one long moment she cannot move, transfixed by the sharp needles of their stares. The space of one heartbeat feels like an age before Juliet bends to retrieve her mask. In that moment the cold claws of dread dig into her throat as a gasp cuts through the hush.

Mask forgotten in unfeeling hands, Juliet straightens. There before her is her cousin, Maria – her pinched face not so far from the cheerless child she once was and lacking none of that girl's sharp regard. Maria Capulet's hand flies to her mouth in horror, but it does nothing to muffle the word that silences the room.

'Juliet?'

149

Fifteen

'What trickery is this?'

The hall descends into chaos as voices burst out from all sides and the musicians falter and stop. Juliet is thrown back by the force of it all while a gaping Maria is thrust aside by Lord Reynard.

'Juliet?' Maria asks again. She is too stunned to say more, but there are few words with more power to swallow all sound in Verona.

Juliet's stomach clenches with fear. The urge to grab uselessly for her mask fills her, but she fights it. The ghost of the girl who fled Verona twenty years previously seems to hang in the air before her – terrified and cowed. At last, Juliet finds the strength to take a breath and that seems to diminish the ghost.

I am not that little girl, she shouts in the privacy of her own mind. *I have fled from assassins, I have brought life into this world! Their words will frighten me no longer.*

'Yes.'

Her throat is hoarse and she barely hears herself over the pulsing cloud of sound that surrounds her, but

Juliet clears her throat and repeats it. No longer a fearful girl, she looks Reynard in the eye as she speaks.

'Yes, it is I.'

A hush, a ripple of quiet that radiates out from her and makes grown men stagger. Then more shouting; animal rage, confusion and disbelief. Juliet lets it wash over her, gaze locked with Lord Reynard who has not spoken. Before he can, another Capulet steps forward and seizes her arm. He drags roughly at her, a man who she does not know but is ten years her senior.

'What is this madness?' the man roars. 'Juliet is dead – dead this twenty year! No swindler with a likeness will live to insult our house by claiming otherwise!'

If they are related, the passage of time has rendered him entirely different to the man she once met. Juliet is struck by the certainty that his first instinct is to drag her outside and she resists his efforts. Before he can move her, others rush forward. Romeo rips the man's hand away and Estelle fights her way through the crowd to throw her arms around her mother and shield her.

'Step back!' roars Francesco as he appears behind Juliet's assailant. 'All of you, withdraw.'

'Lord Governor? You knew of this?' Lord Reynard demands, his anger welling up. 'What deception is afoot here? What scheme plays out around us?'

'There is no deception,' Francesco bellows in reply. 'No swindler besides.'

Before anyone else can respond, Lord Antonio gasps. He advances too, the crowd parting before him.

'But if you are Lady Juliet then... can it be?' He peers at Romeo, incomprehension knitting his brow. 'Cousin?'

Romeo tenses as though stung, but does not immediately respond as he attends his wife. 'Are you

151

hurt?'

Only when Juliet shakes her head does Romeo straighten. Finally, with a great weight on his shoulders to make every movement an effort, he looks Antonio in the eye.

'Yes, cousin, it is I.'

'Murderer! Most base of criminals!' The roar seems to come from all sides at once and the crowd contracts around them. Romeo turns, searching for his accuser, but now it is both Montagues and Capulets who press forward.

Estelle cries out as she is shoved away from Juliet. She falls against a pillar and Francesco is there in a moment. With a snarl he strikes the man who took hold of her and knocks him down, shouting for his guards in the next breath.

Rufus and Aylward appear in moments, Mercutio on their heels with his sword drawn. The threat prompts some guests to produce their own, though Juliet sees yet more shy from Francesco's fury. Soon half of the room are fleeing while the rest prepare to fight.

Before blows can be struck more guards appear, the clatter of boots, shields and mail eclipsing other sound. It is enough to make the guests pause and see the biscione flag of Milan on their livery. Hesitation turns to sense as the soldiers drive a wedge through the crowd to Francesco. It keeps the feuding parties apart from allies as much as enemies, but the distance is enough to win another few breaths. Most are shocked foremost, the habits of their feud ingrained but surprise still reigns.

'How can this be, cousin?' Antonio cries.

'How can Juliet be alive?' Reynard adds. 'What devil's pact has caused this?'

'There was no pact,' Juliet insists, placing herself

between the two lords and her husband. 'A simple ruse when we were young, one never intended to run so far. I took a sleeping draft concocted to escape my obligations – my father's promises of marriage made in ignorance that I was already wed.'

'Already wed?' Reynard gasps. 'To this notary of Milan?'

'To Romeo Montague, trueborn nobleman of Verona.' She can see her retort stings this man who only married into nobility. 'Son and heir of the house of Montague, husband to the only child of Lord Capulet and father to my children.'

Reynard summons a sneer through his surprise. She recognises the look he wears from when he accosted them their first morning home.

'I see only half a man before me; a lackey of Milan who lacks both sword and badge, hiding his face behind a beard. A lawyer well-used to twisting the truth to his own means.'

As Renard adopts practiced contempt, Juliet sees Lord Antonio default to his preferred public face and laughs.

'So speaks a man who wears his wife's name and twists it into his own! Tell me, Lady Isabella, did he offer his hose and braies in exchange or merely his manhood?'

The comment incenses all Capulets and the air is filled with the babble of proud men. Juliet can make out little and cares for less as men grapple and spit their insults. Most of the women have already withdrawn and linger at the fringes of the hall, ready to flee should blood be shed.

Romeo turns his back on it all, intent only on sheltering his family from the press, but he cannot protect them from all sides. Juliet reaches for her children, but Mercutio shrugs her off, his cheeks flush with anger, and Estelle grasps her only feebly.

'Enough!' Francesco shouts above it all and wins a brief moment of respite. 'Stay your swords and still your tongues! Retire and be gone from this place else I choose between irons and steel for your fate.'

The clamour lessens a touch and the struggling mass pulls back. Without the buffeting arms around her, Estelle wavers. Juliet slips her arm around her daughter's waist just as Estelle's knees buckle. One hand fumbling at a bruise on her temple, she lurches in her mother's grip before Mercutio abandons his sword and ducks his head under Estelle's free arm. At the sight, Francesco gives a great roar of fury and draws his sword.

'Guards! Drive these snakes off, cast them out of this place or bleed them!'

With the pommel of his sword Francesco hammers at Antonio. The nobleman staggers under the blow and falls against another Montague. A grinning Aylward brandishes his sword at Lord Reynard and deftly cuts the silk of his tunic. Juliet sees delight on the mercenary's face, enjoying the rare chance to threaten a man of high station without recrimination.

More soldiers join the struggle, presenting a wall of mailed fists and spear shafts that easily throws the erstwhile guests back. There are shrieks from the far side as the non-combatants flee to the courtyard. In the face of a Milanese phalanx, all the men of Montague and Capulet do likewise.

Francesco leads the pursuit like Alexander himself, ready to cut down the first man who resists. Left suddenly alone, watched only by the timid faces of servants at one doorway, Juliet and Mercutio help

Estelle to the ground. She struggles against them for a moment then allows herself to be laid back. Staring up at the ceiling, she only blinks for a long while, until finally her eyes become focused, her breath less ragged. Juliet sees recognition in her eyes and feels a flush of relief.

'Can you sit up?' Romeo asks. Estelle makes a tentative attempt and with some help she manages it.

'I can stand,' she hazards. 'It is passing.'

'Are you certain?'

'I am certain I do not wish to be sat here, splay-legged before the whole castle.'

'It seems her wits are restored,' Mercutio says, sparing a smile for his sister. 'I have heard nothing of more sense from her this past week.'

'Hush your throat,' Romeo commands. 'I heard words of yours not moments ago that I would not call sense, spoken to grown men trained in arms.'

'Come, help her up, Mercutio,' Juliet says. 'Let us retire to our rooms. We are the spark of discord here tonight, let us remove that from the embers at least.'

'And Francesco?' Estelle asks.

'Do not worry for him, the Lord Governor is surrounded by his men.'

'And full of fire,' Mercutio adds. 'Such a rage I have rarely seen upon him. I should only have a care for he who struck you.'

'Enough of your chatter, Mercutio. Retrieve your sword and let us be off. Francesco will know to find us there – come now.'

*

The night passes in fitful pretence of rest. A quilt of prickling worry settles over Juliet as she sits at Estelle's bedside. Fatigue drags at her limbs, but she knows she will not submit to sleep tonight of all nights, even if she was not tasked with keeping her daughter awake.

Francesco comes to Estelle's bedside not long after they had reached it, proving awkward and formal before their whole family. Once Juliet sends Romeo and Mercutio away he relaxes somewhat, but still the clatter of emotion within him renders him frustrated. Juliet chases him back to his duties as swiftly as she can. There will be time later for private words between the pair, for now Francesco is the Lord Governor of a city teetering on the brink of conflict.

The discordant sound of night-time activity rings throughout the castle as mother and daughter make occasional, inconsequential talk. The blow to her head has left Estelle weak and unsteady. Though the dizziness and pain has subsided, Francesco was at pains to insist Juliet not let her sleep yet. He has seen it many times in his years of soldiering, blows to the head that a man will shake off only to never rise from his sleep.

Instead, propped up by pillows, Estelle sits and talks to her mother of the life she has left in Pavia, where the duke holds court. The family have lived recent years in a village within the duke's private hunting ground, enjoying the security it affords. There are the usual court intrigues and gossip of any centre of power, but both Estelle and Mercutio were afforded the run of a beautiful stretch of countryside. Her life is shared between Pavia and the near-deserted woodlands and streams around their village, an idyll fitting to the duke's splendour.

As light threatens the horizon and the first warbling chorus of dawn is spent, Juliet lets Estelle wriggle down in the blankets and settle for a few hours' sleep. For a long while she sits with her daughter in a way she has not for many years. Not since Estelle was a girl and struck down with a fever has Juliet watched over her in this way.

In the early years of their life she and Romeo spent many hours doing just that, marvelling at each serene, sleep-bound smile. The child of then is never closer than when her beautiful daughter sleeps, Juliet realises. The cares and uncertainties of the world fall away, restoring that perfect state of bliss a parent wishes for their child.

Once the dull shine of cloud tells her the sun is risen, Juliet submits to her urge to move – to do more than stand sentinel when there is work yet to be done. She summons a servant and instructs the woman to stay with Estelle, listening to her breathing, before leaving in search of her husband and the governor.

'My lords, is there news?' she asks when she finds them in Francesco's offices.

'None, Lady Juliet,' Francesco replies. His gaze darts to the door, though he asks nothing further. He is dressed for war now, in gambeson and mail.

'She is well, Francesco,' she reassures him. 'The dizziness is passed and Estelle sleeps normally. She needs but rest now. Is there nothing of the city?'

'I have sent orders to San Pietro and the citadel; the garrisons are roused and patrols walk the city. There is no news of disorder, but under cover of dark I have been loath to send them far. We can only hope that day unveils no act of violence, neither house exploiting this moment for the petty demands of their feud. Romeo believes it will be so, that with the morning comes words and not deeds.'

Romeo bows his head. 'Ugly words, though,

157

brandished like spears by lawyers marching upon our door perhaps. A murder of lawyers, circling.'

'Antonio and Reynard must both be concerned for their legitimacy,' Juliet says, 'but do they strengthen their foundations first or undermine ours?'

He smiles weakly. 'I suspect even in this regard, they cannot agree a course to both chart.'

'Your claim to the House of Montague is surely unassailable lest your kin unite to refuse you. Your claim to the House of Capulet is less certain, but it exists and takes the same winding path of marriage that Reynard's does.'

'So Antonio is better served to fortify his position and leave Reynard to attack yours,' Francesco agrees. 'He who holds the high ground has no need to care how he attained it, only use it to attack before the moment is wasted.'

Juliet goes to the window and looks out over the courtyard below. Other than the enclosed garden, there is light and movement everywhere. Two large fires still burn though the torches are now doused. A dozen archers remain on the wall overlooking the street, men-at-arms stationed at every gate.

'They surely cannot attack us,' Juliet says, watching the soldiers below.

'Not unless madness has overtaken them. Better men have done worse in the heat of passion, however.'

'But they must recall that yesterday they lacked the power to defy Milan. Nothing has changed there, for all that there is change.'

'Milan is not their enemy,' Romeo says. 'They will be cautious of making it so. *We* are their enemy – that we reside under Milan's protection is no more than an obstacle in their path.'

158

'I shall make it a mountain,' declares Francesco.

'One they shall endeavour to walk around. Our existence causes unrest in their world – I would expect them to visit that unrest upon the whole of Verona until the city's master considers us more a problem than solution. We serve at our lord's sufferance, my Lord Governor. While he may have further use for you if this ends in disaster, I doubt Juliet or I have great value beyond this city.'

'So we must ensure the matter of Verona does not vex him further, however—' Before Juliet can continue there is a cry from the gatehouse, just as the threads of sunlight begin to pierce the clouds above. One of the archers calls out orders, summoning more men to the wall, while another roars for the Lord Governor to be summoned. Before a man can be dispatched, Francesco is already moving.

Sixteen

Francesco marches toward the gatehouse, voice raised in question but expecting no answer as men-at-arms clatter past. That he is heard is enough; a leader must be prominent in uncertain times.

Behind him follow Juliet and Romeo, unarmed but ready to be called upon. They stay at the base of the stair while Francesco ascends two steps at a time. In moments he stands at the top, looking down over the open ground beyond.

The street is still in grey gloom, but he can see a tide of movement approaching. Clearly this is no attack, but nor is it peaceful. There are voices rising from the mass, shouts of anger. The families have roused their own and more; he spies women and children, noble and commoner, advancing on the castle.

'What lies have they told to summon numbers like this? They cannot have so quickly roused every retainer, dependent and tradesman tied to their house.'

'Lies don't breach walls, my Lord,' Aylward comments from Francesco's side. The archer has his bow strung, but stands relaxed at the crenelations. 'Let them come.'

'Lies undermine walls and we are not at war here, Aylward. We cannot offer peace through threats of violence alone.'

'They will see their choices narrowed quick enough. In a few days the Great Houses must realise your goodwill is all that stands between them and destruction.'

'But who fights harder than an army assured of slaughter in defeat? No, they will struggle to the last and care not who suffers. This is their city, not mine. The mob is a fickle beast when roused. Before reason is restored it might tear this city apart and it is easier to follow the devil you know.'

'By my father's ten finger bones! One good thing has come of this, my Lord,' Aylward says, peering forward into the gloom below. 'Look – you have succeeded in bringing together the Lords of Capulet and Montague. I fancy I see red liveries coming from the east.'

'United in their hate,' Francesco spits. 'What happy news you bring, my friend! It will not last long, just enough to see these cobbles splashed with blood.' He leans forward as far as the walls permit and calls out in a booming voice.

'Come no further! Who marches upon this place?'

'The citizens of Verona!' is the reply that follows. 'We come for justice!'

'You come in force and bearing arms! Is that the justice you seek?'

'We seek an audience with the Lord Governor – here before the eyes of the city.'

'Step forward only those who would speak for you.'

There is a moment of shifting sands within the tide. It is no great piazza there. The shore-side of Scaliger Castle occupies a broad street facing stone-built houses and the remnants of the old city wall behind. The gatehouse itself stands at the junction of streets. Dawn's gleam reveals Lord Antonio Montague at the fore of his House arriving from the north, Capulets from the east.

Antonio and a detachment of knights move ahead of the crowd – armed and without their usual finery, but not wearing armour at least. There is a little uncertainty when they come in line with the Capulet delegation. The mob behind pulses and stirs, but the watch-captain calls orders to his archers in response. Upon hearing this they draw back a way, watching with resentful eyes.

'My Lord Governor, we come as citizens of this fair Verona in search of justice,' Lord Antonio cries out. 'Will you hear us honestly where all may see you, or ignore us from your walls in the manner of a tyrant?'

'I will hear you,' Francesco replies, 'if you truly come with peace and justice in your hearts. If you bring mischief in their place, my forbearance will vanish like the promises of Florence.'

He turns to leave but pauses at Aylward's side. 'Should the mood turn ugly and they attempt to take me, have no care of my person nor regard to their station. Neither man is Richard of England, neither deserves greater respect.'

He descends to the courtyard where Rufus is waiting for him at the postern gate. Francesco seeks Romeo out in the courtyard before he goes, however.

'Bide here, my friend, your time will come soon enough. I will not enrage these vultures with sight of you yet.'

Outside, Francesco pauses at the gate and looks around at the crowds gathered there, distinct by the spots of colour, blue and red, within them. As he suspected there are many from all walks of life. A noble house holds sway of many below it and in Verona that is all the more pronounced. Criminals and upstanding citizens alike have been swallowed by the leviathans of this feud, leaving no spare ground between.

'It has not been long since I welcomed you as my guests, Lord Capulet, Lord Montague. Was your enjoyment of the ball such you hasten to reprise it?'

'We come in protest,' Lord Antonio replies. 'You harbour a murderer behind those walls.'

'There are many fighting men within those walls, would you demand them come to confess their sins one by one?'

'You know of whom I speak.'

'On matters such as murder I choose not to guess.'

'The man who calls himself Romeo Montague.'

'The same Montague who is rightful lord of House Montague?'

Antonio purples. 'No murderer may claim such a right.'

'Again, you make this accusation, but I am a fighting man. *I* have killed, as have many within my company, yet you do not call them murderers.'

'You killed in battle.'

'On occasion, it is true.'

'To cut a man down in the street,' Reynard exclaims, 'to do to death in a graveyard – neither is battle. What then would you call it?'

'I confess the latter sounds more efficient than many of my efforts, but then I am a working man and spare a thought for the labour I may cause others.'

'You would joke about a man's death? It is sinful to insult those who cannot answer your words.'

Francesco raises an eyebrow. 'You defend the memory of one you did not know? You who revolts against the insult of the dead, yet casts accusations upon the living and rouses a portion of the city in outrage with them?'

'Then bring him out, let him defend his actions. Tybalt would have been cousin of mine by marriage had he not been slain.'

'Do you now defy the law? There was much wrong done during the course of the feud, but all is covered by amnesty. Would you choose to have it lifted and expose what lies beneath? There were darker deeds that the death of one man in a fair fight.'

'Not all his deeds are so expunged,' Antonio declares. 'This you know full well. Count Paris was of neither Capulet nor Montague, yet he died at Romeo's hand.'

'You have a witness to this?'

'All of Verona knows it, history itself stands witness to the crime.'

Francesco laughs loudly. 'That shifting reptile called history, which may shed its skin one day and be coloured anew by the dawn light. I would no more trust the word of history than he who had most to profit by that word.'

'Do you now insult my honour?'

'That you do yourself, my Lord, should you feign to be an impartial servant of justice in this matter.'

'I would repeat the claim,' Reynard says. 'Each Montague is the same to me and worth as little as any other. Bring your pet lawyer out in this dawning light. Let him claim what he will and defend what he may before God and Verona.'

'You make demands with a mob at your back.'

'Justice does not favour the weak in this life,' Reynard replies. 'Just as godliness does not favour the poor. You see a mob, I see the people of Verona come to add their voices to the clamour. There is no riot here, no threat to your person or the rule of Milan – only witnesses to your actions.'

'And if I refuse?'

'I do not direct this crowd, I do not dictate its actions.'

Francesco looks back at the gate behind him, silent as he considers the question before him. 'My charge is to establish a lasting peace in Verona,' he says at last. 'She is a slippery and fragile creature compared to my usual trade. I will bring him out, you may speak to him, but have a care, gentlemen. My patience runs thin when there are demands placed upon it. Rufus, fetch my advisor.'

Romeo comes swiftly, having expected the call. Francesco watches him stride out through the gate, head high. For the first time he pictures Romeo as the youth who fled Verona. Not the careworn father he has more often seen, nor the quiet and studious official he is known as in Milan and Pavia. Instead there is a spark in his eye that deepens Francesco's affection for him. Romeo carries no sword, but he now returns to the assured step of a man fearlessly meeting his peers.

'My Lord Governor,' Romeo says with a bow, 'my Lords Capulet and Montague.'

'Now you address me such?' Antonio replies coldly. 'It is a few scant hours since your wife proclaimed you my replacement.'

'Juliet stated a fact, Lord Antonio, nothing more. You have served House Montague since my father's death and she does not contend it was illegally done.'

'Only that it is at an end. You have been absent these past twenty years, you are a stranger to Verona. Do you expect the family to accept you as head of our house now? You who have not fought for us all these years, not bled or lost in Montague's name.'

'Not lost?' Romeo exclaims. 'My family was lost to me, my children lived under threat of murder by their own kin! Do not speak to me of your loss when you have been party to the ruin of our home. You who have invited mercenaries into our halls and families, who has gleefully conspired with all those looking only to profit from this feud—'

'A feud made worse a hundred-fold by your deeds!' Antonio roars. 'By your crimes, by your failings and weakness of character!'

'My own part in this feud I do admit. The unwitting actions of a love-struck youth were a fresh spark to the embers, yet others deliberately heaped fuel atop the heap after.'

'He admits his guilt,' Reynard steps in. 'By his own admission there is fault there and it is your duty, Lord Governor, to investigate further.'

'What man is without fault?' Romeo replies. 'What man is without sin? Do you cast your stones at me, Reynard Capulet?'

'I cast no stones, Messer. I ask only that the fair hand of justice extends across this whole city. A man was killed, a man whose death is not absolved by Milan's amnesty nor erased by the overthrow of the house of Escalus.'

Reynard steps back and spreads his arms to encompass the crowds of Capulets and Montagues behind. 'I ask in the name of the city that you, Romeo Montague, be put to trial for what you have done so that the truth may out.'

'The decision is not yours to make!' Francesco

roars. 'You overstep, Messer!'

'I do not decide, my Lord Governor, only ask in the name of the city. Whatever your views of me, I represent a goodly portion of this city in the name of House Capulet.'

'And I in the name of Montague,' adds Antonio loudly, as the murmurs start to build in the crowd behind. 'We both ask – do all people of Verona shelter beneath your protection or suffer under your glove?'

'The rule of law is for all,' Francesco replies.

'Then I ask you now, will you convene a public trial? You claim your mission is to bring a lasting peace to Verona. That cannot come about until the events of that night are finally known. Perhaps we have heard only lies these past twenty years and my cousin bears no blame. Perhaps the truth in all its darkling robes shall be admitted to all. I do not claim to know, but before this rift can heal the wound must be exposed to the air.'

'Then it must be so,' Romeo says before Francesco is able to reply.

His words silence the other men and Francesco stares at him, aghast. Romeo looks from one to the other with iron resolve in his eyes.

'You would comply with their demands?' Francesco asks.

'I would. I returned to Verona to set it upon a new path, but they are correct. Before we can move forward we must cut the debris of our past away. What honest peace can there otherwise be?'

'I...' Francesco is at a loss what to say at first, but as the silence grows around them he realises he cannot hesitate now. 'So be it,' he says with a heavy heart. 'Rufus, take him into the castle – confine him to his quarters. My Lords Capulet and Montague, take your people and return to your homes.'

Without a word, both men bow and retire, triumph
on their faces but well aware of the growing anger within
Francesco. He watches them go then turns to follow
Romeo.

'Oh my friend, what have you done?'

Seventeen

'How could this happen?'

Juliet stands in the middle of their chamber, hands raised to the heavens as she looms over her seated husband. By contrast Romeo is calm, strangely accepting of what has transpired. When she receives no answer she turns her glower upon Francesco instead.

'How did you allow this, my Lord Governor?'

He blinks. 'They gave me no choice!'

'No choice? You are governor of the city! You have troops at your disposal and the full authority of the duke of Milan.'

Under the weight of her fury he feels himself edging back and is forced to rally his spirit. 'Had I warning of your husband's intent to surrender, I would have never offered battle! I did not expect them to be in agreement, my Lady – Montague and Capulet perhaps, but Romeo was co-conspirator in this deed.'

'Did they trick you? My heart, why did you agree to such a thing?'

Finally Romeo turns and looks from Francesco to his wife. 'It was my duty,' he says at last. 'Our goal is peace in Verona, an end to the feud that plagues it.'

'So you offer your own life for the sins of all others? Husband of mine, king of my heart – you take on a burden no mortal man could bear! You cannot undo the past, that is in God's hands alone. You wish a better future for all Verona, this I understand, but you will not find it on the sword-tips of your enemies. Why then do you cast yourself upon them?'

'I do not.'

'Do you have then some cunning stratagem? Devised in the moments between leaving my side and passing through that gate?' Juliet knees at his side and takes her husband's hand. 'Romeo, please tell me why. A crown of thorns ill suits you, my heart. After all we have risked, all we have survived, why would you deliver yourself into their hands?'

'Because I must,' he says firmly. He looks up at his wife, his face strangely serene.

'Because Verona is greater than you or I. Because my children and my wife are what I care about above all things. My actions twenty years ago have caused such hurt and so many problems they cannot be ignored. No – hush your words, my love. I do not willingly scale the gibbet here. I intend to defend myself and trust to the justice of man and God's mercy both.'

'But the risk?'

He shakes his head. 'The risk must be embraced. We are here to change Verona's future, but you cannot alter course by words alone. A ship does not obey the tiller perfectly and here, the tide is against us, my love. If we ignore that we shall break it and be left adrift to the vagaries of a cold and uncaring sea. My deeds have hung above us all for too long. We must remove that sword of Damocles before there can be any change in Verona.'

'You do not remove it, Romeo, by sawing at the

thread that holds it!'

'No, my love, you do not. But if the blade is the only part within reach, you must grasp it and risk what follows.'

There comes a knock on the door before Juliet can summon the words to reply. It opens and the castle steward, Felipe, peers through.

'My Lord Governor, I apologise for the interruption. The Chief Magistrate has sent a messenger.'

Francesco nods and makes to offer some parting shot towards Romeo, but then shakes his head. 'I will do what I can.'

He leaves and heads towards his office with Felipe trailing in his wake. Before he has gone a dozen paces however, Estelle emerges from a side passage and blocks his path. Despite her paleness the young woman wears an expression he has all too recently seen.

'Estelle, why are you out of your bed?'

'My head is sound, Francesco,' she replies. 'Could you expect me to stay and rest after the news Mercutio has brought?'

'Felipe,' Francesco says, 'Escort the messenger to my office, I will attend presently.'

The man bows and disappears down the corridor, leaving Estelle and Francesco alone.

'How can this be?' Estelle begins as soon as Felipe is out of sight. 'How could you permit this?'

'I? This was far from what I intended – my power is not so absolute.'

'You are the city's governor, Francesco. How is it they can force your hand so?'

'Estelle, this is not an army, my word is not law. Even amongst fighting men I cannot order rifts healed or hearts changed. The divide in this city cannot be papered over with parchment laws.'

'Yet your solution is a trial?'

'Not by my choice, look to your own for that particular wisdom. Your father's mind is set however and...' He sighs and shakes his head. 'And if I am forced to see this from the office I hold, I must concede his point is valid.'

'The decision is a fool's choice! All reason demands you see that and overrule him. You are the governor, not he.'

Francesco takes her hands. 'This I know, but Romeo is a wiser man than I. Of the two of us, it is his destiny to rule Verona, not mine. I steer the course for now, but he must be the one to chart it.'

Her hands tighten on his and Estelle pulls him closer so their lips are almost pressed together.

'You must find a way,' she pleads. 'My father feels the guilt of consequences so heavily I fear for what he might be willing to accept. You, Francesco, you must be the soldier here and raise a shield to defend him against all attacks when he is too weary of his burden to do so.'

Francesco bows his head. 'I will fight for him, I swear it. What soldier could call himself such if he did not struggle alongside his friend? What man could I be if I did not strive to protect the father of one I cherish above all others?'

'Then I thank you and I bid you God's favour.'

He kisses her hand and releases her. 'Go, be with your family. Let that sweet face remind your father of all he has yet to fight for.'

*

'It is time.'

172

Francesco steps out of his carriage and into the daylight of the piazza. Above them is the high shriek of birds, their voices full of outrage and condemnation. He takes a moment to survey the crowd assembled. The whole variety of common people line the piazza, from fat merchants to the emaciated beggars that linger on every one of Verona's street corners. These last are the only individuals unconcerned with the fate of Romeo Montague, but it is the silence greeting him that has Francesco's attention for now.

There is an anxiety in the city, one that has built over the course of the last day since Romeo was bound to trial. The Podesta of Verona attended Francesco that very afternoon and made himself clear as no great friend of Milan nor the feuding houses. He is a choleric and aging man with a bald pate and thick beard; unimpressed with a Lord Governor one third his own age and well-aware of his worth to Verona's signore. As chief magistrate he is not a native of the city, by tradition and Milanese law, but nor is he a man of Milan as Romeo is. Once the office would have been held by the city's ruler, but his is a position much diminished beside the governor and captain-general.

'All I can promise you,' Francesco murmurs to Juliet as she steps down beside him, 'is that the podesta's mind will not be swayed by any man. He will rule as he sees fit or is compelled by edict, nothing less.'

'You do not reassure me if that is what you seek, my Lord Governor,' Juliet replies. 'This all then depends on one old man's disposition. My husband may lie a poor night's sleep away from execution.'

As she speaks Juliet inspects the assembled crowd, eyes coming to rest on one beggar who stands out from the rest. He stands motionless, face half-obscured by the tattered hood of a friar's habit. All eyes seem to be upon her though she stands in Francesco's shadow. Several point and whisper, while Lawrence appears unmoved by the sight. Here he stands witness as is his custom. The chatter of citizens disturbs him no more than the breeze that ripples his habit.

Inside the courtroom it is crowded. Black-clad bailiffs with cudgels loom over the press to keep the people in order. It is largely the nobility inside, crowded upon benches while the podesta sits high on his dais and awaits the governor's presence. When Francesco takes his seat the podesta makes no comment, only begins the proceedings with a curt summary of the charge laid against Romeo.

Romeo himself sits in one isolated corner, shielded by a pair of bailiffs and the further large presence of Rufus, who has occupied the nearest seat by dint of his Milanese livery. Francesco's man wears no weapon in the courtroom, but gauntlets and a mail hauberk make him a fearsome sight nonetheless. Romeo sits with hands folded in his lap, head slightly bowed. He looks up at Juliet's arrival and finds her across the room. His gaze contains no fear, only a strange calm that she does not know whether to read as acceptance or determination.

'This court shall now hear the account of Romeo Montague,' declares the podesta. 'There shall be no interruptions save my own or the court shall be cleared. If the truth of this matter can be separated from the fog of twenty years, it is by testimony alone. Hearsay and the city's own myths have no place here.'

There is a murmur among the benches but nothing more and the podesta continues in a tone that cuts it short. 'Romeo Montague,' he commands. 'Stand and deliver your account of the night in question. Bailiff, place his hand upon the holy book and keep it firm there.'

Romeo stands, head bowed for a moment before it too rises. He allows the bailiff to take his right hand and put it flat upon the bible that is offered before himself, placing the left on top also. Romeo bends and kisses the bible's binding to affirm his oath.

'Before God and this courtroom, I swear that my testimony here today shall be true,' he begins solemnly. 'My Lord Magistrate, I was banished from this city for my part in the death of Tybalt, this much you know. Few knew, however, that his day of death was also of my rebirth, for scant hours before I had been wed.

'My bride was his cousin and I strove to keep the quarrel down, but it did not end that way and two men were dead at the finish. None knew of our marriage and Lord Capulet made clear his intention to wed Juliet to Count Paris. To avoid this sacrilegious union and the rage of her father, Juliet conceived to feign death with the assistance of one other.'

'The conspirator's name, Messer?'

Romeo hesitates, but only for a moment. 'Friar Lawrence, my good friend and the man who wed us. His duty was to then write to me and inform me of their plans, but plague barred the letter's path. When news reached me, it was only that the one star of my heavens had gone out.'

'So why then return to Verona – under threat of death?'

'My goal was to die at my love's side. What threat can there be when it is your one remaining wish? I bought poison in Mantua and resolved to lay myself down with Juliet, to sleep forever in her arms. I fear

175

Count Paris's affection for Juliet ran deeper than I knew, however. That night he had come to pray for her soul, as a man of honour might.'

'And you killed him? How came this about? The exact circumstances – I must hear it all and without hesitation for this is at the heart of the matter. God looks down upon us. Bear your witness false and there shall follow a punishment far greater than any I can bestow.'

'I understand, my Lord. I made my way to the tomb, only for Count Paris to accost me—'

'Accost?'

'With words at first, my Lord. He thought me intent upon desecration, one last vengeance upon the House of Capulet, as did all who came upon that scene later.'

'Did any witness these words?'

'His page perhaps, I do not know. I learned later he saw us clash steel and had run to fetch the watch before the fatal blow, but I saw nothing of him. If he was close enough to hear us, he was well hidden indeed for I never knew of his presence even. My servant Balthasar was nearby, too, but well apart for I had sent him to my father with a letter. He disobeyed, fearing my mood and intent, but fell asleep soon after. The clash of battle invaded his dreams, but he feared to discover the truth until later.'

'Where is Balthasar then?'

'Dead these past three years. He served me faithfully all my time in Milan, but the plague took him when last it struck the city.'

'This we shall verify with our lord's servants. Very well, tell me now what words were spoken between you and Paris?'

'I begged him to let me pass – the exactness I cannot recall now or even the morning following that night. I was heavy with grief by then, caring for nothing more than my own destruction. He would not let me go, he declared he would arrest me and I must die.'

'You refused Count Paris once?'

'Several times, though at that time I knew not it was Paris. The haze of grief was upon me, I saw only a man of gentle birth. Only when he was dead did I know his face and recognise him as kinsman to my closest friend, Mercutio.'

'You refused and he drew his sword?'

'He drew as I came upon him, before words were spoken.'

'And you?'

'Soon after, for what nobleman would react in another way?'

'But you struck the first blow?'

'Only one blow was struck, but the first pass was mine. Some men are ill-adept at swordplay and may be driven off, but Count Paris was not such a man. After that first pass we fought in earnest and grief turned to red rage in my heart.'

'So you struck him down in rage.'

'I fought in blind rage it is true, I had no care for my own life and could see only death around me. I remember little of the fight, not even the death wound. Only when I knelt at his side and heard his final words did the clouds part.'

'What words did he speak?'

'He abjured me to lay him alongside Juliet and I swore that I would do so.'

'You did this alone?'

'It is so. Balthasar was still hidden and half-sleeping. I took Count Paris alone to the tomb and laid him in some semblance of dignity. I drank my poison and sat beside my lady love as I waited for it to work.'

'Yet it did not?'

'I was played false by the apothecary I bought it from. He stole from me my money and with it bought not only my life but more besides. Juliet woke presently and told me all, just as Balthasar and Friar Lawrence pursued me inside the tomb. They knew the watch was close upon us and we fled.'

'And what became of Friar Lawrence? The plague also?'

'No, lord, he lives yet.'

'Where is he then? His testimony would be crucial – I must hear his account without delay.'

'You can hear nothing from him I fear. He was ill-used by Lord Capulet when he brought word on our behalf. He will never speak again.'

'If he hath reason still, he must be brought before me,' the podesta demands.

Romeo bows his head in acknowledgement. 'Then I ask you send your bailiff out into the piazza. I expect Friar Lawrence stands without.'

Eighteen

Romeo feels the weight of the podesta's silent regard as they wait for Friar Lawrence. The people in the courtroom whisper freely, but do not dare break the magistrate's contemplation of the accused. Before Lawrence can be compelled inside, however, the podesta clears his throat and straightens.

'You claim the friar is without, but can you verify it is truly him? Not least when you say he cannot speak.'

'The dowager Lady Capulet will vouch for his identity. Send for her if you doubt my word.'

'Disturb a lady at her grief? Is there no end to the troubles you will cause?'

Romeo bows his head. 'I pray those will all soon end and I may devote myself to the advantage of all Verona. Perhaps a messenger to the Lady Capulet should you be in any doubt? She is aware of her daughter's return. She will easily inform you of Lawrence's appearance and afflictions – there could be no mistake made.'

The podesta nods his head. 'I shall do so – your credibility is all here. Any word to the contrary by Lady Capulet and this trial shall be swiftly closed.'

As he confers with one of his clerks there is a

commotion in the hallway beyond. Romeo sees Juliet leap from her seat and head towards the sound. In mere moments the noise abates and presently she returns to view, leading Lawrence as one might a new-born lamb. The babble of noise in the courtroom rises, the whispers no longer furtive as they recognise who Lawrence has become, but all falls quiet as the podesta bangs his fist upon the table before him.

'There will be quiet,' he booms before looking from Friar Lawrence, frozen in startlement despite Juliet's gentle urging. 'This is the man?' he demands of Romeo. 'This mad monk can testify what occurred?'

'What he can tell you, my Lord, I cannot say. He was driven mad by the furious actions of Lord Capulet. His tongue was cut out for speaking a truth that proved too difficult to hear. I beg you to be gentle with him in your questioning, for terror of a powerful man may rend what remains of his wits.'

'I understand you. Now, Messer – this man informs me you were once known as Friar Lawrence, do you confirm this?'

Lawrence shrinks back when spoken to in such patrician tones, but under the gentle soothing of Juliet's hand he finally summons the strength to look the podesta in the eye. A bailiff advances upon them with a bible and, to Romeo's surprise, Lawrence does not withdraw. Instead he reaches for the good book with the fervour of a drowning man and takes it from the bailiff. There is no need to hold his hand against it; Lawrence kisses the book three times before pressing it close against his chest.

With an effort the magistrate quells his impatience and asks his question again. This time Lawrence nods hesitantly.

'Do you testify that by your hand this man was married to Juliet Capulet and later you did assist her in her scheme to avoid marriage to Count Paris? And furthermore accompanied them into exile before your return here?'

A nod.

'Did you witness the struggle between this man and Count Paris, twenty years past?'

A shake of the head.

'You were not present? You came upon them later?'

Lawrence stares uncomprehending at the podesta for a while before giving the briefest of nods.

'You are renowned within the city of Verona – a man apart from the disputes of this world whose faith surpasses that even of the white penitents. Yet you remain loyal to this man whom you wed to that lady at your side, do you not?'

Another nod.

'Then I do not know what I may make of your testimony. All of Verona has seen you stand between soldiers of the two houses. That is not the bravery of the battlefield but of faith, yet I must question where your allegiance lies. Let us first have more of your account, Friar. You came to the graveyard not long after Romeo Montague and encountered his servant? Good. Did that man describe the fight his master had engaged in? No account of what preceded it? No mention of who drew steel first?'

A long shake of the head then a hesitant gesture, almost childlike in its manner, where Lawrence tilted his head to one side with a hand beneath it to indicate sleep.

'Did you find Count Paris outside the entrance of the tomb? No? Within, then? And there also Romeo Montague. Was he armed still?'

181

A pause then a shake of the head.

'His sword was gone?'

Another shake.

The podesta turns to Romeo briefly. 'Where was your sword?'

'I had cast it upon the floor, it had brought more ruin than I could bear. I swore to surrender myself before I let Juliet be threatened with violence by the watchmen. I have kept my vow never to carry a sword ever since.'

'You feel guilt over these deaths?'

Romeo is slow in his reply, but his gaze does not waver. 'Men died upon my sword. I am no theologian, but I believe that is against the word of God whatever the circumstance. I shall answer for it upon my day of judgement. God shall know the truth of my reasons and weigh them accordingly.'

'Yet you now forego the wearing of a sword, a right afforded by your birth whatever your current position?'

'I killed one man on my wedding day,' Romeo replies. 'A second on the night my lost love was returned to life. The joy of each day is sullied by my actions. I desire that no other day is so marred.'

'But still you claim you killed only with justification.'

'I do. For many years I believed I would never see Verona again, but circumstance has brought me here once more. With my own eyes I see my actions have marred far more than my memories. I bear the guilt of so much more than those two deaths upon my soul, however much I believe I could not have avoided seeing those two men slain.

'The years of conflict Verona has witnessed, the loss and privations suffered by many here – all is consequence of my actions to some degree. I have returned to make what amends I can, to repair what may be, to build a better future for those who may yet suffer.

'My friend, Mercutio, cursed both Tybalt and myself as he died, for our feud had been his death. He called a plague upon both our houses and for my sins I did not heed my friend's warning, for warning I now believe it. This hatred has been carefully kindled by some, but carelessly left to burn by too many more. For my part in this I know there can be no forgiveness. That is a guilt I bear as strongly as the blood that was never fully washed from my hands.'

'You speak nobly, Messer,' the podesta says after a long silence, 'and I have much sympathy for your words even has I have anger too, as a citizen and servant of Verona who has been part of this suffering. But my remit is not one of consequences, nor anger. Those I leave for God alone. My ruling must be according to the laws of Verona, though they too have no certainty when it comes to the matter of noble men fighting fairly.

'Instead I have only your word to the circumstances and precious little more, for all that you do not deny the act itself. I am forced to weigh those circumstances and listen to the manner of your defence. My reading is thus: upon hearing dire news, a grief-stricken youth returns to Verona without care to the threat on his life by the ruling prince. He refuses to lay down his sword when a man attempts to arrest him and kills that man.

'That you did not know who it was you killed matters little. What right you had to defend yourself was expunged by the crime of your return to Verona. Whether or not that crime is since covered by the Lord Governor's amnesty matters not. It was a crime then and supersedes the common privileges of rank. No man of honour can plead grief to excuse his actions, nor claim he knew not that he might be arrested upon sight.

'Romeo Montague, I find you guilty of the murder of Count Paris. Bailiffs, bind the prisoner and take him away.'

Nineteen

'My Lord Governor, might I be permitted to speak?'

Estelle's tone is meekly cold, her voice barely more than a whisper. A mercenary since the age of twelve and veteran of many a bloody battle, Francesco is immediately unmanned by her words.

For a moment he can say nothing, his surprise turning swiftly to dismay as she stands in the doorway and awaits his response. It is late in the evening and Estelle carries a single candle to light her way, staring down at the slender flickering flame.

'Estelle, I will always have time for you,' he gasps finally. 'Please, you are shivering. Come in and stand by the fire.'

'It is not the cold, my Lord.'

'I... I know, but I promise you, I am doing all I can.'

Finally she looks up, but he sees no love in her eyes. 'All you can, my Lord?'

'I beg you, Estelle, do not hate me for the obligations of my office. I cannot simply release Romeo, not in direct violation of the podesta's ruling.'

'I do not hate you, my Lord Governor.'

'Will you not even call me by my name?'

'I—' She takes a long breath and the precarious flame in her hands gutters until Francesco reaches hesitantly out.

When Estelle does not recoil he eases the candle from her hands and ushers her towards the fireplace where the embers are still warm. He places the candle on a table and waits, seeing she is trying to frame the words in her heart.

'Francesco, he is your friend. I know you perform your duties with a heavy heart, but still you perform them. I do not condemn you for that, but he is my father.'

'To hear you call me Lord Governor is more condemnation than I can bear. To see you so distant and reserved is a dagger to my heart.'

'I must beg your forgiveness then, for that is not my goal. I can merely think of nothing while my father is imprisoned and awaiting execution. Not joy nor love, they are but the dim memory of summer during midwinter.'

'Do not let the ice take your heart entirely,' Francesco pleads. 'I have written to my lord in Milan. He sanctioned all that we do here and his word is higher than the law.'

'But will he intervene? We are all but pawns in his great game – to be sacrificed when strategy requires or a gambit fails.'

'I do grant that his affection for Romeo may not outweigh his plans, but neither is he unmoving and cold to those who are close to him. The duke's plan for Verona remains for it to be more than a disruption. It will not serve to indulge the petty contrivances of Montague or Capulet and Romeo remains the end to their charade. For the present I can delay whatever the hot hearts of Verona may demand. If I could open his door and dismiss the guards now, I would do so.'

'Then do so!'

'I cannot. Estelle, precious one, you know I cannot. He is my friend, yet I cannot. Were he a stranger to you I would still desire with all my heart to free him.'

'Do you believe the duke will agree to his release?'

Her simple question drives the air from his lungs. 'I do not know,' Francesco admits. 'We are perhaps tools in the grand vision of Lombardy – Romeo knows this as well as I. But the moods of a city are fickle and we do not yet know how the people may react.'

'You trust my father's life to the changing moods of the mob?' she asks, her voice made small by fear.

'I do not, but I must have reason to do what I will. The two great houses of Verona united in their call for a trial, but never could they remain so for long. When passions are raised, haste is the greatest folly and the keenest demand.

'What of the other families, allied to one or other side? Perhaps they have no great hunger for further bloodshed and will fear the wrath of Milan. The common people can be stirred to passion it is certain, but neither Montague nor Capulet will risk pushing them. Even roused to anger the populace know who is to blame for their woes – not the youth of twenty years past but the thugs and cruel landlords who assail them year after year.'

'And this will be enough to save my father's life? This is what I must trust to?'

He takes her hands. 'Estelle, please trust to me. Trust that I will find a way, that I will not rest until the path is clear. I know there is no place in your heart for affection when it is filled with fear, but I ask that you keep one small ember of faith burning. I will see to your father's freedom and win back your heart.'

'I do have faith in you still,' she says unexpectedly and takes his hands. 'Please, forgive me. It is callous and childish to withhold my feelings as punishment for you. I do not mean to treat you so poorly or offer cheap incentive, as though your heart had been set on any other goal but his freedom.'

Francesco shakes his head and draws her closer. 'To forgive is to agree there was fault and I see no fault in anything you have done. I must be cautious in my actions and to many it will seem over-cautious. It has been long suspected that Florentine influence may have fuelled this feud. Gold and soft words are the bellows that can heat the forge-fire of Verona. If there are agitators here, they will make themselves known soon.'

'This is why you delay?' Estelle demands, aghast. 'To bring such creatures into the light? Is my father to be used as bait?'

'No! Never that, precious one. I mean only that I cannot be sure the demands of the feud are all that drives events. The Florentines do not want a winner in this feud, they do not want Verona to stand strong in any colours.'

'Why have they not yet acted?'

'Fear – they cannot push too hard and they dare not expose themselves. But if their frustration grows, they must soon act. The defeat of the German Emperor means time is short and their paymasters will require success.'

'So they will demand my father's blood and soon.'

'I know not what they will do, but I must remain vigilant.'

'Is there nothing more you can do?'

'Alas, not without pouring oil upon the fire.'

'And if your lord is not moved to help? If the mob demands one man at least is punished for the years of ill-use?'

'Do not ask such questions, Estelle, you will only make yourself sick with worry!'

'I cannot help but ask. I must know, Francesco. If the order is given, will you carry out his sentence?'

He stares at her for a moment that stretches to eternity, the full import of the decision never more strongly looming in his mind. Just as horror begins to build in her eyes he raises her hands to his lips and kisses her fingers.

'Never,' he murmurs, bent low over her hand. 'Never could I give such an order.'

He can hear her breath, fast and shallow, in the silence that follows, but eventually she does the same and kisses his hand.

'Thank you, Francesco,' she whispers. 'Now I must away, the morrow will come all too soon.'

*

Under cover of night, three figures leave Scaliger Castle and slip into the silent streets of Verona. The autumn chill casts thin clouds of breath from each as the moon emerges for a few scant seconds, but then all is dark again. They walk through the city, a woman and two men both wearing swords. Those who see them step away from their path, dissuaded by the purposeful stride of all three. Only a patrol of Milanese soldiers delay them, but a few words is all it requires to be allowed on their way again.

It takes half an hour, but at last they reach their

destination and knock on the kitchen door. They are met with silence and only when they knock again is there a noise from within.

'I come!'

The three wait in silence until a closer, quieter voice calls through the door.

'Who calls at this hour?'

'Your lamb,' the woman says. 'Your ladybird.'

The door opens to a wary face, but in moments that is replaced by joy as Juliet is embraced by her former nurse. 'My faith, come in out of this chill, Lady.'

All three enter and divest themselves of their cloaks while nurse bars the door behind them and goes to light a candle.

'Now I may see you better, my lamb,' she declares in a whisper. 'I beg you three be hushed, though. My employers are kind people, but would fear to be drawn into the feud.'

'We shall be quiet. I wish it was under happier circumstances, too, but I must beg your help.'

'Then you shall have it,' nurse says promptly, 'only first I must demand my price – one good look at this youth beside you. You, Messer,' she adds, looking at the larger of the two men, 'you I do not know, but once might have better acquainted myself with! In old age, however, it is this young man who catches my eye. Come here, stand before me and let me see your colour.

'Yes, as fine a youth as your mother described. A strong jaw, that I like for your father was ever as pretty as any girl in Verona. You, young Mercutio, have the bearing of the grandfather whose reward has only recently come and all too late – nay, not the man who he became, the lord he was in his prime.'

'Nurse, you may inspect his teeth and hooves anon,

first I must speak with you of grave matters.'

The old woman bows her head and releases the startled Mercutio. 'We shall speak of no graves here, my Lady, save for those unneeded.' She gestures around the kitchen where a cot is made up in one corner. 'I can offer little refreshment while we speak, save perhaps some rosehip tea?'

'Hot tea on a cold night would be most welcome,' Juliet agrees. 'Rufus, would you set the kettle over the fire for us?'

While the soldier obeys, Juliet ushers her nurse into a chair at the large kitchen table.

'We must be quick,' she begins. 'We should not risk walking the streets too late.'

'Indeed you should not, even with two swords at your side. So speak, my lamb, tell me what service I might perform for you. I know you did not come here so late for sweet reminiscences.'

'I did not, I came to beg your help.'

'There need be no begging, my Lady, whatever you and yours need.'

Juliet holds up a hand. 'Do not be so hasty, it may prove difficult, dangerous.'

'Fie, what is danger to a woman as old as I? And difficult? My heart has few beats remaining to me, let me spend such coin on something of worth. Speak, girl!'

'Very well. My husband is imprisoned, as you know, and our families call for his blood. I do not know what will come, but the governor has written to Milan for the duke's advice. As Milan's representative he must do what is in that city's best interest. At present, only the feuding families have made their voices known, but there is another force in Verona.'

'The people,' nurse says softly. 'But the people are

frightened – this century of woe is all they have ever known.'

'But not ever – it was with the people's consent that Milan first took control of Verona. I ask you to rouse them once more to anger, to indignation. The fires of outrage lie within them already. None love what Verona has become and now they must see that the time for a new dawn has come. The governor endeavours to walk a narrow path to preserve the peace here, but his remit is clear. The Houses know if they offer him any excuse to bring a fist down it will be gratefully received. They cannot afford such a confrontation. Milan does not care if one great House or two dominates the city, only that peace reigns and taxes flow.'

'I do not have the sort of influence...' Nurse trails off as she realises what is being asked. 'You mean Lawrence. You would need him to do this.'

'I would need you to do this,' Juliet repeats, 'and Lawrence to stand at your side. His authority is unimpeachable among the people of Verona, his motives undoubted. But you must be the one to persuade Verona's citizens that their best chance for peace lies with Romeo. That his execution would solve one problem for Milan only to create a legion of others.'

'I do not deny that your husband offers Verona's best chance, but I know not how I might persuade others of this. He is a Montague, who will speak in defence of one who would be lord of their oppressors?'

'One who would be lord, but has never been their oppressor,' Juliet insists. 'One who is married to a Capulet and might rule both Houses, ending the feud and the corruption that has plagued this city. Surely that future for their children outshines the hurts of their past?'

'I fear you think too highly of people,' nurse says, 'or the passage of years has granted you greater esteem for my words than you once held.'

Juliet smiles and pats the arm of her son. 'The young may still recognise wisdom, even if that gives them only more desire to ignore it. I have no fear for your ability to speak to ears that will hear. Do you think the people of Verona will listen? The passion is inside them, but it will take strong words to tease it out.'

'I cannot say. I know some who will listen – others who will only rejoice at the sight of a Montague in the noose. Certainly the city hungers for change, but we have been helpless for too long. They may fear to raise their voices, they may be needing only a spark to set the city alight.'

'A riot would only force the governor to act against them.'

'In their hearts are contained the roiling fury of the oppressed. Unstop that vial and no man may control what is released.'

'It must not come to that!' Juliet begs, 'you must help them see that.'

'I do not say it will happen, only that it might. If I can somehow persuade the people that Romeo Montague is their best hope for the future, there will be no limiting how deeply they believe that. There is no zealot like a convert, no fools like a mob.'

'Remind them of their enemy, then, remind them that it is not Milan. They do not need to flout the law to secure his release, only offer the governor the reason he craves. Surely it is easier to persuade men to side with justice than go against authority?'

'So I shall hope to achieve,' nurse says with a nod. 'Now you must be gone. The hour grows ever later and the streets ever more perilous. Come the morning I shall begin at the market and see what mood I am met with. Delay the governor a day and he may have his reason.'

Twenty

'Black Will, are you here?'

The whisper is met with silence. Arturo Malacrolla looks around the empty warehouse, seeing only darkness broken by such faint lines he cannot fathom their shape. At last he repeats his words and this time there is a scuff of feet from the far end of the room.

'You are alone?'

'I am, I know your rules well enough.'

'Come forward then.'

He shuffles a few blind steps then stops as a lantern is uncovered. Thin light spills over the debris of the floor. The building is long abandoned, its owner dead and the deed lost amid the struggles of the feud. It has served as a meeting place several times before, but this night Malacrolla knows it is different.

With an unconscious motion he smooths his moustache and goes to join Black Will. The man has set his lamp atop a stack of broken wood and watches him come like a cat, unsettling and threatening. They are much of the same height and age, but there the similarities end. Black Will is a lean and scarred man, clean-shaven with his dark hair tied back, Malacrolla a product of better living and a happier life.

'Why did you ask to meet me?' the other man growls.

'I have work for you, my friend, why else?' Malacrolla speaks sharply though the other man is a killer to the bone. Sometimes even killers must be reminded who pays them.

'These are dangerous times for such work.'

'If your work was not dangerous, I would not need to pay you so handsomely.'

'To do dangerous work in dangerous times is folly.'

'To refuse dangerous work when peace might end your employment must also be folly.'

Black Will laughs softly. 'Your small jobs are lucrative I will grant, but I am a mercenary in Italy. Should I live to a hundred and see only victory, I will never be wanting for work here. Between the Vicar of Rome and the Count of Virtue, my bloody business will ever thrive.'

'Be that as it may,' Malacrolla sniffs, 'I have work for you. Will you take my coin?'

'What is the work?'

'I wish you to kill a man.'

'Which man?'

'Romeo Montague.'

There is a long silence as Black Will stonily considers the suggestion.

'A bold request,' he says at long last. 'More than difficult. More than dangerous.'

'And the reward will be in keeping.'

'One hundred ducats.'

Malacrolla gasps. 'A bold demand! I can offer fifty.'

'A hundred.'

'I do not have a hundred to offer. Sixty alone is a

princely sum.'

'Ninety.'

'Seventy.

'Eighty or I cut your throat now and take whatever is in your purse for my trouble.'

The merchant hisses in fear and clutches his throat as he retreats, but Black Will makes no move to make good on the threat.

'Very well,' Malacrolla mutters. 'Eighty it is.'

'Fifty in advance, thirty to follow.'

'Even bolder!'

'The man is well guarded, I risk my life with this.'

'I risk my purse to your good word.'

Black Will laughs again. 'I risk the remaining thirty being offered to other men for my own life, should I cheat you.'

'That you may depend upon, if fifty ducats is your price.'

'My price is eighty.'

'Indeed.' Malacrolla considers the matter a while longer, the tally of his private finances fixed in his head. 'Very well, I agree. I do not have fifty to give you now, though.'

Black Will gives him a cat-like smile, all teeth and unblinking malice. 'If I thought you did, I might have just cut your throat and quietly profited.'

'Please, do not continue to jest about such things. Here, I have twenty. I can bring the rest tomorrow...' He pauses. 'Somewhere more public, perhaps.'

The smile widens as Black Will takes the purse and hefts it. 'Take it to my friend at the tavern; wrapped inside an ox's tongue and sealed mind, or he may choose to investigate it more closely.'

'I will do so. There is no time to lose, however, you

must act quickly. The governor is smitten with Montague's daughter, he will surely pardon her father when he judges the storm has passed.'

'Then you would be better to wait and pay the lesser sum when he is not under guard.'

'No! The delay could establish Montague's position and end the feud. His life means little to me then, his wife and children could as easily bridge the divide if they have time.'

Black Will raises an eyebrow. 'The merchant is keen to give his money away. Very well, it shall be as you wish.'

Before Malacrolla can object, the assassin restores the cover of his storm lantern and the warehouse is plunged into darkness. He hears soft footsteps pad away and has to restrain the urge to cry out. Instead he counts to fifty, refusing to allow some English bully the satisfaction of hearing his fear. Once that is done he turns carefully around and begins to retrace his steps.

*

The following dawn appears only reluctantly, a thing of mourning where there is no glimpse of the sun. A veil of rainclouds is drawn over the city and tears fall unceasingly. Tempers run short as the fires are slow to light and the chores of the day drag interminably, but nurse lifts her chin to it all as she heads to the market that morning. She buys little, though the harvest has begun to swell the meagre offerings, but goes to each stall in turn.

Custom is slow and the old woman is well known there. She sows her seeds without haste, planting within each man and woman a tiny grain of hope for what might be. It is fertile ground, she discovers – not without stones, but many are eager to talk and to hope.

Others can hardly hear such talk; the idea is too unfamiliar when they have grown up knowing only a city under feud. Some will not even hear her, though they have no response to her demands for an alternative. They do not wish to allow the stranger of hope to creep into their hearts, but nor can they admit how entrenched their despair has become.

Those who refuse her she does not press. Nurse knows they still hear her words to others and are not so unmoved as they appear. A lifetime of recalcitrant children and proud parents has taught her those signs of veiled understanding.

From the market she moves on, visiting another then two public wells. At those she is known, but less so. She does not linger long, does not form her thoughts with the same certainty for few have the time to be lectured by an old woman. Afterwards she travels to the shrine where Lawrence passes his nights. He is still there that morning, sheltered from the rain like a stray dog. Huddled up upon the bench, he watches the people pass from within his cowl over which is drawn a tattered blanket. There is little of his face visible, just the darting eyes of an animal long abused by its master.

He watches her approach without moving, expecting nothing but also showing nothing of friendship's shadow that exists between them.

'Will you come with me?' she asks. 'Our service is not yet done.'

Lawrence does not move, but he stares so intently she is certain he understood her words. There are days she cannot reach him, days where the tangled thorns of memory are too dense for him to escape, but this is not one.

'My service is not yet done,' she corrects after a long pause. 'I can demand nothing more of you – neither can Juliet and her Romeo. But still I ask. There is a duty to be performed and perhaps then we may rest easier in this city we love.'

His regard is both accusatory and meek. That stare is all the power he has in truth, a mirror to one's own failings that has stopped many a fool in his tracks. Lawrence makes no sound, not even a grunt in response, but he pulls the blanket from his head and stiffly places one foot on the ground. Each is wrapped in bandages, strips of ragged cloth that keep the worst of the cold away.

When Lawrence stands he cannot straighten fully. Once, he was taller than her and though age has bowed her, greater burdens have meant they are of a height now. He looks smaller to her eye, a bedraggled and pathetic thing, but it is with her that he can be at his weakest. Whether it is faith or duty or something else entirely, she cannot say, but what drives him to walk Verona's streets comes at a great cost. He can rarely bear the touch of any person, but some days he can do little but shiver and mewl like a kitten. On those days she has sat beside him for long hours, just a finger-width away, and her presence has sustained him somehow.

Together they walk north along the bank of the river towards the great fortress of San Pietro. Along the way nurse speaks to a drover, a tanner's wife and her apprentice. They stop because Lawrence walks beside her. They listen because they all hope for better times to come. They nod because an end to the feud glitters like gold to them all. Should it turn out to be a fool's prize instead, the empty promise of hope is better than none at all.

They see many soldiers on the streets when they cross the river and turn towards the heart of the city. The livery of Milan is dominant but many Montagues and Capulets patrol like wolves around their marked territories. She makes off-hand comments to those nearby whenever she is forced to stop. Some ignore her, others look her way and she adds something more. It is only when they have come almost full circle and find themselves in front of the Roman arena that a true audience is gathered. In the shadow of those broken pillars, which surround a floor soaked in the blood of ancient gladiators and modern duellists, she and Lawrence establish themselves.

'Verona's enemies are clear for all to see, but when there is a hope for change, who stirs?' nurse demands of a broad farmer who has scoffed at her.

'What would you have us do?' he replies in a deep and booming voice. 'Turn our ploughshares against their swords?'

'Milan is not our enemy,' she replies. 'Were the days before the biscione flew above us better or did we invite them in to save us from our own?'

He concedes that with a nod. Though they have rebelled once against Milan and been cruelly punished for it, Duke Visconti named himself signore of Verona with the approval of the people. Between a bloodthirsty fool and a tyrant of ambitious cunning there is no choice.

'Who then is our enemy?'

'Those who set us against each other,' she replies. 'Those who squeeze this city of blood and gold, who sacrifice us upon the alter of their feud.'

'The rain is wet, the sky is grey, and old ladies

complain that others do nothing,' he spits back. 'It is ever thus.'

'But where was hope before? What could have been done by us common folk?'

'Where does hope stand now? On the floor of the arena behind you, woman. It weeps in the blood and dust.'

'It stands in the governor's castle,' she insists as more are drawn to listen. 'Whether by God's hand or the returning sins of the Houses, hope has been brought to Verona and the citizens do nothing to grasp it.'

He laughs. 'The Montague boy? What hope lies with him?'

'All the hopes of Verona. It is a story as old as time, the noble-born rule and the commoners' toil. We have no power to end our woes, it takes one of their class to set it in motion.'

'It requires one of their class to care for us, but a Montague will care only for his name.'

'Not this one.'

'How so? Romeo Montague is a greater man than all the rest, is he? Do you ascribe miracles to his passing as well?'

'I do not, I only grant that God has bestowed his gifts upon him.'

'What gifts?'

'A free mind and a loving heart.' She pauses, glancing around at those now watching them and realising she will need a larger audience than this to deliver her message.

'The one he loves is a Capulet, he is heir to Montague. There need be no love of the common people in him to end this feud. In his heart he has ended it already, he who has killed in feud's name is now ready to end it for us all. For that desire they demand his blood, our one remaining hope to be free of their plague, but we do nothing.'

'What would you have us do? March upon Scaliger Castle? Throw our bodies against its walls?'

'March there, yes, but not to fight! Lend our voices to his cause, raise a clamour that even the angels of heaven may hear our pleas!'

'What can we achieve? We have no voices that they can hear.'

'The Lord Governor is a man of low birth, he can hear us. He brought Romeo Montague to Verona to end the feud – now is the time for us to embrace the hope he offers us before it is extinguished!'

'If he brought Montague here, why does he imprison him?'

'Because he must – the pressure of the Houses has forced him to. He has come to restore peace, but we of Verona know there can never be peace while the Houses are set against each other.'

That much the farmer cannot deny; it is as much a fact as the rain and the cloud. He is quiet a while, long enough that nurse knows she has made an inroad and must move on. No man is persuaded in an instant, no man admits to being persuaded in an hour.

She turns to point to the ancient arena behind her, its arches and tunnels harking back to a grander time. Before it, encompassed by her gesture, is Lawrence and he stands impassive in front of all the faces turned his way.

'There, at dusk – let the people gather and hear us. Let all of Verona come and for this one moment decide our fate. Milan is not our enemy, but they will do what they feel they must to keep Verona peaceful. Let us show them that we will not go so quietly into the last days of our city, for if this feud continues we will be none left. How have your harvests been? How high are the rents and the tithes you owe? How many fields and vineyards have been burned?'

'Go – tell your friends, tell your neighbours,' she cries as loudly as she can. 'Verona stands at a crossroad. Tell them to come here and add their voices or forever be imprisoned by this city's sins.'

She marches off through the district with Lawrence at her side, sensing as much as seeing those who left to carry her message further. Through the poorest parts of Verona she walks, avoiding any place that bears the colours of either house, but finding many an ear willing to bend to her words. The morning drags on through a sluggish, disconsolate drizzle, but slowly Verona begins to wake as her message spreads. As she has predicted, there are embers of discontent in Veronese hearts that are soon stirred to greater heat.

As the rain ends it is replaced by a breeze that builds steadily through the afternoon. The city is lit with the pale yellow light of the sun filtered through uncertain storm clouds. The city begins to surge with life as trees stretch and whip their branches, fallen leaves dancing spirals through the sky. Birds chatter excitedly, the city's dogs sit at their posts with ears pricked. Verona's citizens breathe in the strange building energy and come evening, that restless flow draws hundreds to the arena where Friar Lawrence waits.

Twenty-One

As Arturo Malacrolla looks up at the coral-coloured sky above ancient, half-ruined walls, he feels a shiver of foreboding. It is late in the afternoon and the orange sun cuts low across the city. The wind heaves at the sky and tears at the hood he has pulled tight around his head.

Dark shapes flash through the racing air above, rooks calling as they return to their roosts atop the arena walls. He sees them watching him, gleaming eyes amid the darkness – a dozen deliberating heads turned his way. High above them are knife-winged shapes hunting, their cries lost in the wind, while the starlings dance their secret patterns on the plains beyond the city.

There are people streaming into the arena on all sides, many talking in small and furtive groups, but more still huddled and wary. They look around at the crowds, the dark spaces beneath the arena arches and up at the sky – fearing retribution for the thoughts that now bubble through their hearts.

Malacrolla has heard rumours from more than one agent that this is to be the start of some awakening in the city. Some claim the mad monk is to speak to the city, others that a witch will ensorcell all those who come and lead them against the feuding Houses. All he knows is that Romeo Montague's name has been spoken across the city and the common people are drawn here.

There are merchants, too, some wealthy by the cut of their cloth, but knowing not to wear gems or gold in such a place. He passes through the outer arch behind a cluster of grim-faced labourers, all stern reserve and broad shoulders, while ahead of them a gaggle of youths scamper noisily. From both sides he can hear voices and footsteps.

There are stalls set into shadowy nooks and strung between arches, selling pottery and cheap ironware, cups of wine and dried herbs. From higher up he can hear shouts of laughter while in the shadowed corners he glimpses huddled figures in blankets, inured in their misery to the feverish excitement.

The tide brings him out into the open and he is carried on down to the arena floor. A pitted surface of sand lies underfoot, half hidden by the crowd already gathered. There are several hundred people there, a dozen more stalls positioned around the interior and the infernal flicker of flames visible down the wide sloping tunnel ahead. Hundreds more look down from the seating levels. Many are drinking noisily and engaged in furious discussion, as though the secret of what brings the people here is already revealed.

Malacrolla drifts around the arena floor, driven by the swirling wind's flow and listening to the simmering mood. He pauses to catch snatches of talk. Several times he hears that the mad monk will be there and that he carries Verona's last hope in his hands. The last of the day stretches on and torches are lit in the strange twilight, the sky still cast an unsettling yellow and pink as the dull orb of the sun disappears from view.

Finally he stops drifting, settling himself near a large bearded man who stands with thick arms folded and his family arrayed nearby. As more people enter the arena, it does not take Malacrolla long to strike up a conversation with the man, a clothier with a shop on the edge of the Capulet's land.

He does not say that he is allied to the house of Capulet and Malacrolla does not ask. It is obvious and the mood here is against any such associations. The clothier has no choice but to follow their orders, to pay tithes on top of his rent to a Neapolitan brute in red livery who haunts those streets.

Finally there is a stirring up ahead, a swell of movement that drags hundreds forward. Malacrolla is to one side and can merely watch the press of bodies with an observer's eye, though there are a few cries and complaints from those in the belly of the crowd. More torches appear now. The wind surges and swirls around the arena, dragging long streaks of flame and sparks across the darkened sky. Above the tunnel mouth up ahead a figure appears and the crowd again pushes forward.

Malacrolla blinks for a few moments, his sceptic's eye trying to penetrate the shadows of its cowl, but then the figure pushes its hood back and reveals its face. With the light of bonfires nearby and torches carried by a pair of youths, it is clearly the mad monk of Verona and a sigh rustles around the onlookers. They settle, push forward again then stop, the mounting anticipation of the day now contained as one promise is revealed true.

Malacrolla has seen many drinking solidly in the hour he's been waiting. As he looks around now, he sees several with bottles and hears the harsh bursts of raised voice that speaks to drunkenness. The anticipation has been one of skittish concern however, not fervour. The sight of the mad monk calms that, but cannot extinguish it entirely. His presence is a sign of Verona's will, but that has been crushed more than once in their lifetime.

Beside the monk another figure steps forward, a woman this time. The witch some have been speaking of, Malacrolla is sure. She is old with a round, lined face and a servant's dress. There is fatigue in the stoop of her shoulders and for a moment she falters. Then the mad monk takes her arm and steadies her. The small gesture speaks volumes to the crowd and a ripple of whispers runs through it. Malacrolla suppresses the urge to applaud.

She steps forward, nodding her thanks to the monk, and the entire crowd press closer. The babble of voices in the arena dims, but Malacrolla knows it will be a struggle for many to hear her still. She has chosen her position well, the wind is behind her and will bring her words towards them, but Malacrolla joins the push forward to be close enough to hear.

'People of Verona,' she cries out – as loud as she can shout and still be heard perhaps, but Malacrolla only just catches the words. Fortunately she waits a while and he hears people, her own or simply those used to such addresses, repeat it for the sake of those behind.

'I speak as one of you, as a daughter of this once-fair city.

'I have lived here my entire life. I can remember the time before – the days of spring and summer when we lived according to the rhythms of God's earth.

'Many of you have not known this time, you have seen only plague and bloodshed and feud.

'Once-fair Verona, robbed of her dignity by two

households. I see this city, cowed and ever fearful for what the morning may bring.

'But this day there is hope for Verona. The birds of the sky trace a message for us all if we have the strength to lift our heads.'

She waits for a long while as the crowd murmurs restlessly. Malacrolla hears the clothier breathe "*Romeo Montague*" as others do the same across the arena. He does not sound as awed and convinced as many – his whole manner is one of stern disapproval such that only a man of wealth can muster. It is why Malacrolla has stationed himself here and acquainted himself with the man. Such a type possesses an iron certainty. If ever there was a man of Verona to sow the seeds of an idea in his heart, it is one such as this.

'I speak to you of that lost son of Montague,' the old lady continues after a dozen breaths. 'Heir to that once-great House, husband to the child of Capulet.

'People of Verona, do you believe a mercenary can turn the hearts of these households? Do you believe the commands of Milan can break this ancient grudge?

'No – we have all seen the years of uncivil deed, of theft and murder in the name of honour.

'Only one who can truly command the honour of those Houses can end our woe. Only one who has united them in his heart can mend this city, restore us to the great days of Bartolomeo and Cangrande.

'But the sell-swords and cruel lords know the danger he poses. They have forced him into trial for defending his own life. They have coerced a verdict and only time keeps him from the noose.

'People of Verona, our hope hangs by a thread. We must cast off our fear and act before all hope is lost.

'The governor is not our enemy, he is a soldier with

a lord who commands him and a city to control.

'We must show the governor that Verona is more than the voice of two Houses. We must stand before his walls and show him that we choose a future for our children.

'Our fear has always held us back. Our weakness keeps our voice quiet, but no longer!

'They say Milan desires an end to this feud as much as we. If we show our desires align with Milan's, we are stronger together. Peace to work, peace to live – is this not what we all hope for?

'Without peace there are meagre harvests gathered and meagre taxes paid. Let us stand before the castle walls and show him our strength.

'We have no weapons, we have no wealth, but we have our lives. Our strength is counted in our lives alone, and if we lend those to Milan's steel, what can stop us?

'People of Verona, will you march with me? We march not to war but to peace, that long-forgotten place in our hearts.'

The old woman's last words are lost in the swell of sound that builds like a rising tide within the bowl of the arena. Malacrolla feels the surging fervour, a tremble in his bones that he has never witnessed in Verona before.

The old woman lifts a torch from its sconce to a great roar from the crowd and takes the monk's hand. Together they descend to the arena floor and more torches are fetched. Soon an honour guard of light-bearers surrounds them.

'Do we leave our last hope in the hands of Milan?' Malacrolla wonders aloud for the clothier's benefit. 'Would Romeo Montague not be safer in the hands of the city?'

He sees a slight frown cross the man's face, indication that he has at least heard Malacrolla's words, and then they are gone. The clothier is dragged forward by his family and Malacrolla moves through the crowd as it gathers in the old woman's wake. He seeks the young men, the drunkards, the braggarts. Many times he wonders aloud how best they might seize their chance of hope and many times he is ignored. But not every time.

As they head towards the governor's castle, his work is done as best it can be and his thoughts turn elsewhere. To the man he knows as Black Will and the dagger he carries in his belt.

Twenty-Two

The harsh clang of the alarm rattles through the corridors of Scaliger Castle, sending soldiers and servants scurrying. Black Will watches them go from his high post overlooking the river. He is alone and unobserved. A familiar quickening stirs in his belly, the prickling anticipation of a moment offering itself.

He scans the darkening ground beyond the wall and sees nothing then trots to the further part of the wall to wave at a fellow sentry. The man does not notice him until he whistles then with a hiss comes closer. The wind whips across them, gusts that momentarily sweep all sound away and leave a strange stillness in the wake.

'What comes?' Will calls.

'A mob,' comes the reply. 'Townsfolk, peasants.'

'Armed?'

The man just shrugs, unconcerned. Their walls are strong, a mob is no danger to them despite the modest garrison here. Fifty soldiers could hold the castle against hundreds, he knows this as well as the townsfolk. And yet they are here, the perfect distraction to earn his money.

Black Will waves his thanks and returns to his post

on the far side of the castle from the gate. From there he can see nothing, only hear the discordant alarm and the restless ocean sounds of footsteps and voices merging into an unintelligible roar. He bides his time a little longer then slips quietly away to the hatch that leads down. Inside it is quiet and still, light spilling down the flagstone corridor.

Setting his crossbow to one side, he makes his way around to the room where Romeo Montague has been secured. It is not a cell, simply a locked room on the edge of the guest quarters with a guard outside. The cells deep below are no place for a nobleman and a friend of the governor so Black Will meets no opposition until he nears the room and the guard on duty nods a greeting.

'More sparrows chattering at the gate, Will?' the guard asks as he approaches.

Black Will nods, walking with the brisk purpose expected of a soldier, hand well clear of his dagger. 'Townsfolk I hear,' he replies. 'Perhaps they celebrate – at last one nobleman is but a step from the gibbet.'

'A friend of the governor still,' the guard says with a sceptical voice. 'And servant of Milan. For this prisoner I will be keeping a civil tongue while he still holds breath.'

'A wise course to chart,' Will agrees, joining the soldier at his post. 'Until the deed is done and breath is gone, we know our place in this life yet.'

Without waiting for a response Will draws his dagger and stabs the guard – low in the chest and up to his heart. The man manages only a brief gasp, shock and pain mingling on his face, and then he crumples beneath it. Will eases the body down onto the stool that stands in the corner and props it up as best he can. Blood runs down from the wound onto the guard's boots, but in the dimly lit corridor it will not reveal the crime any sooner than an unanswered question.

He takes the key from the guard's belt and checks around, listening for footsteps but hearing none. With deft hands he unlocks the door and enters, pulling it shut behind him. It is a small room, a fireplace on the left across from a high window, a table with three chairs ahead of him and a narrow bed at the far end.

'Yes?'

The man inside is sat at the table scattered with documents. Black Will stares at it in surprise for a moment. He knew Romeo Montague was an official in the large bureaucracy of Milan, but he hadn't expected the man to still be working now.

Montague's eyes drop to the dagger in Black Will's hand and his eyes widen. Before Will can cross the room Montague hurls the glass oil lamp from the table-top at Will. He bats it aside, but as it falls the lamp shatters and flames burst over a chair. Will falters and slews right as fire licks at his clothes. Montague's hand goes to his belt, but he has only an eating knife there. He draws it as he calls for help, but the words wither as Black Will pulls his long fighting dagger and advances again, knife in each hand.

Montague kicks the table up and shoves it across Will's path, but he barges it aside. The nobleman then fetches up a chair and makes to throw it. Will stops instinctively, bracing for the blow, but it never comes. Instead Montague charges forward with it, knife held back as he drives the chair into Will. With it he pins his murderer's arm and keeps solid wood between the dagger and his own flesh. They push and twist together, Montague making no effort to strike Will and merely using his knife to ward off his attacker.

214

Will drops one knife and grasps the chair pressed into his shoulder. He hauls the nobleman forward and scores a bloody line down his shoulder before kicking at his legs while he's reeling. Montague falls and releases the chair, but Will slams it back down on top of him, bludgeoning Romeo with three swift blows. They are clumsy, but the nobleman cries out and abandons his knife as he tries to protect himself.

Black Will pauses and takes a breath, dagger low at his side and prey helpless before him. In that moment an explosion of dark sparks erupts around his head and he is thrown forward by some terrific blow. He falls hard against something before ending up on the floor, the room melting into smears of dark and light.

Before he can recover his senses there are more blows. His dazed mind is scarcely able to recognise them though his body recoils from the abuse it receives. Heavy impacts in his side toss him around like a ship in a storm; sharp blows descend from above like bolts of lightning.

'Enough!' bellows a voice.

While Black Will gasps and moans, the pummelling ends. He remains curled up, arms covering his face. He can see nothing still. His eyes are blurred and sputter with stars that flower and die in brief moments. Just as he thinks the violence is at an end his hand is seized and he realises he is still holding his dagger somehow.

Unable to resist the grip, Will feels his arm twisted and smashed hard on the tabletop until he manages to unpick his fingers.

Disarmed, he is left to cringe on the floor again while voices speak in the background. Distantly he is aware of his prey being seen to, of Montague speaking and then hissing with pain as his cut is probed. Black

Will lolls back on the floor, the searing sting of broken ribs making each breath an agony.

'Pick him up!' commands a voice.

He is roughly grabbed and hoisted up onto feet that will not hold him. As he collapses, the hands take a firmer grip and he is held upright while a dark-haired figure moves into view.

'One of ours?' the figure demands, features hidden behind the blurry stars.

'Aye, my Lord,' comes one of his captors. 'Will of Avon they call him – Black Will on account of his hair, or so I had thought.'

'But it was in fact for his heart,' the lord growls.

Slowly Will starts to recover his wits and he recognises the face before him, though his features are contorted with anger. It is the Lord Governor himself, even bigger up close than Will had thought at a distance.

'And now it shall be for his flesh, but first I would know who sent him. Who ordered Romeo's death.'

'Mercy!' Black Will croaks. 'Mercy, Lord!'

'Mercy? What mercy do you ask?' the governor roars. 'A black-heart offers none. A blackguard deserves none. A traitor gets none.'

'The name!' Will almost wails. 'I will give you the name! Only spare me the rack, spare me the fire!'

'Give it to me now then, delay a further moment and my rage will only grow.'

'Malacrolla, Arturo Malacrolla – a merchant of the town. My Lord Governor, I swear it on my family. He paid me, he orders Montague's death.'

'Why?'

Will coughs, whimpering at the fire down his side. He chokes out the words as best he can – the stink of burning flesh coming all too readily to mind. 'I know

216

not, only that he would not risk your pardon.'

'Who does he serve?'

'I do not know for sure, he never said.'

The Governor seizes him by the throat with both hands and shakes Will like a rat. 'You know!'

'I suspect!' he croaks. 'Florence, he serves Florence! He mentioned a wife, her Guelphic inclinations and her banking friends.'

'Does he deal with the Houses?'

'Not through me, but I think so. He wishes the feud would grow into civil war, that is his dream.'

'Then I will send him to his long sleep and he may dream it for all time!' snarls the Governor. 'Is this mob his doing?'

'I know not, Lord, truly I do not!'

'You know little of use it seems.'

'Please Lord, I have told you all I know! I am a mercenary, he hires me for small deeds only – messages, threats. I had need of the money this time, he knows of my debts.'

'Your debt is now in blood and flame.'

'My Lord! Spare me!'

The Governor releases his grip, but leans closer still. 'I will spare you the flame and the noose, too!'

Before Black Will can feel any relief, the Governor steps back and draws his sword. Will cries out in fear, but then the tip is driven into his heart and the world enfolds him with pain and terror. The light fades. Finally even the pain is absent and Black Will is no more.

Twenty-Three

Juliet watches the mob approach with mounting concern. Jangling fear in her belly echoes the ugly clang of the alarm chimes – rough iron tubes that hang in the guardhouse. One archer continues to hammer at them with an iron-shod cudgel, a tuneless clatter that draws much of the castle to the gate.

In the deep ocean-blue of the evening sky above, she hears the shrieks of birds hunting. As the mob gets closer those cries are drowned out by the rising tide of sound. There is an ominous swell to their voices. Juliet pulls her grey cloak tight around her against the buffeting wind. Her companions are the castle's archers, twenty men of varying nationalities and ages. It does not seem so many now, not compared to the many hundreds arriving at their gate.

'Don't you worry, my Lady,' Aylward calls from his station. 'If they had mischief in mind they would come armed and still we have the numbers to ward them off.'

The broad longbowman wears his usual easy smile as he speaks and has eschewed his steel cap of war. Whether or not it's intended to reassure Juliet, it does and she's glad for the bluff veteran who has hitched his star to Francesco's.

'The devil's mood can take a mob still,' she says. 'Turn protest to rage, sense to violence.'

'Rage will not weather a storm, my Lady,' he counters, raising his strung bow. Beside him one of the garrison nods, a crossbow in his hands.

'The people of Verona have been sorely used these past twenty years, I would not see them suffer your slings and arrows when there are more worthy targets.'

'They must see sense on their own, my Lady. Neither you nor I can do more than shoot it from these walls.'

The crowd thins as they near the castle walls. Most remain cautious and shy from marching on the castle gate, but a knot of fifty-odd bulge forward from the mass. A kernel of the most indignant or drunken drive on regardless and drag others in their wake. This close, Juliet can now make out their cries – demands for justice and the name of her husband mingling freely.

'They are here for an audience,' she says loudly, in case any of the archers are wondering what to do. Looking around she realises there is no officer in command on the wall now Francesco has been called away – for what reason she cannot imagine, but it brings her a moment of indecision.

Aylward leans out and yells down to the figures below, demanding to know their business. Juliet meanwhile scans the group and is dismayed to find nurse and Lawrence are present, penned in at the rear of the gathering. More prominent are younger men with flushed cheeks, merchants and tradesmen who all angrily reply until the largest of them shouts them down.

'We seek an audience with the governor,' he roars back, a great bear of a man in a fox-fur cloak. 'We seek

219

justice for Romeo Montague!'

'Justice?' Aylward replies. 'What form of justice is offered by a mob?'

'Freedom, for Montague and Verona! Freedom from those who oppress us and live as a plague upon this city!'

Slowly the crowd creeps closer behind. Indistinct growls and shouts emanate from its heart.

'Release Montague!' the leader demands as loudly as he can. This time the rest take up his call.

'Release him! Release Montague!'

The words echo around the street and Juliet can feel a wave of passion surging as the main bulk arrives. She looks at Aylward and sees the man's smile has slipped. Now his fingertips brush the feathers of his arrows.

'Go back!' he yells down. 'Withdraw! The Lord Governor will hear of your demands, but you must go from this place.'

'Bring him out! Release Montague!'

'Back I say or blood will spill! See you there the flag of Milan? Assault the stronghold of the Lord Governor and great vengeance will be upon you!'

'Release him! Release him!'

'Aylward,' Juliet cries, hearing the angry voices increase. 'Do not fire upon them!'

'My Lady, if they do not withdraw I will have no choice.'

'Let me speak to them first, it is my husband who they seek to protect. The people have been denied their voice too long, let me go outside and speak to them.'

'I cannot allow it, you must call down.'

Juliet shakes her head. 'Call down to them with archers beside me? When they seek relief from those who oppress them? No, I must stand where they may know me, they will not harm me then. See – there is Friar Lawrence among them. He would never permit such a crime.'

'I see one old man and a host of drunk ruffians, my Lady. These are more my people than yours though I am sired by an Englishman.'

'Sergeant, I am not yours to command, I will go out.'

'My Lady!' Aylward says in dismay, but Juliet is already marching down the steps to the gate below.

In the courtyard the garrison's men-at-arms are assembled before the gate, shields resting at their sides and spears pointing to the heavens. With them stands Mercutio, youngest of them all, but old enough to use the sword he wears. Juliet's son hops forward when he sees her and intercepts her before the gate.

'Mother, where are you going?'

'My nurse and Friar Lawrence are outside. I will speak to the crowd in the governor's absence.'

'You cannot!'

'Cannot?' Juliet shakes her head at her son, the sight of him in battle-dress enough to cast the fear from her heart. 'Cannot? Grown and armed you may be, Mercutio, you are not yet of an age to make such demands.'

'Mother, it is not safe! That is no peaceful delegation come to request an audience.'

'I do not think them so foolish as to lay hands upon a woman of gentle birth, not before the walls of this castle and the arrows of its soldiers. But my safety has never been assured in this city and I might yet do some good. I cannot stand idly by and allow this to play out – not when I had a hand in its genesis.'

'Then let me come with you.'

'No, my son you must not. The risk I bear all comes

from my own past, my actions and my mistakes. I cannot stand aside from such consequences, but nor can I put all I love in danger.'

'Nor can you ask me to hide from it!' he replies. 'You set me before the city as heir to the great Houses of Verona. All this I may one day inherit and with that comes the blessings, rewards and sins of my fathers, too. You wish to give this city a better future and though you would prefer only your life to be at stake, it is not. This future is mine also – and Estelle's and all those beyond these walls. If we are to share that future, we cannot hide from all it entails.'

He turns and demands that the postern door be opened. The soldier at the gate hesitates until Juliet also steps forward then he ducks his head. He unbolts the door and holds it while Mercutio and Juliet step through, not needing to be ordered to close it behind them.

The crowd of people beyond makes Juliet briefly falter; an angry shifting mass within the evening gloom, half-lit by torches but many just shapes in the darkness. She puts a hand on Mercutio's arm and holds him back as the leaders of the mob press forward. They only stop when she advances too and calls out as loudly as she can.

'People of Verona, my name is Juliet Montague – wife to Romeo Montague, daughter of the Lord Capulet and advisor to the Lord Governor. You wish an audience. You wish justice! No ear can hear your concerns with more sympathy than mine. No voice will relay them to the governor as readily.'

'Bring him out to us,' the large man demands. 'He is the best hope for Verona's future, but your Houses do not wish for that future to come. They will see him dead if we stand aside.'

'My husband is not yet dead and while there is breath in my body, he will remain alive. But what you ask I cannot do. The rule of law must be adhered to if there can ever be peace in Verona.'

'While the Houses are set against each other there can be no peace!' the man roars, raising his torch high. The wind streams yellow light above their heads and casts sparks up into the night as more voices shout in support.

'Messer, do you speak for all here? Will you tell me your name?'

'Lady Montague, I will not.' His face is flushed with drink and power, but Juliet sees his wits have not abandoned him yet. 'If you unite the Houses I will kneel to you as a payer of Capulet tithes, but I would not give you my name with the mercenaries of Milan as witness.'

'Very well, I no longer ask it of you. But is there another here whose name I do know? Did I see Friar Lawrence among you? Come forward, Friar, come stand beside one who speaks for you all. None can deny you are devoted to peace, to the end of this feud between Houses.'

The crowd reluctantly parts and Lawrence shuffles forward with nurse in his wake. The friar's face betrays clashing emotions, unease at the crowd around him overlaying the burning purpose that has kept his madness at bay all these years.

'It is good to see you again, Friar Lawrence,' Juliet says with a respectful curtsey. 'Your presence is a reassurance to us all.'

Looking at those who have placed themselves at the head of the crowd, she sees Lawrence's presence has indeed dampened their fire, but it is far from extinguished.

'We demand the release of Romeo Montague,' the leader repeats. 'We demand he is given into custody of the people of Verona. Only with us can he be safe from the claws of those who would preserve the feud for their own profit.'

'This I cannot do!' Juliet exclaims. 'This castle stands apart from the feud, do you think those liveried bandits can breach its walls?'

'They hold the wealth of the city and money creeps through the tightest defence, my Lady. It can corrupt magistrates and sway judgements, open gates and turn whole armies – all this you know to be true. The Lord Governor himself is a condottiero, many of his soldiers too. Are you so certain of them all? Do you trust all of our futures to the honour of Englishmen and Germans after all they have done in Italy?'

'I trust the Lord Governor,' Juliet declares as the rumbles of the crowd begin to build. 'With my husband's life I trust him.'

'Will the duke protect him? Will he go against the will of the court?'

'I will find a way, I have not yet given up hope. What you ask is too drastic!'

'We have been without hope for years. All through your exile we have suffered, we have known nothing but the abuses done under guise of the feud. Murder and arson, kidnapping and theft. Everything of worth has been pillaged by the creatures give free reign by the Houses.'

'And how many among you are free of the influence of the Houses? How many knows the man beside him will not seek a reward from our enemies?'

'We are here to be free of them forever!' the leader

yelled with such fury Mercutio took a step forward, hand on his sword. 'We risk our lives to be here for we are men without title or arms. There is nothing to protect us should vengeance come.'

'There is the protection of Milan – such as I have had these twenty years. All that has kept me alive in exile has been the hand of the duke, the authority that extends over me and my family right now. No citizen of ancient Rome enjoyed greater.'

'You are noble-born,' another man shouts. 'You are like kin to him and useful to his plans. We are neither, we do not exist to a duke save as cattle to be worked. If it suits he will send his armies and ravage us again. We are the ones to suffer and for these twenty years there has been no end to that, until this day. Now we see a spark of hope, of liberation from this slow death and we would risk all to protect it.'

The crowd presses forward and Juliet is forced back to avoid being enveloped. From the wall above she heard voices, Aylward bellowing above the din. She tries to say more, but her words are swallowed by the waves of noise crashing down upon them.

Mercutio takes her by the arm and pulls her aside, calling up to Aylward for the postern to be opened as he does. He hammers his fist against the wood as Juliet can only watch the crowd get closer. At last the door is opened and Mercutio drives her through it, pulling his mother close to him as he does so.

'Mother,' he cries in her ear, 'Mother you must trust me now!'

'What? Mercutio, what are you saying?'

'Trust me – this will end in massacre if we do not act.'

'No, oh merciful God, Mercutio, what do you

intend?'

He stops and looks her straight in the eye as the crowd presses forward and the men-at-arms advance on the door. 'What I must. If I am to be heir to all the woes of Verona, I must act now or see them consume all we hold dear.'

Juliet blinks at him, seeing the man he has become more clearly than ever before. When she says nothing more, Mercutio gives her a grin that is half terror, half excitement, then he pushes her away and places himself in the path of the men-at-arms.

'Hold off, Sergeant!' he roars with all the assurance of one born to lead. 'Hold there, let the gate stay open! Aylward, keep tight your grip upon your arrows and your men! People of Verona – come with me. I tell you now, harm no one or God's vengeance will descend and the serpent will break you in its jaws.

'If you have dreams of pillage, leave them without these gates or there will be a terrible slaughter – but if you still hold true to that hope for Verona's future, follow me. I will lead you to my father's cell and free him. The time has come for you, citizens of Verona – brothers I have been so cruelly denied by feud and fortune. Your fate is in your hands. Hold it with a new-born care, else calamity falls upon us all. Come, we go to free Romeo Montague!'

Twenty-Four

'What noise is this? Mercutio!' Francesco bellows, sword drawn and men-at-arms arrayed behind him. 'What is it that you do here?'

'I do as I must, Lord. Withdraw I beg you and let us pass!'

Francesco stands agape at the great castle door. The gate is closed yet the postern within it opens and a steady stream of citizens comes through. Archers stand with bows bent upon the wall and men-at-arms are ready to charge the scores of rowdy men behind Mercutio.

'Withdraw? What manner of rebellion is this? Do you lead beasts into my house to rob and overturn all natural order?'

'I do not – they come for one thing alone: my father's release.'

Francesco's face darkens. 'Since when has this been your cause? Since when have you and yours turned your hearts against all that you love?'

'I do not, this I swear, Francesco. I made no plans for this and what I do now is yet in the cause of peace.'

'Your methods of peace are strange, young buck. Your following are unarmed, this I grant, but to violate these grounds is a grave act.'

Mercutio kneels before Francesco, sword flat against the ground. 'I beg you forgive me this one violation, for the need of avoiding one greater. Their fears drive them to desperation, seeing my father as their last hope. I feared some greater offence to God and Verona's future if I did not intervene, some act that would sour all of your dreams and those of my parents.'

He raises his arms to those behind him. 'There will be no violence here, no robbery or any similar act – you come with a noble cause, but I will cut down the first man who violates this law.'

'Come Lord,' urges one of Francesco's men. 'They are within the walls, we must attack them now or step aside.'

'Step aside? My honour demands otherwise.'

'Lord Francesco, many times you have told me honour is a poison to this fair Italy,' Mercutio declares. 'That honour is the root of all our worst qualities and prevents something greater being built here. You are a mercenary by trade, my Lord. Your captain has taught you expediency over honour. Let this offence pass, I will answer to you another day when the blood is cooled and the promise of Damocles is not so frayed.'

'My Lord?' asks the man-at-arms.

Francesco scowls, but is not long about his decision. 'Very well, I shall step aside – but do not trouble any person of this castle, nor the goods contained within it. You will answer to this another day, Mercutio. I pray that when you do so all has worked out well and it is but a matter for my own mutable pride.'

Mercutio rises and bows. 'I swear I shall do so most humbly,' the young man says.

'Very well – soldiers of Milan, hear me!' Francesco

calls loudly. He sends one man back to warn the guard then leads the rest clear of the door to let Mercutio pass.

'We will suffer this outrage as Milan's gift to her sister city – a blessing upon her as she is reborn to better times. If there is one step out of turn, one hand raised to those of Milan's service, the gift is lost forever, but for now you will stay your blades and let Romeo Montague pass.'

Down the hall Mercutio leads a delegation of his weapon-less army, now humbled by their surrounds and the words of their governor. The drink is fading from their minds and while some are of a mind to see what rich pickings they might find, wiser heads prevail.

Mercutio, though just a youth of seventeen, leads the way with all the confidence he can summon and does not let his voice falter. Their path is clear, all have heard the herald Francesco sent and only the guard on Romeo's door is visible when they reach it.

The door itself is open and Romeo stands in the doorway, battered and dishevelled. Mercutio sees blood on the floor and runs to him, calling 'Father!' as he goes.

'Do not be frightened, the blood is not mine,' Romeo says, though he is plainly puzzled by the group of unlikely rescuers behind. 'An assassin was sent and used the tumult as cover, but Francesco has killed him.'

'Sent by whom? The Capulets?'

Romeo hesitates. 'The man gave no name,' he says after a moment's pause. 'He was not given the chance, he fought to the death.'

'It must be the Capulets, they have sent assassins before.'

'The assassin is dead, I do not fear him now. But who are your fellows, my son? Why do you come here?'

'We come to rescue you from injustice,' cries the

large man who led the crowd outside. 'You who have been sent by God to end this feud and were betrayed by the lure of silver.'

'You think too much of me, friend, if you would cast me that way. I am but a man and one who is faithful to the Signore of Verona. What do you rescue me from, the protection of these soldiers? The rulings of our lord, the Duke of Milan?'

'From the schemes of the Houses and from others they might send. The people of Verona have hope once more and we will defend that with our lives if we must. The governor himself has been persuaded to stand aside for our cause.'

'Stand aside? Does he release me or do you ask me to become fugitive once more? Mercutio, was this all of your devising? I cannot violate the law of the city further without ruining all hopes of peace.'

'Father, you must come. There is a great crowd at the gates, I fear violence will result if we do not bring you out.'

'Have you threatened the governor with violence?' Romeo asks in shock.

'No, I endeavour to prevent it – to avoid a night that would end all chance of unity within Verona. They are fearful and eager to grasp their own fate, to chart a course for their children that is better than was plotted for themselves.'

'That wish I know with all my heart, but how does this achieve it?'

'It staves off bloody violence between parties that should be allies. I know you love the law, Father, but your duty is to Verona and the future you might assist. Please, come with us. Let us end this night with no orphans made, no widows with reason to curse the flag of Milan.'

Romeo stands for a long while staring at the face of his son and those earnest strangers behind him.

'I had wished not to flee from consequences,' he says at last. 'I have faith yet that the ruling of the podesta could be altered, that some resolution to satisfy all parties could be reached. If I am to become fugitive once more I do not know where this may lead.'

'None of us can know that, Father – only that this night it leads away from death and destruction. I make no further promises, just as you made none to your children when we set out for Verona. That day we agreed we could do nothing but choose what we believe to be right.

'I have no foresight beyond the need to avoid a massacre, no grand scheme to work to – only that this is the choice before us. What may come tomorrow is in God's hands.'

His father bows his head. 'Very well,' he says in a small voice, though it brings a cheer from the onlookers. 'I will come with you. If my honour is to be the price of blood un-spilled then it is cheaply bought. Let night cool the heads of all and sleep soothe their hearts. Come, we must away.'

Romeo allows himself to be swept into Mercutio's entourage. The men cheer and clap him on the back, declare their great victory and propel both Montague men to their fore once more. He walks the corridors with one arm across Mercutio's shoulders, more a protective gesture than comradely as they descend to the torch-lit courtyard.

More cheers greet them, a wall of sound that buffets and startles Romeo. He falters as he takes in the scene, weapons arrayed all around them like thorns. Plumes of light rise from the higher torches as the wind rails and moans over the walls. A cloak is passed to him, plain homespun wool that will disguise him as much as keep him warm.

'Lord Governor,' Romeo calls as the crowd moves towards Mercutio's delegation. 'This shall be made right in the eyes of our lord.'

'So it must!' Francesco replies. His eyes are hard and cheerless, his jaw tight. 'So it shall, but I pray events shall cast a softer light on that morn.'

'As do I. Until that day, know I take all responsibility for this act.'

'You may not take what is not yours, I will not allow it and nor will our lord. Say no more on it. We will speak again when there are fewer hasty hearts and blades present. Kiss your wife and go quick into the night. She must stay, but I give my word she will not be mistreated in any way.'

'I understand, Lord Governor.'

Romeo bows and hurries to his wife, parting the eager crowd with all the strength that is left to him. Eventually he wins through and Juliet rushes past her guards to embrace him. For one moment he forgets everything. With her arms around his neck, Romeo breathes in the scent of her perfume and presses his lips to her neck.

'I am sorry, my heart,' she whispers to him. 'This is my doing, I set this in motion though not to this intended end.'

Romeo blinks at her in surprise. 'Always you do astonish me, my love,' he murmurs. 'You have won the citizens over to our cause? I profess I would not have wished this, but nor would I have imagined it. To flee as a fugitive is something I would never wish for our son, but Francesco could stop it if he so desired. I feel the hand of fate upon my shoulder. Perhaps God's will favours us yet.'

Juliet kisses him without regard to those watching, pulls herself hard against his lips as he hugs her tight. When she releases him, Romeo runs a hand down that smooth, perfect cheek then plants one more kiss on her forehead.

'We will be reunited soon enough,' he says. 'Your strength will see to it, of that I'm certain.'

'Would that I could come with you,' she says with eyes damp. 'We have been in flight together before. Those days I do not miss, but I would never want you to endure more alone.'

'I am not alone, I have Mercutio at my side and you must be at Estelle's. Come, this bluster shall pass and I would have you in safety than anywhere else.'

She nods. 'If I must howl down the storm itself, I will see this past. Be safe, my heart.'

'I will. Adieu, my love.'

With that there are no more words to be said. Romeo catches only one last glimpse of Juliet before the crowd bears him away. Out through the postern they go to be met by great roars from a dark street filled with people. He cannot guess their numbers as he is drawn into the heart of them and a hat set upon his head. From the walls, he imagines, Romeo Montague has vanished into the mass of craftsmen and traders.

He barely sees which direction they head in. The Roman forum appears in the distance before voices start to call for the crowd to part and confound any pursuit. Only then is he presented with the next astonishing sight, the faces of Juliet's nurse and Friar Lawrence emerging from the fractured crowd.

With those allies at his side he is finally able to make his voice heard and some direction given to events. All four are taken by circuitous route to the home of a shopkeeper near the city wall, the owner beaming as though they are a prize won. There, they can finally rest and shake off the breathless mood that has gripped them all. In more intimate surrounds, away from the roars of fools, Romeo sits and lets quiet descend. The shopkeeper's wife timidly offers him a thin soup and dark gritty bread to eat. He mumbles his thanks, glad of both its warmth and the distraction. While the tale of the day is related to him and the wind rages on above, he eats and thinks.

*

'Did you invite them inside the walls?'

Francesco's question is met with silence. Juliet looks him in the eye as she wonders how best to answer, Estelle close beside her. She can feel Estelle's hands trembling slightly, the shock of events returning old childhood fears. Juliet herself can scarcely believe what she has been told and it has been an effort to keep her own composure. The assassin had been one of the guards here, an Englishman of many years' service to the former governor, Ugolotto Biancardo.

'I did not speak the words,' she says at last. 'But I believed them correct. Mercutio saw what threatened and I agreed to his actions.'

'You agreed,' Francesco states in a flat tone. 'And so this stronghold was invaded, a prisoner unlawfully taken.'

She can see the clash of emotion inside him. No doubt if Estelle had been absent his anger would have boiled over, but in the presence of the woman Francesco aspires to, he keeps it in check. It sticks in his throat though, the pressure of head and heart meeting to choke the words he might wish to speak.

'We saw no other choice, when bloodshed might undo all our endeavours.'

'Endeavours that rely upon the power I wield, the authority of control.'

'Authority that remains yours, my Lord Governor. Power that remains yours.' Juliet bows her head slightly. 'It was not done with a glad heart, but the strength of Milan remains behind you. The soldiers of the garrison remain yours to command. Those who see this as a sign of weakness will soon discover themselves mistaken. Those who see this as a gesture of compassion towards a beleaguered citizenry will embrace it and the man who made it.'

'That man was not I!' Francesco roars.

'History will not relate that,' Juliet says. 'You are the Lord Governor of Verona – you chose not to massacre civilians, you chose to permit Romeo's departure.'

'Shall you ask history to relate your words to the duke? Will history be advising the noble Houses of Verona when they decide whether to oppose my will?'

'History will make no decisions in the coming days,' she insists. 'What is yet unwritten shall be determined by us, by your decisions. These events have not yet seen their conclusion, but should Romeo be executed the church bells shall toll for Verona herself. Then history will judge us all.'

'So what is your advice, my Lady?' Francesco snaps. 'If you are still my advisor and have charted this course we follow, what comes next?'

'Calm waters,' she replies. 'A few days without

disturbance permits us all to breathe. There will be cause to pardon Romeo somehow, to undo the sentence that was laid down. Meanwhile the plans we have set to unpick the claws of Capulets and Montagues from this city must be enacted. The regulations and limitations we have devised to lessen their power, this night has proved that the city will welcome them.'

'You do not know what this night proves, you claim too much, Lady. Can you tell me where your husband spends this night? Can you be sure there are no vassals of either family near him? No? When one or other of Lords Antonio or Reynard ask me tomorrow where my prisoner is, can you assure me they will not know more than I?'

'Do not speak to them tomorrow. They remain subjects of the city, should they ask for you they can be delayed.'

'You would have me hide from those I must convince of my power? To enforce these regulations I must have soldiers spread across the city. Either one of the families could ambush them and pick them off well past the point where I could respond. Those bound to the Houses will be forced to choose to follow the devil they have lived in fear of for a generation, or the man who has let unarmed citizens carry off a prisoner in his charge.'

'When we issue the regulations there will be no cause for them to follow those they are bound to.'

'Only if I can enforce them with steel – without that they must do as they always have. The law seldom protects the poor, principle does not shelter or feed those in need.'

'Do you think either would be so bold as to attack your soldiers?'

236

Francesco laughs cruelly at that. 'My Lady, they know that the duke is concerned with greater affairs than Verona. If Lord Reynard strung myself and your family up then took control of the city, compared to the coming war against Bologna and Florence it would be nothing so long as he was careful to pay taxes.'

Juliet feels those words as a knife made of ice, cutting deep into her gut. The threat of violence has been constant these past twenty years, a fact never more so keenly felt than tonight, but to hear it described without consequences is a shock still.

'We must have faith in the people of Verona,' she finds herself saying in a muted voice. 'This night they made their voices heard for the first time in many a year.'

'The people of Verona have this night shown they cannot be fully controlled when they are roused with drink. In the morning we will see what they are made of, but I can have no faith in a herd of confused and fearful beasts.'

Twenty-Five

Romeo lies in a narrow cot with his eyes closed, listening as he waits in vain for sleep to come. Beside him he can hear the heavy, regular breathing of Mercutio, asleep at last, while the shutters creak and someone snores in a room downstairs.

From what he can recall, the street outside is busy during the day. He can hear each pair of boots on the cobbles right now however. His heart jolts whenever there is more than one. The wind ebbs after midnight, finally exhausting its efforts to wrench the shutters away and expose his hiding place. Fatigue drags at him, making his whole body heavy and unwieldy while a tangled knot builds behind his eyes.

Whenever he feels himself drifting towards sleep, some small sound prickles his fears once more and a twitch of his body jerks him back to wakefulness. For much of the time he simply lies there and tries to order his thoughts, to plan for the day to come. His efforts come to nothing, however, ideas darting from his attempts to grasp them, as elusive as the gusts outside.

When pre-dawn begins to blearily describe the window frames, he eases himself up. Romeo wraps his borrowed cloak about him and leaves the room, finding a small terrace overlooking the rear yard. There he sits to watch the last few bats scatter to their roosts and clear the fog of fatigue. His view is an unfamiliar one, south across the district and the sprawl of dwellings beyond. His aching head begins to ease in the fresh morning air, but still he sees no answers to this latest turn of events.

The breeze has turned somnolent. Where he sees hearth smoke rising from the suburbs, it leans in tall towers towards the south. From the trees out past the city he sees a scattering of birds dart up into the dusty grey sky, too distant to make out anything but their movement. The stuttered calls of crows and dogs echo along the street, while the sleepy murmur of pigeons comes from the roof above.

He realises he is not alone and turns to discover Lawrence watching him from the doorway.

'Good morrow, Father, Benedicte.'

The quirk of what might once have been a smile twitches Lawrence's cheek. The hunched friar bobs his head in response and joins Romeo at the balustrade to look out over the city. His habit is stained and much patched, his skin as battered and marked as his clothing. Lawrence's hair is roughly cut, no tonsure now and no thought made to appearance as it was chopped back. Beholding him now in the morning light, Romeo sees how thin and lined Lawrence's face is. Ancient scars and the marks of time are both readily apparent.

The passage of time takes a greater toll on the poor; their youth is stolen all the sooner. 'Verona is peaceful now, I will grant Mercutio that.'

Another nod.

Romeo sighs and bows his head. 'It is what the day may bring that I fear. My son has followed in my sorry tracks and where those lead next, I cannot predict.'

Lawrence makes no reaction, but Romeo feels a pang of shame all the same.

'Oh I do not blame him, what else was there to be done? To quell a riot with force of arms could have turned the city against Francesco – uniting all of Verona into revolt just when I had promised the duke peace. But we move beyond the intended course here and any predictions I might chance are dismal. I do not know what I should do now.'

Lawrence glances towards him then closes his eyes and settles himself against the wall where the balustrade ends.

'You think I should do nothing?'

There is no response; Lawrence merely tilts his face up a little, as though enjoying the sun against his skin.

'Do nothing,' Romeo muses. 'Let events run as they will? But how can I even know what takes place, here in hiding? Our host may bring news, but I would not ask him to play informant to some rebellious exile.'

'But what can I do?' he continues after a pause. 'When re-arrest would only worsen matters and the streets of a city are not so numerous as to be a refuge. Can I do anything but trust my wife's efforts and the honour of my friend?'

Lawrence bows his head, arms wrapped around his body.

'Humility,' Romeo says softly. 'I am one man alone. Father, will you hear my confession?'

The question provokes a flinch and Lawrence draws back, but Romeo does not move to follow.

'If you do not wish it, I will understand, but there is no man of God I would honour more. There... there is no man under God's sky I have greater need to beg for forgiveness.'

Lawrence stays clear, his shoulder pressed against the wall as he watches Romeo out of the corner of his eye. His eyes flicker and dart, his ragged lips silently twitch. It is a long time before the fear and confusion subsides, but at last he calms and offers Romeo a short nod.

Leaning heavily on the balustrade Lawrence eases himself to his knees, fumbling at his hands before remembering he carries no prayer beads. He uses one gnarled and bent hand to steady himself on the balustrade, the other he presses to his lips as Romeo kneels beside him.

'Forgive me Father, for I have sinned.'

*

'The pup is more a Montague than the sire, my Lord.'

Lord Antonio smiles. 'The boy shares much with his sire to my eye, uncle.'

'Chief amongst those qualities being a fugitive spirit?' Sir Paolo says, laughing.

'He was a bold youth, too, as I recall? Hasty, quick to fall in love and as easily quit it, but a young man of heartfelt energy and that I admired. I do not recognise this notary of Milan.'

'Exiles are a plague upon all of Italy,' Paolo replies. 'Even when the city's gates have been opened to outsiders, they still cause turmoil.'

The old, bear-like soldier tears at a crust of bread and paces as he speaks, while Lord Antonio reclines in a chair and faces the morning sun.

'Perhaps then, we should offer him all that he wishes?'

'How so?'

'An exile desires a return to his home, does he not? Now father and son are both fugitives, they may be more inclined to risk accepting the hand of friendship.'

'Would he be so desperate?'

'What man would not feel desperation this morning? A sentence of death lurks in his shadow—' Antonio snorts. 'While his beautiful wife and radiant daughter lie in the care of a handsome young soldier, a man of boldness and few morals. Romeo's plans are in tatters, his children in danger. Liberation may have buoyed his mood while the night lasted, but it is morning now. Any true man will face the sun and recognise what its light reveals as true.'

'The sober light of day makes a man sceptical of gifts,' Paolo cautions.

'This line we must balance is not unfamiliar here. My cousin is not fool enough to believe I will give him everything, nor desperate enough to accept scraps from my table.'

'What is it he desires, then?'

'All of Verona,' Antonio declares. 'His manner may be more lawyerly these days, but those creatures are as hungry as the most envious of exiles.'

'But what will tempt him?'

'Romeo is a nobleman of Verona as much a servant of Milan. He comes here charged with securing peace, there can be no doubt now that this cowherd mercenary was never long for the governorship. Beyond that, he is a man with a family.'

'So he wishes peace and the governorship he was promised. But there remains his birth-right.'

'Something he must know I will never willingly give. Let him have one of the notable families of Verona if he

242

must however; there is another worth less than the House of Montague.'

Paolo laughs. 'You offer him Capulet?'

'I offer him acceptance and my support to the governorship, in return for renouncing his claim to the House of Montague. If he takes Capulet for his son, that is his business, I will not suggest it. Reynard is a foe we know, but I prefer an untested youth as my enemy.'

'Now I am left uncertain whether this is ruse or true! Your suggestion has more than the ring of sense – every church bell in Verona might peal to announce it as our future.'

'And trust the rightful heir or his son would honour it once they ruled Verona?' Lord Antonio demands. 'And be the lesser of the Lords Montague?'

'Now hold, my sharp son-in-law, let us consider further. Reynard must bow down, he could not oppose Milan, the citizens and Montague, too. The governor is a paid official, subject to the whims and needs of his lord's employment. Once peace is secure and the Capulets the lesser force in Verona, a great lord of that city might sway the duke's mind.'

'The House of Capulet might be reduced, but it would remain a force. Reynard is no true-born son of a Capulet, scarcely true-married is that one. For all that they might bear the Montague name, Juliet and Romeo would be Capulets in society and power when their son takes the title from Reynard, as he surely must. Though I would find no greater joy than to watch that House suffer the humiliation of a Montague for their lord, it might lead to our eclipse soon enough.'

'Ah, but you are correct!' Sir Paolo scowls and casts his bread aside. 'My eagerness gets the better of me once more,' he adds with a brief laugh, patting his own belly. 'There can be only one Lord Montague in Verona, to consider more is to go against nature itself.'

'Have a message sent through one of our vassals – in good faith, mind, no offer can be believed if they might have been followed to his lair.'

Sir Paolo bows. 'As you wish, my Lord. I go.'

Twenty-Six

'I hope I find you in restored spirits, my Lady.'

Estelle turns to face Francesco and the anger in her heart melts away. He is shorn of the robes of office and wears the simpler garb of a soldier. A lock of his unruly hair hangs over one eye and she restrains the urge to sweep it back, though she wishes more than anything to hold that face in her hands.

She curtseys which makes Francesco's young face fall, but then Estelle presents her hand. He sweeps it up and kisses it tenderly.

'You do find me so, Francesco. The headaches are gone, the city seems peaceful for the present. The good lord knows there is more that I would wish for, but enough has been granted for this morning.'

'It is my hope that in the afternoon, what God does not provide, I may serve as his agent.'

'How so?'

'I confess, I do not fully know, but I will not see my friend dead or my love in mourning.'

They stand at a tall window that looks north along the riverbank. The pale sky is hardly marked by thin cloud and ten thousand sparkles of sunlight drift away from them on the calm waters. The people at the river's edge go about their daily tasks with no haste or obvious concern. Estelle feels a strange envy that life can continue as normal for them, when for her it has stopped.

'What will you do?' she asks as he joins her at the window.

She leans in as she speaks, resting her shoulder against his. She imagines sliding her hands around his waist and the reassurance of his strong frame, but she knows she cannot. Her arms feel empty as a result and it reminds her of her absent, fugitive family.

'Perhaps this was not meant to be. Perhaps your father must go once more into exile.'

'What? After all this? After a murderer came so close to cutting this throat not twelve hours past you would have him flee from the threat?'

'I would have him wear a sword to defend himself,' Francesco says with a trace of bitterness before his voice softens and he looks at her. 'But there is so much I cannot have at present and I wonder if his guidance is one, at least until the peace is secure.'

'If secured in his absence, it would be threatened by his return.'

'Did you so hate your life in Milan?'

Estelle opens her mouth to reply then shakes it once more. 'Milan is a beautiful city, but Verona is my home – I feel it in my bones. These past few years as my father worked in the duke's court at Pavia, we were permitted a villa in his private hunting park. Yet even there, in that peaceful house where soldiers guarded us at a distance, I felt the call of Verona. I have heard too much of this city. It is a song that echoes in my blood.'

Francesco bows his head and is silent a long while. 'I

have never felt that call,' he admits. 'I crave it and one day I hope to find that place I can truly call home, but my place has only ever been in an army camp. I sometimes dream of returning to Carmagnola a man of wealth and title, but would it then be home?'

She smiles at him. 'I have hope for you yet, my Lord Governor. It may be one day your restless spirit is tamed.'

'As likely a peasant shall become duke of Milan,' he says with a smile. 'But this day, we have other concerns. I have issued instructions to search for your father, but my men are aware of my disposition and will not search too hard. I can afford no more shows of weakness, but a day without success harms nothing.'

'Mother tells me it was Florentine silver that betrayed my father.'

He nods. 'So I believe. Twenty florins were found in the assassin's purse and among his affairs. No doubt more was to be paid upon success. I have known good men killed for far less.'

'Do you search for the man who paid him?'

'No. I do not know what other informants he might have and I intend to take him alive. He was at the ball, we might lure him back here if we are careful, but I can only trust Rufus and Aylward without reserve. Were they familiar with Verona's streets I would task them with keeping a careful watch on this merchant. Only a handful know the assassin confessed and I have made clear their lives will be forfeit if word reaches the man.'

'Can you not simply dispatch soldiers to arrest him?'

'Only if we are certain where he is, otherwise he may slip the net. We will get only one opportunity to take him, no doubt he has prepared boltholes and routes of escape.'

'What of your other plans?'

'The measures against the families? One will be announced today – not enough to provoke great argument, but a measure of authority still. The city must remember who rules it and what he intends to achieve, else the lords are emboldened and the citizens disheartened.'

'The business of the city continues,' Estelle agrees. 'Forgive me, Governor, I must go. I should attend my mother and not leave her to her fears.'

'There is nothing to forgive. After the words spoken last night, I am only glad for the sight of your smile once more.'

She curtseys again and brushes close to him before she leaves. At the door she looks back and sees he is watching her go. Francesco's cheeks pink slightly behind the threads of beard and he turns away, hand on his sword as he surveys the city once more.

*

'Can this message be true?'

Mercutio shakes his head. 'It is a trap, it must be. Father, you must not go.'

'Were he offering to renounce his title, I would be certain, but he states quite clearly he would never do so.' Romeo scratches irritably at his beard. 'Antonio does not offer anything more than reason would require as compromise.'

'What interest has he in compromise?' Mercutio exclaims. 'He has grown as rich as Reynard by this feud, he would not wish it ended!'

'He would profit from winning this war at long last,' Romeo argues. 'With a Montague as Governor, his cousin by blood no less, the Capulets would wither on the vine.'

'You told me once, sense means nothing to a proud man – who could be more so than a lord? Who will guard his position more jealously than one faced with the rightful heir?'

'If he gives all that he offers,' Romeo says, 'he does not lose that position. Instead he enhances it.'

In reply his son hammers his fist on the tabletop in uncharacteristic display of vehemence. 'As sense fails before pride, jealousy eclipses all! Antonio is no fool, but that does not mean he is immune to man's failings.'

Romeo stares at his son. 'Never have you raised your voice to me this way, Mercutio.'

'Never before have I feared you blind to the danger posed, Father,' Mercutio pleads. 'You must not go! If his offer is genuine it will not expire.'

'You fear his great pride yet propose to sting it with a refusal? Lords are not so easily refused and less forgiving when they are. Any true offer might turn swiftly to ashes.'

'You could write a message, send Lawrence to deliver it. A deft apology that you cannot come immediately does not injure the pride of a reasonable man. You argue in false terms, father, to say a man of reason is so easily robbed of it.'

'I will not place Lawrence in any more danger,' Romeo insists, 'nor my only son, for I see those words dancing upon your tongue. In good conscience I can only risk my own neck and if all of this endeavour is for aught, a moment's trust to goodwill must one day come.'

'One day perhaps, but not this day!' Mercutio says. 'Not when you are so easily killed. For all that they may do in the days and months to come, there has been twenty years of murder and kidnap between the Houses. It is their first recourse. Those wise warriors who trained me in arms taught me as much – in desperation a man reaches for what comes most naturally. The hours of cut and thrust make it second nature so when the time comes, your body will obey despite confusion or fatigue.'

'And see how such instincts have served me!' Romeo says with sudden passion. 'See where that path has led me and all of Verona, too! In exile I had the choice what man I was to become, whether to use what I have learned in creation or destruction. There are few choices available to one who has killed twice and finds his young wife pregnant. That other path is a dark one, o son of mine; the way of the condottiero is hard and cold and terrible.

'Death in battle is little more than I perhaps deserve, but Italy has no need of another nobleman to whom violence comes easily. You admire your friend Francesco and so do I, but would you have Facino Cane for your father? Biancardo? Perhaps the English devil, Hawkwood, whose greatest hour came at Verona's expense? Might I have been that rare thing, the honourable mercenary, or a savage who profits from death and destruction?

'No, Mercutio – I am not that man. I will not be that man. I chose to let my sword fall from my hands because I knew the direction it points. Peace was my choice, to accept the power of words and the weight of reason. I shall write a reply to Lord Antonio, I shall accept his offer and have another deliver my words. I shall attend his meeting with due prudence, but to repair all the hurt and mistrust in Verona requires someone to make that first step. As God is my witness I will take that step and trust His grace to ensure there is stone beneath my footing.'

Mercutio is quiet a long time. The room seems to tremble under Romeo's invocation, but neither son nor father stirs until the startled voice of a blackbird breaks the quiet.

'I will bring you paper and ink,' Mercutio says in a quiet voice. 'I pray to God that Lord Antonio will submit to reason also.'

Twenty-Seven

"'Lord Antonio, events conspire against me informing you in person that I agree to your suggestion.'"

Antonio pauses in his reading and looks to his left where Sir Paolo sits. 'He apologises for being unable to be present while agreeing to meet with me. I fear already, Uncle, that there is no help for my cousin. Romeo Montague is irredeemably a lawyer.'

They are in a small tavern on the outskirts of Verona, midway between the Navi Bridge and the east gate of the city. Through the windows comes a cool breeze from a pale blue sky and the sound of many voices, some startled as they are dissuaded from entering the tavern. It is after midday, but other than two guards they are alone in the tavern room.

'Does he insult you in glowing terms, my lord?'

'Ah, no, he does not.'

'Then there is some yet for Romeo to learn,' the aging warrior grunts. 'His art is not yet perfected, but I am sure it will come.'

'Indeed. He continues instead, "I pray you will forgive a fugitive's inability to travel as easily as I might. To you now, however, I say that I will submit to your request for an affidavit" – note, Uncle, how he does not write what he promises to swear to in writing – "and entrust it to the Lord Governor in return for your support regarding the matter of my trial. I wish to settle my family in Verona, to live in peace amongst my own and to leave as my legacy an end to the feud here. My aspirations are to governorship over lordship; to service of the city's needs as a son of Montague and a husband of Capulet, but ruler of neither."'

'Twenty years of marriage might indeed leave some men lord of nothing,' Paolo laughs.

'"For the good of Verona and our ancient name, I beg you to hold faith with this compact. I knew you once and would embrace you as brother and lord in future. Your honour I do not doubt and if this feud may one day end, it will be at your word alone."'

'That much is true,' Antonio adds as he folds the letter and passes it to his father-in-law, 'but if it is by your hand, Romeo, that the feud ends, Verona will see you as being the one to bring Reynard to heel. You will be the one they celebrate and I will be Montague in name only.'

'But he is not here,' Paolo says. 'So what is to be done now?'

'Perhaps I will not be the one to bear Romeo to the governor, but my honour is a soldier's livery. One more stain will make no difference to it. Should he present himself there, he will be arrested and I may easily claim my words were mere coercion to bring about his arrest. Governor Francesco is no wide-eye fool. He will not let himself become embroiled in further argument. That would only undermine him both in the eyes of those he attempts to rule and the one he attempts to serve.'

'You will write a reply then?'

'Yes – give me the paper and wax, I'll embrace my

cousin in words and he will be reassured. You there, fetch in the child who brought this message if he remains without. We will send him back with my note and see what may come.'

As the guard heads outside, Paolo retrieves a bag from the far end of the table. A cup of wine sits before each of them and Antonio takes a long drink while Paolo sets out paper and ink. A block of sealing wax comes next and as Antonio begins to write Paolo goes in search of a lit candle.

'Honoured cousin,' Antonio says aloud as he writes. 'I am pleased that despite your long years of absence the House of Montague remains dear to your heart. Lord Reynard will be denied the opportunities presented by a dispute between us and shall read his own downfall in the result. Send your affidavit to the Lord Governor and I shall visit him this evening to confirm our alliance—'

'Not alliance,' Paolo calls as he emerges from the next room. 'It would sound too close to an alliance of forces. The ears of a peaceful man are ever sensitive to such ideas.'

'Agreement?'

'Much more suited to a lawyer.'

'To confirm our agreement regarding the future of House Montague and my support for any pardon or amnesty the governor is able to grant. Does that serve?'

'They are friends,' Paolo agrees, 'it will serve. Milan's creature will be mindful of either lord dictating events to the Lord Governor.'

'Good.'

Antonio signs the letter and allows it to dry before folding and sealing it with wax. The guard returns with a boy in tow, long-haired and barefoot, who manages some form of bow to Lord Antonio. He ignores the effort while impressing the wax with the seal of the Lord of Montague. A quick inspection of his work shows it to be satisfactory and he finally looks at the boy who quickly lowers his gaze.

'You know where to find Romeo Montague?'

'I... I do not, Lord.'

'But you know those who might get this letter to him quickly?'

'I believe so, yes, Lord.'

'That will serve. Here, take a coin to hasten its passage.'

The boy wastes no time in scampering away and the guard closes the door as Lord Antonio reaches for the wine bottle.

'Come, Uncle, let us not rush away. The best laid traps should not be dismantled in haste.'

'How so, Lord?'

'Were I a cautious man I would not come to a meeting such as this, the risk is too great. But if the offer was genuine I might be waiting close by to see what response came.'

Sir Paolo bows his head in acknowledgement and retakes his seat, more than willing to drink another cup of wine. One of the guards goes to the window and peers out.

'My Lord, there is a crowd out there.'

'Is there indeed? Are their faces known to us?'

'Tradesmen and labourers for the main, none I know.'

'Draw back a shade. Do not let them see a man-at-arms watching too closely.'

They wait in silence for several long minutes. The only interruption is Sir Paolo rising to check on the rear of the tavern where they have stationed half a dozen soldiers. Satisfied all remains in place and undiscovered, he checks on the three others in the next room and returns to his seat. It is several more minutes before the guard near the window stiffens.

'Another group comes,' he whispers. 'There is one leading them – no, two. Their clothes are far better than the others. It is our quarry.'

'Be ready then,' Lord Antonio says. 'Extend them all courtesy, he is the heir of Montague after all.'

Presently there is a rap upon the door and at a nod from his lord, the guard answers.

'Who comes?'

'Romeo Montague,' is the reply.

He opens the door and there indeed is the erstwhile son of Montague, the heir of all at his side. Romeo looks older and more tired than Antonio recalls, in clothes more rumpled and plain than the proud youth he had once been.

'You requested my presence, Lord Montague,' Romeo announces with a bow.

'And you were unable to be present, cousin,' Antonio says with a smile. He rises and offers his hand. 'But it is to our fortune that you were only delayed. A lord does not enjoy an outright refusal, it does not suit the cut of his cloth. Come, join me for a drink, but perhaps this table should be for family only. Your friends might wait outside.'

Romeo glances back at those behind him. There seems to be no leader among those that Antonio can see, where men of some small wealth stand with an old woman servant and a large labourer.

'Wait for me without,' Romeo says at last.

None of his escort have the temerity to speak, though several look unhappy at the instruction. Only the son enters with Romeo, a young man with a fierce look on his face and a hand resting on his hilt.

'Nephew,' Antonio says cordially, 'a cup of wine for you, too?'

There is no response at first then Romeo glances at his son and the boy ducks his head. He is barely a man this one, seventeen at best, but no shrimp to be batted away. Antonio reminds himself that Mercutio has grown up with a threat on his life and, so it appears, condottieri as friends. His schooling at arms will not be honed for the duelling field perhaps, but he is not to be dismissed so easily here.

'Lord Montague,' the youth says at last, as though the words are bitter in his mouth. 'Thank you. With your permission I shall take a cup.'

'I will gladly raise mine to your health,' Antonio declares. 'Now we are met in civilised fashion, might I ask your forgiveness for what has come before? My time as Lord of Montague has been short, but the Capulets have been most bold for much of it. Twice they have come close to killing me and I confess to an instinct of aggression towards any possible threat. It was a policy I should not have extended to those of my own blood.'

'It is forgivable,' Romeo assures him. 'Surprise is rarely welcome to the embattled.'

'I served as aide to your father for many years, we received news of you twice. I knew you still lived, but he felt gravely wounded by your actions. He sought no news and few dared bring your name up in his presence.'

'And I do not begrudge that he groomed another as his successor, for what use was I to the family? It took many years for Duke Visconti to value my work in any way that might have served House Montague.'

'And so we come to the matter at hand,' Antonio says. 'My sole concern is for House Montague and what is best for our family.'

'You think I have another focus?'

'I believe you have wider ambitions and a Capulet wife.'

Antonio nods to the guard nearest the door and the man closes it, dropping a bar across it. Romeo gasps in shock while Mercutio roars and throws himself forward. He grapples with the guard, but lacks the bulk to pull him away while Antonio summons the three men-at-arms from the back room.

'Treachery!' Mercutio yells.

He draws his sword and lunges at the guard who reels out of the way, but cannot avoid a cut to the arm. As the voices outside bellow in response, Mercutio drags the bar from the door. Paolo draws his own weapon, but before he can attack Mercutio, Romeo charges at him. Avoiding the knight's sword, he uses his shoulder to drive Paolo into a table. The pair stagger together, half-fallen across it while chairs tumble. Abandoning the door, Mercutio rushes to defend his father, sword and dagger drawn as the Montague soldiers appear.

'Don't kill them!' Antonio orders as the first of his men lunges at Mercutio.

The young man holds his ground, parrying and slashing to keep the men back for as long as he can. Romeo sprawls across Paolo, punching at the older man's arm to try and force his sword from his hand. Antonio clashes blades with Mercutio and forces his sword down. The youth retreats and cuts wildly with his dagger, seeing a guard close on his left. Mindful of Antonio's order, the man ignores the opening that would have been the death of Mercutio, content to parry the slash with his sword.

Antonio and the man beside him press in, crowding Mercutio against a table and together they pin him, the points of their swords at his breast. Before they can demand his surrender, however, the door bursts open and the mob pours fourth.

Two, five, then eight men surge into the room, blinking at the gloom of within. Mercutio hesitates as he looks back and one guard steps in to punch him hard in the jaw. The blow sends Mercutio staggering as the mob descend upon Romeo and four pairs of hands grab him at once. They pull him away from Paolo as the old soldier struggles up off the tabletop, clawing for purchase at Romeo's tunic.

Antonio shoves one guard towards his father-in-law while he himself kicks Mercutio's sword away. Hauling the young man up, he puts his sword to Mercutio's throat as more of Romeo's supporters enter.

'Back!' he yells, but in the next moment he realises they are not listening.

With Romeo safe in their hands, though he struggles against them, and a cacophony of voices within and without, the men see nothing but the rescue of their anointed. Heedless of his words they pull him out and into the safety of the street. Just as swiftly Antonio realises he must do the same and he drags a stunned Mercutio with him towards the back door. There his remaining men-at-arms are arriving from the alley behind.

The houses crowd against each other here, leaning on their neighbours, and the tavern was chosen so there would be no quick path around. While two men drag a cart across the rear door and terrified onlookers flee, Mercutio is thrown over a horse. Antonio and Paolo both mount with one more of their bodyguards and then they are off – racing back to safer streets while their armed men follow behind. From the rooftops birds rise up, screaming in outrage, while the roar of the mob from the street beyond shakes the wooden houses.

Antonio looks over at his prize, only half in the saddle and forced to grip the horse's mane or risk serious injury in a fall. The reins are held by the bodyguard accompanying them, Antonio's own. He laughs and spurs his horse a little harder.

'You were not my intended prize, boy,' Antonio calls as they near the river. 'But you will serve my purpose well enough.'

There he sees Capulet livery on some and a pair of soldiers wearing the serpent of Milan. He rides on through them all, each man recognising him and none willing to slow or question his passage.

'It is time your family learned this truth – there can be only one Lord of Montague.'

Twenty-Eight

In the hall of Scaliger Castle, Francesco presides over the household's main meal of the day. Platters of trout baked with lemons and almonds sit in ruin down its length. Juliet has merely picked at each course, eating enough to satisfy the stern eyes of her daughter but barely tasting the meal. Dogs prowl and squabble beneath the table, while the servants at the far end provide a constant, muted chatter.

At its head there is quiet. The clerks and officials of the castle make sparse conversation in the presence of a lady sick with worry and lord whose brooding turns to a glower at the smallest intrusion. A single cup of wine has been enough to promote an ache in Juliet's head, but Francesco finds no such obstacle. He drinks freely and frowning, as though each mouthful proves a personal affront he must endure for duty's sake.

Before the kitchen servants can clear the empty plates away, a muffled shout comes from the courtyard. Francesco looks up with a hunger in his eyes that the meal has not satisfied. He nods to Rufus as the man casts him a look and the large man-at-arms rises without a word. As he reaches the door to the courtyard there are more calls outside, words spoken in argument then one brief clattering peal of the alarm.

Francesco jumps to his feet, snatching his sword and belt from the back of his chair and buckling it around his waist, cheeks spotted pink with rising anger. Rufus is already outside, closely followed by the other fighting men, but Juliet forces her way towards Francesco. They spill into the courtyard and all of a sudden, swords are being drawn, men-at-arms running in from the right with spears levelled.

Juliet looks past the flattening line of soldiers in front of Francesco and feels a jolt in her gut. Through the main gate come soldiers in Montague livery, also drawing their weapons and advancing with Lord Antonio at their fore. Beside him stumbles a battered figure with hands bound, but one she recognises all too well.

'Mercutio!' Juliet shrieks, bolting forward until Francesco himself catches her at the waist and prevents her from breaking the line. She struggles a moment against him then her mind reasserts dominion over instinct once more. Juliet has to fight it with every lurch of her heart, but she does not press forward. Some part of her curses and rages inside, but she does not move. Her son is a prisoner in the hands of her enemy and a mother's terror will not change that.

'My Lord Governor,' Lord Antonio roars above the clamour echoing around the courtyard walls. 'I bring you a prize!'

'A prize?' Juliet gasps, the words striking like a punch.

Francesco steps forward from the line his troops have formed.

'You dare bring armed men into my castle?' he shouts back as more men-at-arms gather behind the

Lord of Montague. 'Hold there, my Lord, or I will see Crécy be played out again for my own entertainment!'

With this he raises an arm and the archers on the walls either side of the gate nock arrows. The Montagues falter at this threat, encircled by weapons, but Lord Antonio drags Mercutio forward with him.

'You offer a poor welcome to one who brings you a criminal your own men could not find,' Antonio says, stopping a dozen paces short. 'A poorer welcome than this insurrectionist with his mob received only yesterday, my Lord.'

'My forbearance has been exhausted for unwelcome guests,' Francesco replies. 'Henceforth there shall be a sharp welcome to any who tries to force entry here. Aylward, do you hear me? Your sharpest welcome!'

'I am glad my Lord Governor has found his claws,' says Antonio. 'For this one here should not be toyed with as his sire was. It appears the security of this castle is lax and I would not wish justice to be cheated.'

'You demand my son's blood now?' Juliet roars, shaking off those who would prevent her from advancing into the open. 'What next? My own life? Perhaps the hand of my daughter is to your fancy?'

'I would not marry a girl of Capulet blood,' Antonio sneers. 'Nor would any true Montague stain his family's honour by doing so.'

'Hold that tongue of yours,' says Francesco. 'Or you may lose it and more besides. There are other men who can take the title of lord. Do not feel so secure in this stronghold.'

'I have spoken with one such man this very hour. He tells me he is willing to give up all claim he might have for a chance to save his neck. Such a man is unworthy of this great house, such a man is unworthy of this city.'

Antonio spits his words now, untroubled by Francesco's threats.

'That man is worthier than you can know,' Juliet says. 'That man puts pride aside for the good of others; something you could never do and the whole city suffers for it.'

'Forgetting those of his own blood,' Antonio adds angrily. 'Forgetting the pride and the ties of those who raised him – those whom he expects to raise him high. No, Lady, he is no true son of Montague but a sorry note amid our symphony. The sooner he is brought to justice the better for all of Verona – perhaps with the exception of the Capulets he so clearly favours.'

'Turn the boy over to me,' Francesco commands. 'This justice is mine to dispense, this household is mine to rule.'

'But do you rule it? Can you truly dispense justice, my Lord Governor? I am not so certain. I suggest he be strung up here and now, in the interests of Milan as well as Verona. My men will ensure no mob interferes since clearly your mercenaries cannot be relied upon.'

'Your men will trot out of my gate like fat little ponies, or be stuck like pigs where they stand.'

'Do you offer violence upon your citizens in the name of Milan or your own capricious self?' Antonio cries.

'Pick whichever you will. Imagine the livery of your choice upon my breast as I drive you from this place.'

'While another of this faithless family is let free?'

'He will go to the cells – guard, take him – but you will not decide his fate, Lord Antonio. The right and the duty are mine.'

'You must hang him for what he did,' Antonio warns, though he gives up his prisoner freely when a soldier comes forward. 'Elsewise you overthrow station and convention to your own ends and that cannot be endured.'

Francesco steps forward, his sword shining in the light of day. 'You do not tell me my duty,' he declares. 'Nor make demands upon my actions.'

Antonio does not respond immediately. The two men face each other, one with sword drawn and the other not. They circle slowly, a duel not yet called but in their eyes there is violent delight; a crackle of energy in the air. Francesco paces like a leopard, brimming with restless strength, while Antonio faces him with a tigerish glare.

'Does the law now preside over Verona or is it merely another form of oppression?' Antonio asks.

'You do not decide the law,' Francesco counters.

'I have not. The law is written and you yourself were witness to his crime.'

'Still you make demands above your place.'

Antonio laughs. 'Above my place? I am the Lord Montague, it is my place to offer such advice to the ruler of my city.' He pauses. 'And were that ruler here, he would listen. You are merely a servant of his, you are the one who overreaches.'

'You presume too much,' Francesco says coldly. 'You predict the actions of a man who has so often defied prediction.'

'Do you imagine he would ever hesitate in your place? Are your thoughts stained by sentiment, my Lord Governor?'

'You imagine my thoughts to be as simple and base as your own.'

With each barb Juliet sees the resolve hardening on each man's face. Distracted by the sight of Mercutio being led away to the cells, she has been no more than a spectator, but time and again has she seen where the pride of men leads. She steps inside the circle they trace and drags their unwilling gaze from their opponent.

'My Lords, what is it you do here? Do you truly mean to fight? Is there no man in Verona capable of another thought? Brawl with your fists perhaps until the bile inside you is exhausted? Clash blades and draw blood? What sympathy then from the duke?'

'Quiet, my Lady, I would not hear more from you or your kin today.'

'You will hear more from me, Lord Antonio! Do not think you can threaten my son and slander my family without a word from me!'

'Juliet,' Francesco warns. 'Step back. I do not wish further discussion here, nor do I ask your advice. Lord Antonio will retire or he will draw his sword and let God decide.'

Antonio cocks his head as Juliet hesitates then steps back. 'You may be governor of this city, but you are not of noble blood. Just as your archers will refrain from shooting at their betters, you should have a greater care for what you threaten.'

'Go now, or draw,' Francesco says.

'My Lords,' Juliet interjects. 'This is below both your stations. All of Verona watches and the victor will earn only scorn in the city's eyes.'

Antonio looks around at the men-at-arms on all sides and gives a curt nod. 'I withdraw,' he says after a pause. 'There shall be a better time to resolve this discussion. My men will take station beyond the walls, ready to face down any fresh mob that might be stirred up.'

'Their presence is not required.'

'We shall see, my Lord. I pray that justice and the law will prevail this day over myrmidon aggression.'

He turns and with a gesture his followers lower their weapons, parting for Antonio to lead them out of the gate once more. Francesco watches them go without moving. Only when they are all disappeared from view does he sheath his sword. Then he sweeps round, fixes Juliet with a look and nods for them to retire inside.

'The gate stays barred,' he calls over his shoulder. 'Should these peacocks offer threat to any party, citizens or soldiers, remind them with fresh plumage who alone has that right. Lady Juliet, you will attend me.'

*

Juliet follows him to his private office, Francesco marching ahead with long inpatient strides. She walks at a measured pace, reminding herself and him of composure. The first time he waits for her with only irritation, but by the second the flush is gone from his face.

'My Lady, you do astonish me at times,' he murmurs.

'A man with his blood up may be easily astonished.'

He gives her words a tired smile. 'I will delay you only a short while, I know you will need to go to your son.'

'I do,' she says. 'But my own feelings must wait. I can better serve him here for the time being and that is what I must do.'

When they reach the office Francesco throws himself into a chair then immediately bounds up, unable to sit. Instead he paces around the confines of the opulent room, his fingers running along the top of his great desk as he passes it.

'I wish he had not pressed me so hard there. He draws a line on matters better left uncertain.'

'I wish many things were different,' Juliet says, her chiding tone making him glance over. 'Among those are your willingness to kill a lord of Verona.'

'Should I allow such a challenge to go unanswered?'

'Perhaps you might have answered it with a little less eagerness? No matter now, it is done. We must concern ourselves with what we make of it.'

'What can we? Do I acquiesce and appear weak or refuse and appear no better than the fools I intend to come to heel?'

'What would our lord the duke do?'

He snorts. 'I do not believe I am better suited than Lord Antonio to know that.'

'It would be something unexpected,' Juliet says slowly, teasing her thoughts like thread. 'Something that might not immediately appear as it truly is.'

'The duke is but a man,' Francesco reminds her, 'take care you do not ascribe too much to him.'

'It is what he would hope to do,' Juliet corrects herself. 'The constraints of life may hinder that of course, but let us still consider it. What would be unexpected from you, my Lord Governor?'

He shrugs. 'Some might suggest I was not as humble as I so loudly claim. Lord Antonio does not know me however, only that I am a soldier. He would not expect a soldier to back down when they have the greater numbers at hand.'

'Indeed. Perhaps we should embrace your new-found meekness, my Lord? That would surprise him.'

'Meekness harms our cause. If I am weak, I cannot impose my authority upon these troublesome houses of yours.'

'Unless it serves a purpose. My Lord, what are your goals this day or the next? Not a lasting peace but those desires more immediately to hand?'

'A reason to release Mercutio,' he says hesitantly. 'A reason to pardon Romeo. A reason to hang Lord Antonio by his ankles and whip the—'

'My Lord!' she interrupts. 'There is one other more pressing desire than that, I believe.'

He frowns at her for a moment then realisation dawns across his face. The rogue's smile returns to where it is most suited. 'The spy!'

'Indeed. Securing him would be of great worth. Enough perhaps to bring down other figures in this city, certainly to distract the nobility from their present concerns. Perhaps Mercutio's actions could have been part of your own plan, in obedience to your commands even? If victory is achieved, the victor may write his own account of how it was secured.'

'That much I like,' Francesco says. He takes her hands as though he was her younger brother rather than governor of a city and hopeful suitor of her daughter.

'But how? How do I feign meekness and claim victory?'

Gently she slips his hands and turns to pace as she speaks her thoughts. 'We must draw him out. Without being able to trust who is in his pay, we cannot identify and take him without being certain we will lose our quarry. If he comes to us and steps within these walls, however, there is a trap that can close about him. I will recognise his face if none other here can.'

'But how do we bring him here? No official invite will bring him, no ball or state function will tempt a man who does not know for certain what his assassin said.'

'Indeed not,' Juliet agrees, 'which is why you must embrace that quality of meekness you have been hiding under a bushel for so long.'

'Lady, how?'

'My Lord Governor, you must dangle bait that he cannot resist – offer a spectacle that will drag in the Houses, and all interested parties will not consider ignoring.

'Francesco, you must hang my son.'

Twenty-Nine

Voices stir Estelle from her torpor. She moves to the window where she can see the castle courtyard just as the gate creaks open. A pair of horsemen ride in; not soldiers, but under thick dark cloaks she can discern no more than that. The guards are brisk about their duty, but without urgency or alarm as they close the gate behind the arrivals.

Grooms hold the horses steady while the riders dismount and finally she sees who has come. A cold nausea fills her belly as she recognises the older man – the Podesta of Verona. His expression is blank, but his body betrays discomfort and displeasure.

'His heart was flintily set even when in his own domain,' Estelle breathes. 'Now he is summoned here, Mercutio will be afforded no greater care from this old philosopher.'

'Never had I thought to see the day,' says a voice from beyond the open doorway.

The sound startles Estelle and she draws back as Francesco comes into view. He is alone, dressed once more as a man of politics in a rich green tunic.

'Which day was that, my Lord Governor?' Estelle

asks.

'When I would hear such dismal talk from your sweet self, while I am the one possessed yet of hope.'

'There is hope yet?'

'There is, Estelle.' He walks to the window and looks out briefly at the arriving magistrate. 'Old for certain, wedded to the letter of his laws perhaps, the man is no fool and he is a good and faithful servant of Verona.'

'Tell me plain, I beg of you, Francesco.'

'I can tell you nothing,' he says. 'For all that I would hide nothing, I must beg your indulgence still.'

He takes her hand and draws it to his chest. There is an imploring look in his eye, but Estelle sees something more. A flicker of the warrior who stirs her heart, the fire and spirit that lends him authority beyond his years. She takes a long breath and her fingers tighten around his.

'Speak it and I will give it freely.'

'That you do not judge me too soon this night. I can tell you no more, we all have our part to play in what may come. Yours is loving sister and loyal daughter, I can tell you know more.'

'You tell me nothing!'

'I know. It is as it must be. All I ask is that you do not harden your heart against me; that you do not poison the well of all I love until this tale is ended.'

'You ask for trust yet give none in return. That well may one day run dry.'

'That risk is the price of my duty,' Francesco says with a grave nod of the head, a flicker of pain in his eyes as he speaks. He releases her hand and turns. 'Now I must go, soon I will not be able to bear the scrutiny of your eyes.'

'Why? What do you mean?'

Her calls bring no answer as Francesco departs, his footsteps beating a swift retreat as he goes to greet the podesta and settle whatever business is between them. Estelle stays a while longer, confused and frightened by the unknown, but then more voices come from the courtyard. Servants this time, a team labouring together to drive a cart in through the main gate. The men-at-arms watch them with a strange stillness as the cart is moved towards the main castle door. Estelle joins their vigil with a growing disquiet, but it is only when the cart stops and its wheels are locked in place that she truly understands.

A fist clamps around her heart as Estelle watches timbers being unloaded from the cart. Soon a dozen men are hard at work, constructing a gibbet in full view of the castle. A chill descends as the pale autumn light begins to fade and evening approaches, but still Estelle finds she cannot move. Ensnared by the ugly, rough lines of her brother's executioner and the clatter that surrounds it, she sees nothing else. Torches are lit and people begin to move in and out of the courtyard with urgency, but the growing gloom and dancing shadows only tighten the sensation in her chest. Even Francesco's words, distantly recalled, cannot relieve the pressure – not when he could no longer bear to look her in the eye.

The gibbet takes on monstrous proportions in her mind, a demon that leers and threatens when finally the noose is swung over. Its eye lurches forward and back, searching for prey. Only when her mother, Juliet, comes to usher her away do the tears start to fall. Then the dam breaks and grief tears at her – at them both. The pair stand in the dark and cry for longer than Estelle knows, until at last her mother pushes them apart and wipes her daughter's tears from her cheek.

'Mercutio is not lost to us yet,' she declares. 'Have courage my love, though all of Italy may seem against us, we are not done yet. Now come, the lords arrive.'

*

Juliet leads her daughter to the ground floor of the castle just as four servants emerge from a side room bearing a large square table. She watches them carry it outside with a growing sense of resolve, her fears cried out and now set aside.

I will weep no more this night, Juliet promises herself. *While there is breath yet in my body, I shall spend it without tears.*

A crowd is assembling in the courtyard. The gate is no longer closed to the citizens of Verona and news of the gibbet has drawn many. Among those is Lord Reynard with a large contingent of Capulets. There are several women among them and Juliet finds her breath catch when she sees her mother at their heart. Lady Capulet stands stately and swathed in mourning cloth, but Juliet can do no more than catch her mother's eye. To move closer might be to spark a confrontation and for now she must dance to Francesco's tune.

Lord Antonio has already claimed his place near the gibbet, the notable shape of Sir Paolo at the fore of a dozen soldiers. He does not spare her more than a disdainful glance and Juliet finds her nails digging into her palms as she avoids calling to him. He is barely ten yards from her and an urge to cross that ground fills her heart. Her feet even begin to move before she overrules them and anchors herself more firmly to her daughter's side.

Of the others, many are common citizens – priests and the richest merchants at their fore. Most of the latter are clear in their loyalties and keep to their allotted side as the Capulets take position opposite the Montagues. Each family stares across at the other with barely restrained hostility while the servants place the table before the gibbet. From a side door the castle steward ushers six musicians, dragged from local taverns perhaps and startled at their summons. He establishes them close to the gibbet on the Capulet side. Their presence draws many curious looks, but the musicians have no answers and merely busy themselves with their instruments.

A square of empty ground has formed before the gibbet, twenty yards across. As ever in Verona it is defined by where Montagues and Capulets stand, the common folk caught between. There are scores of citizens in the crowd facing the gibbet with more arriving each minute; rich and poor, old and young. Juliet spies the unmistakable figure of Lawrence near their fore, afforded the privilege alongside those of wealth or physical size. She has no doubt that the diminutive figure of her former nurse will be somewhere there, too.

Juliet looks for her husband's shape amid that crowd, trusting to twenty years of marriage to recognise his form however his head may be covered. She sees no one to match him, however. Many of those present have been drinking and there is a restless energy to the press and swell within the crowd. The gates remain open and she finds herself casting looks in that direction, as though Romeo might make a dramatic entrance.

Indeed he yet might, though I pray he does not think I would stand so meekly and watch our son die.

'Wait for me here,' she whispers to her daughter and

slips her hand free.

Estelle gives her a look of puzzlement, but does not question her mother's actions. Juliet pulls her shawl over her head against the chill and begins to skirt around the back of the crowd. Though Lord Antonio notices her move, his eyes do not linger. With the bustle of people around the courtyard and servants bringing the notable guests wine, one woman in dark and modest clothes attracts little attention.

Juliet searches the faces as she goes, trying not to stare, but the assembled mass is now well over a hundred with more trickling in. Juliet walks on, briefly shaking her head to Rufus who stands at the gate in hauberk and helm, then continuing around to make note of the Capulets present.

As Juliet walks she can hear the last of the season's swallows hunt, their cries punctuating the murmurs below. Soon the bats will descend as the gloaming's shadow overlays the whole scene, despite every lamp and torch that can be spared from inside the castle. The servants set out more tables behind the noble groups – food and wine to be sampled at their leisure while a halo of light is described around events. A barrel of ale is rolled out to the gatehouse and it draws many citizens towards it, lessening the press of the crowd and with luck ensuring no impatience forces any hand.

Juliet walks quicker, aware the shadows will only make her task more difficult and forced to stare more intently at each man she sees. It does not matter however, for at that moment there is a rise in the mutterings. The castle steward announces Lord Francesco to the courtyard and all eyes are drawn towards him. Juliet is free to scrutinise faces in side profile, but against the autumn chill many wear hoods or caps.

With a hiss of frustration she slips around and inside the castle, making for higher ground to secure her advantage. Behind her the booming voice of Francesco greets those assembled and the first act of their play begins.

Thirty

'My Lords and Ladies of Verona. Good people of this city and representatives of mother Church, too, welcome. Rumour is indeed fleet of foot, but I am glad of all who feel compelled to attend me this evening. No doubt the call of justice ringing in your hearts. First, however, I have business to conduct. I trust you will share in our drink and afford your governor a few moments more to see to his duty.'

With that unusual pronouncement, Francesco approaches the table set out before the gibbet as servants bring chairs to it. Behind him, moving uncomfortably, walks the podesta and a look from Francesco is all it takes to bring Antonio and Reynard forward. The crowd watches in near silence, but it is curiosity on their faces. In the presence of the city's powers, they are not so easily roused to anger and Francesco's generosity has distracted those most prone.

Francesco inspects the faces around them. He has soldiers stationed on each side, a pace inside the square of open ground to dissuade any from coming closer. He does not want all the city to hear their words; they are here to witness how it ends instead. Without a signal from him, the castle steward, Felipe, directs the musicians to play. They are uncertain and ragged, incongruous in the shadow of a noose, but Francesco nods all the same. The noise is all he requires, a veil of privacy for this conversation conducted in plain view.

'What is this now?' Lord Reynard asks as he joins Francesco.

'This? A table, my lord.' Francesco smiles. 'Sturdy, but unremarkable. I feel it does not warrant the suspicion you regard it with.'

Reynard's eyes dart from Antonio to Francesco, then the gibbet. 'My wariness is not for the table, but the strangeness of these proceedings.'

'The new addition to my courtyard does not find your favour? Do not worry, it is only a temporary feature.'

'You make unseemly jests, my Lord Governor,' Antonio breaks in, 'in the shadow of the noose.'

'That is where a soldier's humour is usually to be found, Lord Antonio.' There is an edge to his tone that they all mark, but the Lord of the Montagues does not demur.

'We are not on a battlefield, my Lord Governor. Do you suggest any of us stand in the shadow of death, from which such black humour rises? You make jest while your servants make music, but there is grave business to be discussed.'

'That there is,' Francesco agrees. 'Of such gravity that I have asked the city's chief magistrate to attend as witness.'

He raises one hand and a clerk advances to join them, a leather wallet in his hands. This he gives to Francesco and retreats without further instruction. Without haste the governor unties the wallet and withdraws several pieces of parchment. He places them in the centre of the table and both Antonio and Reynard tilt their heads to read what they can of the document. Francesco offers a copy to each and remains silent for a while as they read.

'My lords, the stars align only rarely, but pay your astrologer well and wonderous things can result. Our interests orbit this city on separate paths and it shall ever be thus, but I propose we declare an alignment and dare any to contradict us.'

'I see a contract, not charts, before me,' Antonio says, 'and our learned friend here is no astrologer.'

'As the passage of the stars obey certain laws, so we must obey the city's. Without laws to chart our progress, all may fall into hellish anarchy – do you not agree?'

'Do you expect us to follow your star across the sky, my Lord Governor? To drag us in your wake perhaps?'

'What you describe is not alignment, but domination. Had I chosen that path I would not be here, sat with you both and my gates open to all. This document might then have been a decree nailed to your door, but he who seeks peace must allow for peace.'

'What do you know of seeking peace?' Reynard asks. 'I mean no insult there, my Lord, but you are a young man who tells us of peace. Perhaps you are not cut from the same cloth as your captain, Cane, but you are a mercenary still. Your livelihood is war, not peace. An English brigand you may not be, but no mercenary in Italy has ever truly strived to secure a lasting peace.'

'That much is true, but as you say, I am a young man. I seek glory as well as riches, I am not content to live all my remaining years in Lombardy helping to grind it to dust beneath petty disputes and skirmishes. There will be war enough for my appetite, of that I am certain.

A good warrior wins the fight before him, but that does not prove he will make a good general. A general secures the objective he is instructed to, whether it is a castle, a city or a lasting peace.'

'Then you offer something in return?'

'The good magistrate here has agreed that, rather than initiating a lengthy trial, offences committed against the representative of Milan in this city might fall under my jurisdiction. The matter of Mercutio Montague is easily placed at my discretion.'

'Does your document mention him?'

Francesco smiles. 'Young and inexperienced I may be, I did not need my advisors to explain how such a thing is not possible.'

'Your advisors, yes,' Antonio says. 'What do they say about what you propose?'

'I have not discussed it with them, as you might imagine. What conclusions they might have drawn from this gibbet is their own concern, but only one of them is currently in my service. The other remains a fugitive – his name may once have presented certain opportunities, but it is not crucial to my orders.'

'And his daughter?' Reynard asks pointedly. 'A most beautiful young woman, if you might permit.'

'Of that we are in agreement, as gentle and graceful as a husband might wish. However, she is not possessed of any fortune to assist a man of ambition, nor does her family name carry any great weight in Milan – if you will forgive the observation, Lord Antonio.'

'A general of Milan might be better served with a Visconti bride, recent history tells us as much,' Antonio says as he nods his acknowledgement. 'Only a governor of Verona will find value in a name of Verona.'

'Indeed, my Lord.'

'This deed will strike her hard. I recall an ancient tale of this city – the barbarian Alboin who made his wife drink wine from her own father's skull.'

Francesco raises an eyebrow. 'I promise nothing so dramatic, my Lord Antonio.'

'The point remains, power must be seen. It is good you do not falter at what must be done.'

'What then do we commit to here?' Reynard asks.

'Obedience,' Francesco says simply. 'An assurance to obey the dictates of Milan's steward and maintain the peace of the city. In past years much has been overlooked – murder, kidnapping and raiding proving commonplace in Verona. There must be no duels or brawls between Montague and Capulet men, no harming of the interests of the other party or widening of your family's influence by threatening means.'

'All this has been announced by edict already.'

'A reminder of the established law and pronounced across the city, yes,' Francesco agrees. 'But in this place, away from polite society and the indignant citizenry, might we not be afforded the chance to speak frankly as men? Men of money, men of power, men of arms – the law does not always hold us in perfect observance as the hours of light and dark. We may agree what we choose and command the world to conform to our will.'

Antonio points to the parchment, turning one page to better see the words written there. 'Here it appears you command alone and we conform.'

'You are not men easily cowed, but nor are you fools. You know the power I can bring to bear, I need not lay it upon the table.'

'There is no lasting peace if you destroy one or both of us.'

'There would be peace of another kind, but it is not

one that would serve Milan. To take that path would be to turn on you with force, to strip the wealth of your houses in lieu of those taxes our lord intends to reap over the years to come. That would be a troublesome course and one that does not serve the future our lord envisages. Better to be strong and united to the benefit of all.'

'And you offer young Montague's life in return.'

'As much a symbol as anything. His continued existence is a threat to each of your positions. Without him you are more secure and his parents, also threats, become more distant from my lord's plans. They are not people to understand his loss as acceptable and thus they become of less use to the greater scheme.'

'It will not be so simply done for you.'

Francesco shrugs. 'No great concern once the cards are played. You have your Houses in order, none will break from your side to join them against Milan. One remains under threat of justice. The others are women who no doubt can enter the House of their mother to live quietly – or a nunnery to live in quiet.'

Antonio touches the paper before him. 'If we are to speak as men unfettered by the law and in private, I note the imbalance of this document goes beyond the imbalance of power between us. There is nothing here to assure us of your benevolent regard. It was not so long ago that we spoke in more combative tones, my Lord Governor.'

'You came to make demands upon me,' Francesco says. 'Do you think I would stand for it so meekly? You marched boldly into my domain and I will not treat with a man if I am unsure of his mettle. This document will be signed and displayed in both your Houses – that is my price. All of Montague and Capulet will read it and see the penalties laid out, should they fail to maintain what you have promised to me. The law may be as mutable as the seasons, but your obligations to me shall be iron. All who serve you will know it or regret.'

'And Mercutio goes to the gibbet this very night? Or tomorrow, or another day? Promises spoken are merely breath and last only as long as the speaker chooses.'

'You wish to see the boy?'

'I wish to have some assurance before I commit my pen.'

'No man of sense could expect less.' Francesco turns and beckons over Felipe who scurries to his master's side. 'Have the boy brought out for his final bow.'

'The podesta shall serve as witness to our signatures and more besides,' Francesco says once his steward is gone. 'You know his adherence to the law; his reputation must serve as no small collateral here.'

'I do not call your words into question, my Lord,' Antonio says carefully, 'but I will admit the magistrate's presence is a reassuring one. However, you have not yet spoken, Messer. Do you verify what my Lord Governor tells us?'

The podesta coughs and blinks at Antonio before answering, clearly surprised at being called upon.

'In so far as my power and knowledge extends, I can confirm all that has been said. Some is beyond my remit, but Lord Francesco consulted with me before you came and secured my agreement – both to my role and my discretion in everything spoken here.'

'It is nobly said,' Reynard declares. He looks once more at the parchment, eyes roving down the lines of text and lips moving slightly. 'I for one am content. A new age has come to Verona, that much I see. It will not be easy to keep a check on so many hot-blooded souls, but you state here that our Houses will remain preeminent in the state of Verona, our council valued above all others.'

'That is so. Upheaval and revolt is all too common in Italy and rarely does it bring benefit. Milan's strength will remain the power in Verona, but that can only keep control of the city. To see it prosper and become the jewel our lord wishes shall require the consent and effort of you both.'

'Then bring me a quill, I shall make my sign.'

'The triumvirates of Rome fared poorly,' Antonio points out as Francesco beckons Felipe forward once more.

'Three men all competing for control, how could they not?' Francesco says simply. 'Here, the deciding vote shall be Milan's, the military power shall be Milan's – but when power is exerted at a remove, the balance shall be easier to find. You both must work together, no doubt through myself at first, to the enrichment of you both. Fight for control and you will lose, my Lords, but strive to make each of your Houses greater for the generations to come and all three parties shall be satisfied.'

'It is a strange balance we must strike.'

'What other balance is there in politics?'

Antonio nods, reluctant at first but once Reynard has signed all three parchments and offered the quill he does not hesitate.

'You have a compact, my Lord.'

Antonio signs and Felipe scatters sand over each signature to ensure they are dry before Francesco presents each man his copy.

'I thank you, my Lords Capulet and Montague.' Francesco pauses as there comes a murmur of discontent from the crowd. 'I believe our young lordling has appeared. Perhaps we should now withdraw. The more public part of proceedings is upon us.'

The young Montague looks dazed and frightened as he steps out into the courtyard. His cheek is bruised, courtesy of Francesco's own hand, and now he is far from the confident youth who led his father's liberation. Now he is a boy who flinches at the dark flash of a bat swooping close to his head, who stares fearfully at the fluttering torch flames that ring the courtyard.

The voices rise to a swell and with the lords moved aside, Verona's citizens press forward. A line of steel greets them, soldiers in mail and helms who push their shields forward to halt the crowd. Hemmed in by armed noblemen and half their number distracted by drink, they respond meekly enough and no angry words are spoken.

Francesco can see the resentment on their faces, the disbelief at hopes dashed once more, but he spares them little time. His search is for Juliet and he cannot see her until he looks back at Mercutio. There she stands on a balcony behind, small and elegant in a dress of red and blue. Juliet wears a dark cloak around her shoulders and leans over the balustrade as she watches the crowd. When she sees Francesco, Juliet makes a small downward gesture.

She has found our man? He resists the urge to look around, knowing Juliet would shout if she wanted him taken yet. *We must play our roles a little longer – all of us.*

He looks away, catching sight of Estelle standing alone at the far side of the gibbet. Her face is pale, but there is more disbelief in her eyes than anything.

It is time for you to drink, my love, he thinks sadly. *I*

*must force this Alboin's cup upon you or they may not
yet believe.*

He beckons over Felipe while Mercutio is driven up
the steps to the gibbet. The young man shakes his head
and whispers protests but is too shocked to fight.

'Have the gate closed,' Francesco whispers in his
steward's ear. 'Tell Rufus to attend me.

'People of Verona!' Francesco calls as Felipe walks
away. He ascends to the gibbet platform as he speaks
and the wood creaks under his feet. Nearby the noose
sways silently like a cobra's head. Mercutio flinches from
it, but he is escorted by a pair of men-at-arms and they
keep a firm grip. 'You are here to witness justice.'

'What justice is this?' shouts an anonymous man in
the crowd. 'What trial was there?'

'There is no need of a trial – I witnessed the offence
myself as did all this castle. His guilt is assured and the
podesta has ceded all claim to punishment to me.'

'This is not justice!'

The speaker's impertinence prompts a rough
response from the line of soldiers who drive forward
with their shields. Several citizens cry out in pain, but it
emboldens the growls of discontent from the rest of the
crowd.

'The authority of Milan has been offended,'
Francesco roars. 'Such insult cannot be overlooked.
Whatever noble spirit inspired it, the act was treasonous.
If this city is to see peace, it must be clear to all men that
our lord's authority cannot be challenged without violent
end.'

As he speaks he spares one last glance for Estelle.
The look breaks her tremulous spirit. With one high
cut-off cry that pierces both Francesco's heart and the
evening sky, Estelle turns and flees inside.

Thirty-One

For all that she has expected them, Juliet feels Francesco's words land like blows; the rough hands of her father when on childish occasion she incurred his wrath. For a moment she is dizzy and bends low over the balustrade, but she forces herself upright.

Below, her Mercutio is driven forward to the noose. The sight twists a knife of primal fear inside Juliet, one against which the armour of reason and sense offers little protection. The sight of him in the place of the condemned is near-unbearable, but she tears her gaze away. The man she sought has not moved, his position set, and it tells a story they had all suspected.

Before anything more can happen, however, someone else in the crowd pushes back his homespun hood and steps forward against the line of shields.

'My Lord Francesco,' Romeo shouts. 'I say again this is not justice – but if this is the price of peace then let me be the one to pay it.'

Keep calm, my heart, Juliet pleads silently. *Do not let the fear drive you even now.*

'Messer Romeo, you have come to join your son's final dance?' Francesco replies, playing his role so well it chills Juliet's heart.

All of a sudden Juliet is stricken by the notion that Francesco is not playing, that he is truly a mercenary of the same ilk as his captain, and it sickens her. Worse has been done for less profit over the years of her life, the scars of such horror scattered the length of Europe. Frantic thoughts race through her mind, searching for any clue in his manner earlier and advantage to such treachery.

'I offer to stand in his place,' Romeo says. 'Spare my son the wages of his father's sin. All this can be traced back to my hand. If your peace must be sealed in blood, let mine be spilled upon that parchment and the seals of each great House impressed upon it.'

'My Lord Governor!' Antonio breaks in, now standing at the head of the Montagues. 'Romeo is already convicted, he is a fugitive to be taken no matter what punishment you give this pup.'

Francesco ignores Antonio for the moment, directing his men to open and permit Romeo forward into the space before the gibbet. Juliet watches her quarry worm his way right to the elbow of Lord Reynard and whisper urgently. There is a brief reply, the parchment thrust in his direction.

'How much blood is required?' Romeo asks. 'What will it take to douse these flames? You know, my Lord Governor, that Mercutio acted as he did to prevent a riot. There was no malice in his actions, no insult to Milan, only ever an eye to preserving the peace you demand. Where then is his sin? Where then is the offence that requires his death?'

As Romeo speaks, Friar Lawrence works his way to the fore as well. He stands right up against the line of soldiers and after a few heartbeats one man concedes the ground and lets him through. Lawrence takes position beside Romeo and the sight stills the crowd.

Juliet looks up and sees the main gate closed, Rufus already marching towards them with Aylward at his side. A knot of five mailed men-at-arms comes close behind. She gestures to them, directing the group to the Capulet side of the crowd and Rufus nods, making up the ground as quickly as he can without causing alarm.

'I am minded to accept,' Francesco continues amid scattered cries of dismay from the citizens behind. 'We seek a new beginning here today. Though perhaps this covenant must be sealed by the noose, what worth is there in a second death? Lord Romeo is convicted too, but his gesture is most honourable. What greater sacrifice can there be than one's own life in the place of a child? What true man could refuse such nobility?'

Before Antonio can reply, Reynard pushes forward away from those surrounding him and adds his voice to proceedings. 'If this is your judgement, my Lord Governor, then I accept and support it. The time of blood is almost at an end.'

'Are you certain, my Lord?' Francesco says. 'Not all of your party seem so pleased at the turn of events.'

'They are not Lord of the Capulets,' Reynard says firmly.

Before anyone else can speak Friar Lawrence puts himself in front of Romeo. His back is straighter now, his manner strong and purposeful. He advances on the gibbet and ascends the stair. The guards there do not stop him. Juliet finds the breath has caught in her chest as she watches Lawrence walk with God's will flowing through him, outside of time and mortal concerns.

Ragged and dirty, a small man without shoes or voice, Lawrence bears a majesty that even Francesco cannot resist. He watches Lawrence as though every child's tale told about him is true and the spirit of Verona indeed walks among them. Without hesitation Lawrence walks up to Mercutio and gently pushes him back, away from the noose. Once the way is clear Lawrence settles the rope around his own neck and looks out over the crowd with a terrible calm in his eyes.

Finally Francesco finds his wits again and he steps forward, placing a gentle hand on the friar's arm.

'No, my friend,' he says. 'Yours will not be the sacrifice here today.'

Lawrence faces him without emotion and removes Francesco's hand from him. Though he cannot speak, the action could be no clearer and Juliet hears from somewhere in the crowd a gasp and a sob.

Francesco shakes his head. 'Not this day, it is not required of you. Faithful servant of this city you are – soul of the city you must remain for this peace to hold. This burden is not yours to bear.'

Juliet is transfixed, but movement draws her eye and she sees Rufus has paid no mind to what goes on around the gibbet. She blinks and seeks her prey again before gasping.

'There!' Juliet cries, 'Rufus, before you, him!'

There is a flurry of movement. The Capulets roar with alarm and outrage, but Rufus is quick and large. With mailed fists he rushes forward and seizes the merchant Malacrolla. The man writhes and howls in outrage, but Rufus shakes him like a rat until he stops. The soldiers behind push forward and the startled Capulets, seeing Malacrolla is not one of their own, quickly give way.

'My Lord of Capulet,' Juliet calls down from her balcony. 'You should have a greater care for the company you keep.'

Reynard stares up at her then steps back as Rufus drives his prey forward and dumps him onto the ground before the gibbet.

'This man is a stranger to my company,' Reynard says as Malacrolla struggles to his feet only to receive a punch to the ribs from the great fist of Rufus. 'He came and asked the terms of Lord Francesco's covenant.'

'And you were most obliging, see he still holds it in his hands.'

Reynard blinks at the moaning man before him then darts forward and snatches the parchment from Malacrolla's hand. 'The words are not secret, it seemed best to let him read it and be rid of his pestering.'

'Your friend did not appear pleased with what he read,' Juliet presses.

'He is no friend of mine or my House,' Reynard replies sharply. 'I do not care what pleases a man I did not know before this night.'

'Is that so? What of you, Lord Antonio? Is he known to you?'

The Lord of the Montagues advances with a look of suspicion. As he peers at the wheezing merchant, Rufus hauls the man bodily up and displays his face for Antonio with all the care of a butcher at his trade.

'His face I have seen before, a merchant I believe.' Antonio steps back. 'I cannot recall his name, but he made overtures of a sort - bringing gifts and bribes in the hope of securing some minor favour. His manner offended me and his offers were too generous. I had him thrown out.'

'It is well that you did, my Lord,' Francesco says. 'For this man is a spy of Florence - my Lady Juliet, you can confirm his identity?'

She bows her head. 'That is he, Arturo Malacrolla. I am certain.'

'That is the name,' Antonio confirms. 'That is the one he gave.'

'And that is the name spoken by the assassin as his employer,' Francesco declares. 'Bind his hands.'

'My Lord Governor!' Malacrolla wails. 'I did nothing, I swear it! I know no assassin, I am no spy!'

'Will you not admit it even now?' Francesco roars, face scarlet with sudden fury. 'Save yourself the misery of what awaits you? I will have more from you than denials, that much I promise. This gibbet offers a swift death and that I can promise if you tell us all – it will wait for you a day, a week, a month. But I warn you, after such time you shall beg for its tight embrace.'

The merchant collapses, fainting dead away at the prospect of torture, and so two men grasp him roughly by the arms and begin to drag him away.

'Rufus, seize Lord Reynard also,' Juliet shouts. 'He is a traitor to Verona.'

Astonishment swiftly turns to outrage and several Capulets move to protect Reynard, but the soldiers turn their way and those few quickly find themselves faced with a dozen shields and swords.

'What is the meaning of this?' Reynard splutters. 'Because this alleged spy asked to read a document, you accuse me of collusion? Of treason? If you were a man I would cut you down for the offence.'

'But I am no man,' Juliet replies angrily, 'and a woman will always be reminded thus. A woman watches her step and those around her. She uses her mind where a man marches forward with only the force of his arm employed. You declared to the Lord Governor you did not know the spy, but I saw you Reynard – I saw the whispers you shared with him at the ball when my identity was revealed. Before the magistrate of this city, before the lords of Verona and the very incarnation of its soul, you lied. You knew this man – this spy who ordered the murder of my husband.'

'Mere carelessness of speech!' Reynard protests. 'The man spoke a few words to me there too, so small an incident I thought nothing more of it since.'

Up on the gibbet Lawrence stirs, his face contorting with emotion for a few moments. When he recovers himself he lifts the noose from around his head. With the strange quirk of a smile on his lips he offers it forward to Reynard. Several within the crowd begin to laugh, not all of them Montagues. Francesco raises his hands for quiet and the courtyard swiftly falls silent.

'We will discover the truth of this,' he declares, 'but not this night. Reynard of House Capulet, I do not know if you are an inveterate liar or an honest fool. One makes you a traitor to this city and the state of Milan, the other merely unworthy of your station. Until the truth is learned, you will be detained here under guard.'

'This is an outrage!' Reynard bellows and draws his sword, but again his House are reluctant to be so bold.

The threatening slither of steel on leather comes only twice more, both from mercenaries who, like Reynard, have married to earn their Capulet name. When they see they are alone and faced with swords on all sides they soon withdraw and sheath their blades again.

'You lie, Reynard,' another Capulet says, as loud as the cracked and thin voice of an old woman can manage. Lady Capulet herself steps forward and fixes him with her cold regard. 'I have seen this man before, in my husband's company. If he is a spy of Florence, you are indeed either a fool or a traitor. Whichever is the truth, the House of Capulet has no need of you.'

'Do not fear, Reynard,' Lord Antonio adds, ever happy to torment his adversary. 'I will be glad to oversee your trial and ensure you get what you deserve.'

Rufus cautiously advances on the Capulet, removing his sword and dagger from his belt then taking hold of Reynard's wrists. The man angrily shakes him off, but before it can come to violence Francesco intervenes.

'No, he remains a nobleman, he may go without binding. Take him to the room which so recently held Romeo and set a guard upon the door.'

'You make an enemy here tonight!' Reynard snarls as he is ushered away.

'We were already enemies if you serve the will of Florence,' Francesco replies. 'Do you think Malacrolla is a man to stand much torture?'

'A disciple of Cane must know such a man will say anything to avoid torture.'

'That I am counting on,' Francesco says with cold certainty. 'Malacrolla is a merchant by trade and merchants keep good records. There will be evidence of the truth and he will get his swift mercy once he leads us to it.'

Reynard's face pales and Juliet sees the guilt writ plain upon his face. He casts left and right but his allies are gone, as scarce as his chances of escape. The soldiers, fearing he will fight all the same, take him by the arms and this time he is so defeated he does not resist as they lead him away.

Once Reynard is gone, Francesco lets out a laugh that startles most of those watching.

'A happy end to events I feel, yet I have no cup to toast this. Felipe, bring me my cup damn you!'

'End, my Lord Governor?' Antonio asks pointedly. 'What has ended here? Is there not the matter of justice to be served?'

He points to the gibbet and steps forward so he is no more than three paces from Romeo.

'Justice?' Francesco throws wide his arms. 'Justice is mine to dispense, if you recall. I am now in a greater mood of benevolence.'

'The rule of law must still apply, you said as much yourself a few scant minutes ago.'

'As I did. However, in this instance I am minded to forgive the boy his sins and so there is no place for Romeo to step into.'

'Forgive an offence against the state of Milan?'

'Forgive an act he chose to avoid the deaths of innocents. One he deemed likely to assist in drawing out a Florentine agitator intent on keeping you, Lord Antonio, and your counterpart at war with each other.'

Antonio gapes at him for a moment, but soon recovers his wits, Mercutio's never having been the death he sought. 'Be that as it may, my Lord, Romeo remains under sentence of death for his killing of Count Paris.'

'Indeed he is.' Francesco cocks his head to one side and makes a show of observing his friend on the courtyard floor. 'And there we are, my friend.'

Romeo gives him a level look in return. Juliet sees the confusion on her husband's face, shock at the pace of events and abrupt change in Francesco's manner. A man who is quick to anger does not change, this much she knows, but her life with Romeo has seen him learn to control that anger. To hide it from the world behind considered words and formal manners.

Francesco takes a long breath and looks around at

the face present. 'I see no baying mob here,' he announces. 'No thirst for death or punishment. In the faces before me I see a tired citizenry, one that scarcely dares hope for the peace I'm promised.'

No voices rise in argument, the nobles cowed and the common folk nodding at what they hear.

'It is as I thought. The Lords of Capulet and Montague have pledged themselves to the peace I offer, the peace I demand, and I see the mood of the city here in the faces of you all. But should such an age of peace be bought with blood? What precedent does that set for the future, my friends? If old hurts make fresh wounds, where then is the end to the feud that plagued these streets?

'A feud lives only in the hearts of those present. It may be painful to end that feud, it may be difficult to live alongside an enemy and call him now a friend, but what other choice must there be? You children shall inherit this earth and all that you give them – will that be the bitterness in your hearts or the dream of a better world?'

Francesco shakes his head and looks over at Mercutio, nodding at the young man's bonds which are swiftly cut.

'I say to you now, this night we end the feud of Verona. I am a man of war, schooled only in bloodshed, yet I choose another path and I ask you all to walk it with me. The killing is at an end. We are done with it all and will wake to the new dawn as a city of hope once more.'

'NO!' Lord Antonio bellows.

He strides forward and before anyone can stop him he swings the back of his hand across Romeo's face. Romeo staggers under the blow, but recovers and straightens to look Antonio in the eye once more.

'Will that satisfy you, my Lord?' Romeo asks with dignity. He touches one finger to his lip and offers the blood that has trickled out. 'Is my blood so precious to you? Will this much suffice? I will cut my own hand if you require enough to sign your covenant.'

'I require more than that of you,' Antonio declares. 'You bleed and yet I call you bloodless. A cur who licks for scraps, a man who has killed to defend his honour yet casts honour upon the pyre! You are unworthy of the name Montague and I will not stand idle as you claim it still.'

He brandishes his finger at all those present, turning in a circle so all may see him. 'Hear me now, this peace is not yet won. One final death was foretold, one final corpse promised. I swear it now, peace may come with the dawn but this night, one more among us must die.'

Thirty-Two

Romeo looks at the blood on his fingers a long time before saying any more. Antonio's cheeks are pink with anger, his feet set in a duellist's stance though his blade remains sheathed.

'Cousin, can you truly not bear my face that you would prefer the blood we share upon your sword?' Romeo asks softly. 'Our lives have been lived apart, but we are kin still. After all you have endured, all you have fought for, would you now strike down your own?'

'You are no true kin of mine,' Antonio replies. 'No true man of noble blood. I see a notary before me and a notary's hand in that document offered to me today. I know your ways and I curse you for the cowardice of them. A hundred paper cuts to weaken your prey, a hundred strokes of the pen to bring a man to his knees, a hundred threads of silk to tangle and bind.'

'You convict me for what you imagine I might do. Is there any defence permitted for this? Have my offers to renounce all claims been mere ruse?'

'Likely so – your son did not make such an offer and a coward prefers to rule by proxy. You have offended me and the honour of the House I rule. You must face me now with steel in your hand and allow God to judge.'

'You speak of cowardice yet demand to fight a man who carries no sword, who has renounced martial ways these twenty years.'

'You hide behind your cowardice,' Antonio spits. 'I would expect nothing less, but you are trained in the arts and have proved your skill before. What nobleman should be permitted to hide by abandoning the ways of his class?'

'I do not hide,' Romeo replies firmly. 'Nor do I accept your challenge. I swore before God I would not use a sword again, not risk another wasted life through my own ill temper.'

'You must accept – you have harmed the honour of our House by your failings and you must answer this challenge.'

Romeo pauses and looks over towards the podesta. The man stands hunched and unhappy, beleaguered both by age and those who act past the boundaries of the law.

'What say you, Magistrate? Must I answer this myself? Am I the culprit or the offended party here?'

The podesta narrows his eyes and clears his throat as he considers each man. 'Romeo Montague has been charged with no offence to you Lord Antonio, nor to the House of Montague,' he says cautiously.

'He has stained the honour of my House!' Antonio roars. 'By murder of a noble man who was not our enemy, by marriage to our greatest hate and flight from all duties and obligations. He is the only son of the last Lord Montague and his claim is strongest, but I say again he has failed in all he has inherited and cannot live in Verona while I still draw breath as lord.'

'Such disputes are not matters for the law,' the

podesta says with a weary shake of the head. 'Romeo Montague is not the offending party here. Insulted and publicly struck, he may accept or decline your offer of a duel as he chooses, but is not obliged to answer it himself.'

'Not himself?' Francesco interjects. 'Well now – if only he had a friend willing to face such a seasoned campaigner, what then might Romeo do?'

'A second is permitted to defend the injured party.'

'What say you, Lord Antonio? Will you withdraw your charge and apologise, or must I take a few moments out from my newly won peace to kill you?'

'Francesco, no!' Romeo says. 'I do not accept his challenge on my part or yours. I will not have either of you die on this of all nights.'

'My friend, you have no choice.'

'How so?'

'Because peace depends upon it. Reynard was confirmed as Lord of the Capulets in lieu of any legitimate heir, but there is one who has a greater claim than any man here.'

Francesco points to Mercutio who stands at the far end of the gibbet. The young man's face is red with anger, his fists balled, only Friar Lawrence's hand preventing him from advancing.

'If this matter is not settled, I fancy the heir-apparent to the House of Capulet shall fight the Lord of Montague to the death. This I cannot permit.'

To punctuate the matter Antonio spits at the feet of Romeo. 'You are exposed in your cowardice before all of Verona. Will you stand or let your pup fight in your place? He is keen, he strains at the leash there for he knows this matter cannot stand. There must not be two lords of Montague in Verona. Fetch you a sword and let this end as it must.'

'I will not fight you.'

'Then let slip the growling pup.'

'Father!' Mercutio shouts, unable to restrain himself any longer. 'I will kill him!'

'You will not fight!' Romeo bellows in sudden fury. 'I would rather Antonio pierce my heart than see you fight him in my stead.'

'Then take your son's sword,' Antonio demands contemptuously, 'and remind yourself of your manhood – or does your Capulet wife keep that in a purse?'

Francesco drops down from the platform and forcibly pushes Romeo away from Antonio. 'Romeo, you will not fight and nor shall your son. Name me your second and we will be done with this.'

'Francesco, the law I hold more sacred than honour. It is second only to my wife and children.'

'Who he insults too.'

'I have been goaded before, it will not happen again.'

Antonio turns to the remaining Montagues and spreads his arms out wide. 'Do you see what sort of a man would put himself at your head? The pet of a Capulet woman, the sire of one barking pup and one—'

In a flash Francesco has turned and drawn his sword. 'One more word from you, Lord, and there shall be no need for a second.'

A sneer appears on Antonio's face. 'So now the truth comes out! The Lord Governor is also in thrall to a Capulet lady. And this is the peace we are offered? This is the way it shall be, with soft words and delicate hands guiding all of Verona to the Capulet cause. Tell me, Lord Governor, does she lead you with promises of advancement or by her warm embrace?'

'You insult a lady of good name and the Lord

Governor of Verona. You will offer apologies or die for it.'

'You are perhaps confused, my Lord Governor, for a man of your birth has no such recourse.'

'But I do!' Mercutio shouts, stepping down and holding out his hand for Antonio's sword. 'You cannot refuse me, Lord Antonio.'

'No!' Romeo thunders. 'You will not.'

'I must, Father, else this will forever hang over our heads!'

Romeo bows his head. The moment stretches out, the courtyard silent and taut. Finally he looks up and speaks.

'Then I name Francesco my second and beg him answer this claim on my behalf.'

'And you, Lord Antonio?' Francesco says, pointing at the man with his sword. 'Do you withdraw?'

'I do not. I am not so old that I am frightened of a common mercenary.'

'All the better – we shall have an end of this tonight and none will call me common again.'

Francesco steps away and directs his soldiers to give them room as he sheaths his sword again and begins to pull off his tunic. With that discarded, Francesco removes his shirt too and reveals the thick muscles of his arms. Antonio does the same and the older man looks older still in comparison, but he is neither small nor run to fat. What advantage Francesco has in height and strength may easily be countered by experience and training.

Each man unbuckles his sword belt, Rufus advancing to take Francesco's while his lord pulls sword and dagger from their sheaths. Francesco's other faithful servant, Aylward, barges his way through the crowd and bellows bloodthirsty encouragement in the manner of all Englishmen. The words put a smile on Francesco's face as he whirls his weapons through the air to loosen his wrists.

Lord Antonio watches the flamboyant act carefully, himself turning one brief circle with each weapon and settling his feet.

'Will you not end this foolishness?' Romeo asks, refusing to relinquish the ground until he has tried once more.

'I will not, Messer,' Antonio says stiffly. 'Retire or take your place.'

'My Lord Governor,' the podesta interrupts. 'Do you mean to ignore all usual formality? This is more brawl than duel between men of honour.'

'It is honour that has been questioned,' Francesco replies with a laugh, 'and I am in a hurry. We are resolved to fight, there is no reason to delay. Your place here, magistrate, is to sanction what you see as legal, nothing more. Do you have reason to object to this dual?'

'As a man of reason I must,' comes the reply, 'yet as an officer of the law I cannot, other than to state that the terms of the duel are not yet agreed.'

'One of us will be dead,' Francesco breaks in. 'We may then be beyond apologies!'

'If it is I,' Antonio says in a more serious tone, 'Romeo shall be Lord of Montague and the House shall be his to rule. If the governor falls or yields, Romeo and Mercutio must leave Verona and never return or exert any influence over the House of Montague.'

Francesco nods. 'Agreed – there, are you happy now? May we be at our business?'

'I withdraw. You must find another to official here.'

Francesco points to a merchant from the centre of the crowd, neither of the Capulet nor Montague camps. 'You Messer, will you serve? We fight to the death or yield – the work shall be simple and brief, but my household shall give you ten ducats for you to call us forward and ensure it is done honourably.'

The merchant blinks at each of the men, but eventually he nods his agreement and steps forward. He is a large man with a mass of dark curling hair and a long wooden staff in his hands, no soldier perhaps but not a stranger to violence, Romeo guesses.

'Very good. Romeo, please retire and let this be done.'

Francesco directs him away with his sword and finally Romeo does yield the ground. The soldiers of the castle make one last effort to push the crowd back. With the prospect of steel and blood they allow themselves to be driven until the duellists stand inside a square twenty yards across.

'My Lords, there can be no resolution?' asks the merchant in a gruff voice.

Both men answer that there cannot.

'Will you not make confession?'

'It has not been so long since my last,' Francesco declares. 'I have done little enough of note since then.'

Antonio shakes his head. 'I will not leave the notary time to find further excuse.'

'Very well.' The merchant levels his staff between them. 'Take your places.'

The two men take position opposite each other, each with his sword half-extended and his dagger held closer.

'My Lords, at arms!'

Francesco presses his attack from the outset, quick

cuts at Antonio's sword to push it aside. The older man rides the battering and slashes at eye-height, but falls short. They circle, Francesco advancing in quick bursts and Antonio defending, waiting for a mistake. Romeo's eye for combat has long since gone unused, but every young nobleman learns to fight as a matter of vital course. The speed of his large friend surprises him, and Antonio too. In the blink of an eye Francesco scores an unexpected nick on his opponent's calf with a low flick and darts back from the riposte.

The wound is slight, but still Antonio winces as the blood begins to trickle. He does not throw himself forward though. It is not so grave a cut as to slow him down, but the older man now begins to vary his stance. He brings his dagger first high, then wide as he turns his hips towards Francesco. Each step is neat and assured, the product of decades, and it shows the flaws in Francesco's own movement.

Romeo feels a flicker of fear as he sees how Francesco's weight drags at his feet, but when Antonio comes forward the younger man's speed saves him. Back and forth they move, swift and economical. A dozen staccato exchanges flash by in seconds. Francesco is cut on his left arm, a larger wound than Antonio's, but he merely licks up the trickle of blood and laughs it away.

The crash of steel heralds them coming together, both men squirming and twisting as they vie to bring their daggers to bear and avoid the edge of the other. Francesco's height and strength wins it and he slices into Antonio's shoulder. Lord Montague cries out and stumbles back, one foot catching underneath him to make him tumble.

The onlookers gasp as he falls, but Francesco does

not pursue him. Instead the mercenary retreats
courteously.

'This is not a battlefield, I will not kill you on the
ground. Please, Lord Antonio, take your feet again.'

Antonio grunts acknowledgement and wastes little
time in getting up. He takes a moment to shake the dust
from his body and inspect his sword, but then he adopts
his guard position. Francesco nods and lets the man
advance. Again they clash, neither man pressing hastily
for all that a long lunge from Francesco pricks the skin
of Antonio's breast.

A scream breaks the quiet. Both men draw back as
the entire crowd looks around in alarm. Romeo follows
the eyes of those ahead of him and turns, looking up to
the balcony behind their heads. His stomach clenches at
the sight awaiting him as a roar cuts across the courtyard.

'Ever the cowardly Montague! Can you do nothing
without your mercenary protector?'

On the balcony of the governor's office stands
Reynard, one arm clamped across the chest of Estelle
while in his other he holds a dagger. Estelle's cry is cut
off as he shakes her and tightens his grip, brandishing
the dagger before her eyes wide with terror. Her fingers
dig onto Reynard's forearm but cannot loosen the hold
he has on her.

There is a scrape down Reynard's cheek and his
sleeve is partly torn, but the man wears a cruel smile on
his face as he seeks out Romeo in the crowd.

'I commend your desire to kill Lord Antonio, few
could wish it more than I! However, there is one man I
would see die before him. If you will not fight to protect
your honour, what will you sacrifice to preserve?'

'What madness is this, Reynard?' Francesco shouts
furiously, his fight forgotten. He vaults up onto the

gibbet platform and points his sword up at them. 'If you harm her, your death will be more terrible than any man in Italy has dreamed of!'

'Enough of your idiot bluster! One more word from your fool's hole and I'll prick her pretty cheek, let the red run for all to see!'

Romeo feels his head swim in terror and he grasps his son's shoulder as his legs threaten to betray him. In the dim periphery of his vision he sees Aylward and Rufus run inside at the head of a group of soldiers. Reynard is in the governor's own study though – there are heavy bolts on the door and Romeo knows they cannot break it down quickly.

'What do you want, Reynard?' he forces himself to say in reply.

The man's eyes gleam with malice, but as he turns his attention back to Romeo he at least points with the dagger instead of pressing it to Estelle's face.

'The death of all Montagues!' he shouts back. 'But I will settle for only one. You, Romeo – I would see you dead before this night is much older or you will see your oldest child no more!'

Thirty-Three

Black spots appear before Juliet's eyes as the breath is stolen from her body. She fights the urge to shriek, to scream in terror and rage at the man just a scant half-dozen yards away, but reason overrules all.

Estelle squirms in Reynard's grip then whimpers as he pulls her head cruelly back. Laughing, he plants a kiss on her cheek, dagger still at her throat, then spits over the balcony at Romeo below.

'Delay and it is her life, I swear it!'

'And when I obey?' Romeo calls with all the dignity he can muster, though Juliet sees her own terror mirrored in his face. 'Will you release her? She is innocent of all things.'

'Her very existence is an insult,' Reynard replies. 'Product of a union that should never have been, of parents who should have died long ago!'

'She has done nothing!' Juliet cries, dragging his attention round to her. 'It is my blood you want, take me instead.'

'A man must take as life offers. Yes, it is your blood I desire, but that runs in her veins, too. If I must spill some to see that man dead as all laws demand, so be it.'

'What then? You cannot escape, the gates are closed.'

'They will open for a pretty face, I have no doubt of that. Two horses or a promise to open her up. This accursed place shall see the back of me and I'll bring her too. If I see the Lord Governor behind I will cut her and he can choose to take me or save her.'

'Will you take me instead? I will go without a fight, I swear, if you only release Estelle.'

Reynard laughs loudly. 'Marriage to a Montague has left many a woman willing to offer herself wherever she can. No, I will not – her life is more precious to you and the governor both, I think, and a tastier treat besides.'

'I will have your head on a pike, Reynard!' Francesco shouts, sword still drawn, blood dripping unnoticed from his wounds. 'Poxed wretch, I swear it will be so!'

'Have a care, my Lord Cowherd,' Reynard shouts back. 'As yet she is untouched – cease your lowing or I shall spoil her for all men here in front of you!'

'Francesco, I beg you!' Juliet cries. 'Have a care what you say when there is a blade at her throat!'

'You would do well to listen to a Capulet,' Reynard says. He cocks his head to one side as the hollow drum of men-at-arms beating at his chamber door. 'I hear your herd trampling away, but those bolts are strong. You best warn your cows that should they enter, this calf shall be sacrificed long before they reach me.'

Francesco's wits are robbed and he can only stare up at Reynard, but Romeo is quick to call for Felipe. 'Tell them to hold off, none must enter without their lord's word.'

The steward looks briefly at Francesco then scampers away. Juliet does the same as Reynard savours

310

the sight of both men so helpless before him. She is first to the soldiers, but her voice goes unnoticed at first. Aylward and Rufus are at their fore, the big men lending their shoulders together in great crashing blows against the door.

Juliet fights her way through the rest and drags at Aylward's arm. 'Hold, hold off! He will kill her if you enter.'

The archer turns in confusion, hardly hearing her in his determination. 'My Lady?'

'Aylward, you must stop – he will murder her before you can ever get close.'

That stops the both of them and the broad archer's face falls, his usual merriment turned to anguish, while dark Rufus merely grows darker still.

'What can we do then?'

'We must find another way, come with me.'

She leads Aylward back to the balcony she had occupied. Estelle is still captive, so close Juliet can almost touch her, but she forces herself to ignore the pleading look in her daughter's eye. The traitor does not notice Juliet, he is too busy shouting curses down at those on the ground. She looks quickly down and sees Lawrence has barred Romeo's way, placing the noose over his own neck as offered sacrifice.

'Is your mind so still as your tongue, priest?' Reynard yells angrily. 'Your life is worth nothing to me. It is Romeo I would see die – quit his stage or I will carve a fresh tongue for your head!'

Juliet turns and stops Aylward from coming out onto the balcony. 'Could you shoot him?' she whispers.

He leans out and peeks over her head before ducking back in.

'I cannot, not with certainty,' he says regretfully. 'At

such range an arrow would pass through them both. I dare not risk her.'

Juliet shudders at the thought, but she nods and raises a hand to him. 'Wait here, be ready for my signal.'

'My Lady, the risk is too great!'

'He will kill or maim her once he is escaped,' she hisses back, and Aylward shrinks from the anger on her face. 'I will not risk her life, but you must stand ready for any moment to save her!'

Eyes downcast he readies his bow and nocks an arrow, ready to draw. 'As you command, my Lady.'

As Juliet turns her attention back to Reynard she hears his tone grow angrier.

'My patience is at an end, Montague! Do as I order or offer the child your empty prayers.'

'I will obey,' Romeo calls out in reply. 'All I ask is your word? Can you offer as much?'

'You ask his word?' Francesco roars. 'Damned fool, what worth is in that? Any Capulet's word to a Montague would be of less worth than the breath spent upon it. This man knows only lies and hatred.'

'This Capulet is no fool,' Reynard replies. 'A lord of Verona may not pursue me wherever I go, nor Milan's dog himself, but you I think, Francesco, you would avenge the girl beyond Babylon itself if I killed her.'

'I swear it on my blood!' Francesco shouts, setting the edge of his sword to his bare chest until a red line appears across his breast. 'In life and death I would avenge her. To hell and beyond I would lead the worst of men to find you!'

'So I shall be content, Montague – you have your promise, secured by the cowherd's vow. Unless I might be forced to wound her and leave her as distraction to my pursuers, I shall not harm her, but first you must kick your last.'

Estelle struggles once more, stamping on Reynard's feet and hauling at his arm. She comes close to freedom as her captor grunts in pain, but then he snatches a fistful of Estelle's hair and drags her back to him.

'Not now, pretty one,' he laughs. 'You are not free yet.'

'You cannot make her watch this!' Juliet cries. 'The shock would be too much for her – she might fall!'

'I have a good grip, never fear, whore!' Reynard snaps back. 'She will live to see me safe!'

'And if she faints? Will you carry her?'

'As I must, this girl weighs little – the governor's horse may bear us both with ease.' Reynard dismisses Juliet with a slash of the dagger and turns back to Romeo. 'No more delay, Montague – take your stage and dance for me!'

With heavy footsteps Romeo does as he is told, each sound echoing like a pounding nail in Juliet's own coffin. Her heart beats furiously in her ears and her head swims but she grips the balustrade for support. Silently she pleads for her daughter to look her way, but Estelle cannot take her gaze from her father at first. She begins to wail and Reynard seems to heed Juliet's warning, shifting the young woman from one arm to the other.

Facing away from the gibbet, Estelle shudders and twists but still cannot break his grip. In the next moment her eyes lock with her mother's. Juliet gestures as furiously as she dares, trying to banish the blind panic from Estelle's face. At first it does nothing, but then Romeo's footsteps halt and the absence of sound strikes her like a slap.

Juliet holds one hand up for Estelle to stay still and

tries not to look down. Romeo – whether he sees her or not – is moving fearfully and slow, but he has reached the gibbet and taken the noose in his hands. Juliet puts the back of her hand up to her forehead and sees Estelle blink once, some measure of understanding passing between them. Juliet looks down and sees Romeo has the noose around his neck. He stands at the edge of the platform, staring down at the short drop off the edge that will nonetheless kill him.

Juliet moves to one side and hisses for her companion as she signals Estelle.

'Aylward!'

As the archer appears beside her, bow bending as he comes, Estelle gives a gasp and falls limp. With her legs gone beneath her, she falls like a doll and Reynard's grip is not enough to stop her fully. He bends as he is dragged half down, but releases Estelle in his surprise. As he reaches to grab her again Aylward loses his arrow.

In the dark Juliet sees only a blink of movement, but the force of the arrow throws Reynard staggering. There are screams all around. Estelle adds to her mother's own before Reynard lets loose a howl. It drowns out all other sound and time stands still as he lurches forward over the balustrade.

Estelle shrieks again as he scrabbles at her, fighting for any sort of grip as he begins to tip and then he is falling. The arrowhead has passed right through his chest, buried up to the feathers. As he falls he makes one last desperate effort and somehow catches Estelle's dress collar. Over the edge he goes, dragging Estelle in his wake and the young girl is slammed against the balustrade. She screams again, in pain now more than fear, and clings desperately at the stonework.

Reynard's weight shifts her and Estelle jerks forward.

Bent over the balustrade, she only has one hand keeping her from falling. The other flaps madly but can only brush the stonework while Reynard twists violently beneath her. The movement halts Estelle's cries suddenly as his grip becomes a tourniquet around her neck. Aylward shoots again and it strikes Reynard in the belly, but his hand is twisted into the cloth of Estelle's collar and he cannot release his hold as he cries again.

'No!' Juliet screams, throwing herself forward. 'Break the door down!' she howls, a cry that Aylward takes up with all the force of his great lungs.

Juliet looks at the gap between balconies. They are so close but suddenly it seems like a league of distance. She cannot jump so many yards, but then she sees the stonework of the wall.

'Aylward, look,' Juliet cries, pointing. There is a ridge that runs down the wall, barely enough for a toe-hold, but it is something at least.

'I cannot balance there,' he groans, pausing when already half-over the balustrade. 'It is too small.'

'I can,' Juliet says as Estelle's strangled whimpers tear at her soul. 'Stay there, hold your bow out.'

'My Lady, you must not!'

'No more words,' Juliet rages as she clambers over. Using the great archer as an anchor she works her way around him and to the wall, setting one toe on the thin line of stone. 'Use your bow to steady me!'

'Wait,' Aylward calls before shouting down. 'You, your spear!'

The spear is raised high then tossed up for him to catch. Aylward then does as ordered, holding the spear behind the blade and keeping it as steady as he can. Juliet presses herself flat against the wall and shuffles along as fast as she dares, the spear's butt pushed hard into the small of her back.

'I can reach no further!' Aylward shouts when she is a little over halfway. Juliet pauses. There are almost two yards still to go – a small thing on the ground but up here a yawning chasm.

I cannot make it.

Juliet looks up once more and sees Estelle moving ever further over the edge. Below her Reynard gasps and croaks as blood stains his hose. His hand remains hidden within a twisted bunch of cloth and the slow turn of his body only strangles her harder.

I must.

Without thinking any more Juliet reaches one last step and throws herself the remaining distance. She hits the stone balustrade heavily, arms thrown over it as pain bursts across her chest. Her feet scrabble and she feels herself slip for a moment until one toe catches a hold and she manages to clamber over.

Before her is the dagger Reynard used to threaten Estelle. Juliet snatches it up and begins to saw at the cloth wrapped around Reynard's fist. He howls as she slices his skin, but it is Estelle's silent choking that terrifies Juliet. She cuts as furiously as she can without harming her daughter.

There is a rip and a tear. Estelle gasps in relief as the bind around her throat lessens but Reynard gives a croak of rage and with his free hand snatches at Juliet's arm. The weight of him yanks Juliet forward and she hits the stone edge with a crack of pain in her shoulder.

'I will have one of you,' he hisses.

Juliet cannot see for pain. Dark stars burst before her eyes, the torches of the courtyard are mere smears of yellow against the looming black. She feels a jolt as the last threads of Estelle's collar part and her daughter is freed. For one sweet moment she feels the kiss of peace, the knowledge that her daughter is saved, then Reynard's full weight hauls at her.

'Mother!' Estelle cries and wraps herself around Juliet's legs.

The pain is intolerable, the stone balustrade driving into Juliet's pelvis with enough force to make her scream. Her moment of peace turns to memories of childbirth – terror and clamping pain, joy and such hope her heart seemed it would burst. The recollection fills her with strength. The pain surges through her body and turns trembling muscles to oak.

'You will have nothing,' Juliet rasps. 'A lonely grave and no more.'

Reynard's face is contorted by rage as he tries to swing and drag her off with his remaining strength. Juliet pulls him closer with all she has left and grabs at the arrow protruding from his shoulder. Reynard screams as she twists it, but then the wood snaps and she is left with the broad steel head.

Reynard roars and tries to grab her with his free arm, but Juliet slashes at it with the arrowhead. The pain in her shoulder and belly sharpens and she sobs, but she has strength yet.

'You get nothing,' she whispers, 'just a heart of iron.'

With that she stabs the arrowhead into his eye.

Reynard screams. The image of his agony is all she can see and then he releases her, hands clawing at his eye even as he falls. Juliet watches him drop and slam into the paved ground below. Reynard's head splits and blood splashes – the lord of the Capulets dead in an instance.

Estelle hauls her back away from the awful sight, but Juliet can do nothing to help. Even when she is pulled back and her daughter envelops her in a heaving embrace, for a moment Juliet sees nothing. Then her breath returns and she lets out one huge sob which contains every emotion she knows. They sink to the floor, hugging and wincing then laughing through their tears.

Juliet runs shaking hands over her daughter's face then her body, looking for injuries, but gives up when Estelle pushes her away. She is too weak and pained to resist. Together they turn and look out over the balcony. The noose is empty, the crowd in the courtyard scattered.

The hammering begins again at the door, this time with the voices of Romeo and Francesco raised above the sound.

'Anon, I come!' Juliet calls, wheezing as she struggles to her feet. With Estelle's help she stands and they support each other to the door where the creaking bolts are soon eased open. The door is flung back and Romeo surges forward to envelop both in his arms.

'Are you hurt?' he cries, his voice muffled as he presses his face against Juliet.

'No great wound, we will live I think.'

There is a thump as Mercutio, no proud warrior now, throws himself onto them and hugs them all as close as he can.

'We will live,' Romeo echoes and pulls them all tighter still.

Epilogue

A diffuse dawn light spreads over the city of Verona. A morning veil of mist shines white and gold on the fields beyond the city. Soft spectres linger at the mouths of streets as the sun rises, waiting to be banished. Their chill hangs in the air, muting the smoke and stink of any city, while a low circlet of cloud overlays the palest blue sky.

Juliet and Romeo do not speak as they wake together. Instead they turn to face each other and lie in silence, so close that their lips can touch with only the slightest effort. Juliet winces as she shifts, her bruised and overtaxed body complaining in a dozen ways. Romeo brushes his fingers gently down her injured shoulder and up to the line of her jaw.

What a sight I must be, Juliet thinks with a smile.

The expression is echoed by Romeo, as though he has guessed what is in her mind. Unconsciously he pulls the blanket away from his neck, discomforted by its presence against his throat. Juliet leans forward despite her stiffness and kisses her husband there, once, twice.

Romeo responds in kind, hands sliding over her hips and around to the small of her back before he places delicate kisses on her nose, her cheek, her forehead. Then discomfort makes them rise together and go quietly out to the corridor, blankets around their shoulders. Mercutio and Estelle sleep soundly in the adjoining chamber, the door only half-closed between. Knowing the room beyond is unused, the pair go in there to watch the emerging sun. Juliet nestles herself inside Romeo's warm embrace, his chin resting against the side of her head. Their breathing and the hopeful voices of dawn are the only sounds as they look across the sleeping rooftops.

The night just gone feels a dream already. Everything after Estelle's rescue is a blur in Juliet's mind, unimportant and half-forgotten. Francesco's restless and bloodied form looms heavily in her memory, by turns snarling with frustrated anger and rendered dumb with relief. His duel was forgotten, Lord Antonio having not pressed the matter further. There was blood enough spilled for all tastes; none had the desire for more.

The crowd had dispersed quickly, the Capulets leaving Reynard's body where it fell. Juliet recalls orders shouted, a bier fetched. Rufus had tended their injuries as best he could until a doctor could be summoned, the knowledge of such things being superior in his native land.

'Is it over?' Romeo whispers into her hair. 'Are we finally home?'

Juliet pulls his arms tighter against her. 'We are home, king of my heart,' she says. 'Whatever else may come, we are home.'

They stand a long while, but eventually the sounds of movement remind them the castle is waking and they return to their room to dress and prepare for the day. When they descend to the great hall, the servants are all most careful and courteous around them – as would befit a lord and lady within their own domain. There they find Francesco, attended by his steward and several men-at-arms as well as a man in Montague livery.

'Sir Paolo,' Romeo says in surprise as the Montague turns. 'What brings you here this morning?'

'My Lord Romeo,' the knight says with a respectful bow. 'My Lady Capulet.'

'He has brought a letter from Lord Antonio,' Francesco says, brandishing a piece of paper. 'A formal apology.'

'My Lord Montague withdraws all demands he has made, in the spirit of peace,' Sir Paolo adds. 'A new dawn is upon Verona and our Houses shall be reconciled.'

'My Lady Capulet?' Juliet says enquiringly. 'Do you forget I am married, Sir Paolo?'

Francesco shakes his head and answers for the man. 'A letter has also come from your mother. It is the will of all Capulets that you are confirmed your father's heir and inheritor of all estates and wealth as might be permitted a woman – in addition to holding in trust all else that may one day be passed to your son at a time of your choosing.'

'*All* Capulets?' Juliet repeats with a smile.

He laughs, though she sees the movement causes him some small discomfort. 'None are so foolish as to oppose her desire. So she wills it, as do all Capulets. The messenger said something to the regard of her wearing an arrow in her belt when she left her chambers this morning.'

Juliet closes her eyes at that, the memory of agony and fear, of blood and death, still strong in her mind. Her hands tighten as her stomach clenches, but she fights the sickness she feels welling up in her belly.

'And Lord Antonio?' Romeo asks while she stands still and silent. 'What is his will?'

'To hear yours, my Lord Romeo,' Paolo says smoothly, 'such as might then serve as accommodation between you.'

'Let it be this then – I renounce all claim I have to the title and inheritance of House Montague. Lord Antonio shall serve the House as he has before and after my father's death, but Mercutio shall be named his legal heir. Upon Lord Antonio's death, which I trust shall not come soon, all titles and estates shall pass to Mercutio and his line.'

Sir Paolo bows. 'I am sure that will be acceptable to Lord Antonio.'

'See that it is,' Francesco says harshly. 'I am sore and cut this morning, but I doubt a man twice my age shall be any keener to contest matters.'

'My Lord Antonio holds his signed obligations most precious, as he trusts does any Capulet to follow Lord Reynard.'

'My signature shall be added to the agreement,' Juliet agrees. 'My second act shall be to tear down the walls and gates that enclose the dwellings of the Capulet family.'

'Lord Antonio has issued similar orders.' Sir Paolo bows once more and gathers up his gloves and hat. 'I shall leave you all to your day then and instruct the notaries to draw up such documents as we may require.'

Once Sir Paolo is gone, Francesco dismisses the servants and sits alone with Juliet and Romeo. He eats freshly baked bread as he considers them. The smell fills the room and Juliet feels a rare hunger.

'It appears our task is complete,' Francesco says at

last. 'The great Houses of Verona are tamed.'

'Far from tame, my Lord Governor,' Juliet replies. 'Belligerence and antipathy are woven into their fabric. Men of war have married in and taken the name of both. There will be many difficulties yet, I have no doubt.'

'Those I do not mind. Some may be encouraged to take contracts with Milan and win glory and riches for their House. I will invite my captain, Facino Cane, to feast here with me soon and many will be drawn to the prospect of war to come. If Montague and Capulet no longer patrol their claimed streets, if Romeo Montague himself can walk freely into his wife's new home, then our work is done.'

'And you? Will you go to Tuscany with Cane?'

'I shall go where I am ordered, my contract with Milan runs through winter, spring and summer. Come autumn again, who knows where we shall stand? I have had no orders but to govern here my whole term of employment.'

'You have no hope to join what may be the greatest and most lucrative campaign in recent memory?'

Francesco smiles. 'There shall be rewards in Lombardy too, of that I am sure. The Lord of Padua is a bold and constant enemy, I have no doubt he shall attempt to take advantage of any campaign Milan may wage.' He pauses for a short while. 'There are also other reasons that keep me close by.'

Juliet raises an eyebrow. 'Is that so? I hope they do not number so many. Some may dislike sharing such regard.'

His cheeks pink. 'There is but one, of which I believe my Lady Capulet knows already.' Francesco's shoulders droop as he speaks. Where the great warrior was so fierce and strong when faced with danger, now he becomes meek and unsure. Juliet suppresses the urge to laugh and stroke his cheek as she might a child.

'A lady of good birth would never comment on something yet unspoken,' she says. 'However birth is not all, as my own love attests.'

'Worthiness comes in many ways,' Romeo agrees, taking his wife's hand. 'Through word and deed may a man's true worth be better measured.'

'So speaks a man of considerable wealth.'

'We cannot determine the fortunes of our birth,' Juliet concedes. 'Only strive to make best of what the years bring. You will not end your life in the same condition as you began it, I fancy.'

'That much I swear!' Francesco declares, banging his fist on the tabletop. 'By my blood, so it shall be.'

He freezes as he speaks the last word, attention caught elsewhere. Juliet turns to see her daughter at the doorway, watching them all with a gentle smile upon her face.

'Romeo, my heart,' she says, standing. Juliet takes her husband's hand and he rises too. 'I feel an urge to walk Verona's streets in the new day's light.'

'Gladly will I accompany you, my love. With my Lord Governor's permission?'

They leave arm in arm, the sun on their faces and a pair of guards following discreetly along behind. The business of the new day is well underway by then. Even the bustling starlings ignore them as the pair slowly walk to the riverbank and look out over the Adige.

There is no ragged-robed figure in sight. Only fishermen and children splashing at the water's edge, servants hurrying past with laden baskets and carts rumbling into view with the last of the city's meagre harvest.

'We are home, my love,' Romeo breathes.

Overhead a cloud of starlings rises as one, wheeling and crying. They watch the birds sweep up and around through the clear sky, a long spiral that encompasses the entire city.

'Yes, my heart,' Juliet says. 'Home at last. Our debt fulfilled, our future secure.'

'There is much to do before I consider my debt cleared.'

'It is cleared,' she insists. 'Though there is certainly more to do, we are but two people. We can bring peace to the city. Bring a chance of this new dawn to the citizens who yearn for it. Our endeavours will not end, but the debt is done. What we do now we do for love.'

'For love then. There can be no better reason for our labours.'

'Never shall there be.'

Acknowledgements

The seed of this book (unsurprisingly) came from watching a performance of Romeo and Juliet with my wife, discussed over whisky afterwards and breakfast the next day. It's fair to say that without her brains at the start and support throughout, I might never have even written this, so thank you Fi — for everything as always.

When you have a slightly mad idea that you want to explore (even if it's just a way to avoid writing the book you're meant to be writing), the support of others makes all the difference. So thank you also to Simon Kavanagh for such cheerful enthusiasm at the early chapters and ideas, my whole family for their thoughts and encouragement throughout, in addition to KV Johansen, Liv Chapman and Xander Cansell for help and advice. I can't even list all of the wider network of relations, friends and colleagues who were so generous about it, but you all made the process all the better for your assistance. Finally, Stuart Debar too — who's taken a chance on someone writing outside of his usual field, but hasn't blinked at the challenge.

SRL Publishing don't just publish books, we also do our best in keeping this world sustainable. In the UK alone, over 77 million books are destroyed each year, unsold and unread, due to overproduction and bigger profit margins.

Our business model is inherently sustainable by only printing what we sell. While this means our cost price is much higher, it means we have minimum waste and minimum returns. We made a public promise in 2020 to never overprint our books just for the sake of profit.

We give back to our planet by calculating the number of trees used for our products so we can then replace. We also calculate our carbon emissions and support projects which reduce CO_2. These same projects also support the United Nations Sustainable Development Goals.

The way we operate means we knowingly waive our profit margins for the sake of the environment. Every book sold via the SRL website plants at least one tree.

To find out more, please visit
www.srlpublishing.co.uk/responsibility

Ingram Content Group UK Ltd.
Milton Keynes UK
UKHW041847040723
424529UK00001B/6

9 781915 073129